PINE LAKES

Christopher Motz

First Edition
Pine Lakes ©2017, Christopher Motz
All Rights Reserved
ISBN: 154678926X
ISBN-13: 978-1546789260

Typesetting & Cover Design: RDB Interactive, llc

OTHER WORKS

The Darkening (2016)
The Farm, A Novella (2017)

Magic Awaits (2017)
Short story published in "Collected Easter Horror Shorts"

ACKNOWLEDGEMENTS

Special thanks go out to my wife, LeeAnn, and Bernie Alonge for helping with early critiques and corrections. God knows I can't find them all myself. Also, a huge thanks to all of those who helped spread the word on social media and get my name out there. My biggest thanks go out to Robert Bardall, who tirelessly spent hours getting this into shape, selflessly finding time to help me in any way possible.

And of course, you, the reader. Without your support, there would have never been a second novel.

My deepest gratitude to you all.

For my wife LeeAnn, who has saved me from the darkness more times than I can count.

I

Ted and Susan Merchant were twenty miles from the Pine Lakes Resort when the sky clouded over and rain splattered the road.

Ted's restored Barracuda cruised up the winding lane, surrounded by tall trees and thick brush on either side. A thin guardrail separated the road from a forty foot drop to the forest floor. Susan looked out the rain-speckled window into the darkness as she reached into her purse for a cigarette. This stretch of road always made her nervous, now compounded by the sudden gloom and rain that quickly slicked the asphalt surface. She lit her cigarette and blew out a cloud of white smoke, filling the interior of the car. She cracked the window and took another deep drag.

"Don't worry, babe," Ted said. "I know this road like the back of my hand."

"You say that every year, but it still makes me nervous," Susan replied.

Ted placed his hand on his wife's thigh and patted soothingly. They'd been coming to the Pine Lakes Resort once a year since they met, when they were both still in high school. It had been Ted's idea.

His family had been vacationing in Pine Lakes for as long as he could remember, and when it came time for him to start a family of his own, the tradition continued. Susan fell in love with the place immediately, but the ride up the mountain was a different story. Driving in general scared her to death. She hadn't had a license in years, not since her second year in college, not since the night on Interstate 81 when everything changed.

"I thought you'd be used to it by now," Ted said. "We've driven this road enough times to have it memorized."

Susan shrugged. They had a similar conversation every year, but familiarity didn't change the way she felt. She held the cigarette out to her husband and Ted took a quick drag, waving the cloud of smoke from his field of vision. The Cuda had taken the better part of a decade to restore, and smoking in her was generally forbidden, but knowing how Susan got on these trips, he let it slide.

"We have everything, right?" Susan asked. "Reservations? Clothes? Money? Your shampoo?"

Ted laughed and nodded. "I don't know about money or clothing, as long as you packed my Breck." It was one of Ted's many foibles. Special shampoo, special brand of socks, a specific type of soft drink. His habits were deep-seated and impossible to change, but he was perfectly happy with the way things were. Change was a four letter word.

"My man is a strange one," Susan joked.

"That's why you love me!"

Susan leaned over and kissed him on the cheek. Love wasn't a strong enough word; she absolutely adored him with every ounce of her being. When their eyes met, she still felt that little tingle, that butterfly flitting around in her stomach like it was the first time they'd met. Twenty years later that strange magic was still working. They'd ditched their Prom dates, taking a drive to Tuscarora Lake and sharing a flask of whiskey Ted had stolen from his father's liquor cabinet. They just *clicked*, the kind of relationship seen only in the romantic comedies Susan was so fond of watching. Their divorced friends watched them carefully, wondering what had gone wrong in their own lives, but Ted and Susan only shrugged it off. Some things were meant to be, and some weren't. One of life's simplest lessons.

"Cabin 105?" Susan asked.

"As always," Ted said. It was another of their traditions; same cabin every year as if they'd claimed ownership. Every summer Ted scratched a hash mark in the wood beneath the cabin's bed, along with their initials and a crudely carved heart. So far, no one had noticed their eighteen scratches, soon to be nineteen. It was always the first thing Ted did when they arrived at the cabin.

"Are you going to try writing this year?" Susan asked.

"I don't know," Ted sighed. "No one wants to hear what I have to say."

"How will you know if you don't try?"

Ted laughed and patted her thigh again. "Maybe one day."

Ted worked at the same distribution center for nearly a decade. He didn't love his job by any means, but it paid the bills. He'd flirted with the idea of writing a novel since high school, but he never had the time, the ambition, or the belief in himself that anyone would ever want to read it. Several drafts of the nearly completed manuscript sat on the closet shelf collecting dust for the better part of his adult life.

Rain lashed the windshield and dripped in through Susan's open window, splashing her arm. She cranked the window closed and fidgeted with the cuff of her blouse. Damn, she hated this road. She'd tried to get over it for years, but as soon as she thought her fear was under control, she looked into the forest speeding by and instantly lost her resolve. The forest was creepy at night; she couldn't imagine anyone arguing that point. *The Blair Witch Project* had really done a number on her. She knew it was just a movie, a work of fiction, but having lived near the woods her entire life, it had suddenly taken on a much more sinister tone. Who knows what kind of baddies lurked in the shadows?

"It always feels amazing coming up here," Ted said, flicking the cigarette out the window. "A week away from work, away from the neighbors!"

"Don't even get me started," Susan laughed. "Crazy Anne was on her front porch having a conversation with a stuffed parrot yesterday."

Ted laughed loudly and nodded. "I heard her scolding her garbage can last week."

"No!"

"I'm serious. She dragged it up the driveway and cursed at it for poor hygiene. You can't make this stuff up."

They both laughed and Susan's nerves quieted. Ted always knew how to make her laugh, even when she didn't want to. He had a knack for bringing her back from the edge; without him, she'd likely be in a padded cell by now.

They chatted back and forth as the sky grew darker and rain

threatened to wash out sections of the road. Susan clicked on the radio and bobbed her head along to the newest Imagine Dragons track as Ted poked fun at her for her taste in music. Ted was Black Sabbath, Metallica, and Opeth all the way. New music hurt his ears; auto-tune made him cringe, and the sound of sampled drum tracks was enough to send him into a diatribe on the lost art of creativity.

"Lars Ulrich," Ted yelled, "now *he* was a drummer. These other guys are still trying to catch up."

"Lars looks like my Uncle Barry and plays drums about as well, which is to say he *doesn't*."

"The old stuff," Ted said. "You can't hold his age against him."

"You're only as good as your last drum fill, dear."

Ted laughed and agreed. "Times change."

"You're not kidding," she said. "I noticed lines around my eyes last week. We need to change that bathroom mirror before I break it."

"Your lines are beautiful," Ted chuckled, "all of them." He slid his hand over and squeezed her inner thigh playfully. She swatted it away and giggled.

"Eyes on the road, Romeo."

Ted stared ahead dramatically, watching as the rain passed through the twin sets of headlights. "Just imagine what we'll look like in twenty years," he said. "I'll be pushing sixty, likely bald, with a big beer belly hanging over my belt."

"And I'll be three-hundred pounds with a big old ass to match."

"You'll *still* be beautiful," he said. "More to love."

She slapped his arm and snorted laughter. Her face wrinkled as the radio switched to an old Lynyrd Skynyrd song. She reached out to switch the station as Ted grabbed her hand and pulled it away.

"No you don't," he said. "You never change Skynyrd."

"I've heard this song a million times," she said.

"One million and one will be just as good. Classic rock is like a fine wine; it only gets better with age." Ted turned the volume knob and sang along to "Simple Man" discordantly as Susan laughed and covered her ears.

"Keep your day job, this one isn't working out."

The Cuda turned a sharp corner, the rear tires hydroplaning in a river of muddy runoff. Susan grabbed the door handle and pressed her feet tightly to the floor as Ted let off the accelerator, continuing at a slightly slower pace.

"It's getting bad out here," he said.

"Bad? Are you *trying* to kill us?"

"No worries, I know how to drive."

"Slow down, you know I hate this road."

"Already done Suzie dear. Relax. We'll be at the lodge in fifteen minutes and you can drown your sorrows in a bottle of Pinot."

"We can share a bottle," she said, "or two."

"Whatever you like. We have a week without worry or responsibility."

The Cuda hit another deep puddle and slid across the road, skewing sideways over the center line. Susan moaned, reaching out for the dashboard as Ted spun the wheel wildly. The vehicle swung around, tires squealing on the wet road, nose pointed at the thick trees on their right. They punched through the guardrail at forty-five miles an hour; the front of the car crumpled as the hood swung up, smashing into the windshield and cracking it in a series of thick lines. Susan lifted from her seat as the car soared into open space and gravity equalized. For just a second, she felt like an astronaut aboard the space station, and realized the sensation wasn't a pleasant one. Branches scraped the undercarriage and thumped loudly against the doors as the car rocketed through dark space. She watched as the side mirror shattered and flew off into the night. The engine's low rumble became a shrill scream.

Ted shouted unintelligibly and gripped the steering wheel with white knuckles, his mouth an 'o' of surprise. Everything ran in slow motion as the car bounced through the trees in a cacophony of wrenching metal and breaking glass. The weight of the engine pulled the front of the car down, turning it into a speeding missile; the G-force pushed Susan back into her seat and stole the breath from her lungs. She lost consciousness before the Cuda slammed into the forest floor with a final, loud crump.

Susan sank deeper and deeper into the murky waters of unconsciousness.

***

Susan opened her eyes and gazed around the shattered interior of the car. It *wasn't* Ted's Barracuda, it was her roommate Barron's Toyota Tercel, and it wasn't 2017, but 1999. The steaming Toyota rested crookedly down the embankment along the passing lane of Interstate 81. Susan and Barron were on their way to a Spin Doctors concert in Wilkes-Barre when they were forced off the road by a swerving eighteen-wheeler, pushing them over the grassy stretch between the northbound and southbound lanes. The car slammed into a tree, engaging the airbags and causing Susan to black out at the moment of impact.

They'd been planning the trip for months, Barron having purchased tickets the day they went on sale. The band's popularity had waned since the early nineties, but Barron remained one of their most faithful fans, seeing them several times a year on each of their tours. Susan remembered "Two Princes" from the radio, but was ignorant of most of the band's recorded output. She'd only agreed to go because Barron wouldn't let her hear the end of it.

"You're going to love it," Barron had said. "Their singer's last name is my first name," she'd squeal, "and he's so sexy."

"It's the band with the bee girl in their video, right?" Susan asked.

"No, no, no! That was Blind Melon! They're garbage!"

Barron took her music seriously.

The band's latest album was on the CD player when the car careened off the side of the highway; Barron had been singing along loudly when the trailer merged into their lane and pushed them onto the rocky shoulder. It literally went downhill from there.

When Susan came to, she pushed the deflated airbag aside and looked at her feet, taking stock, rubbing her hands over her legs, arms, and ribs, making sure she was still in one piece. She'd be sore for a while, and likely have a hell of a headache, but otherwise no damage done.

"Where'd you learn how to drive?" Susan croaked.

Barron didn't respond, didn't move. Her eyes stared forward and the side of her head bulged freakishly. A thin trickle of blood ran from her nostrils; her mouth hung open in a final, silent shout.

"Oh, Barron, no," Susan said shakily. "No, no, you can't."

Susan reached out a trembling hand and touched Barron's arm. She hissed and pulled away, tucking her arm close to her chest. Barron's skin had an unfamiliar texture. Cool. Lifeless.

"Oh, no. No, no, I don't fucking *accept* this," Susan screamed. "Wake up, damn you. Wake up, please," she cried, "we're going to be late for the concert."

Blood dripped from Barron's nose and spotted her white, concert t-shirt as Susan hugged herself and wailed piercingly. She hadn't even known Barron before college, but in the short time they'd shared a room, they'd gotten close. This went against everything right in the world, everything natural.

"Move goddamn you," Susan shouted. "Stop playing around, I know you're okay! You *have* to be!"

Barron didn't move, and she was certainly not okay. There was nothing Susan could do to change that.

Susan grabbed her friend's shoulder and shook lightly; Barron's head tilted and thumped against the broken driver's side window, resting in the crater her skull had created during the collision. Susan screamed again and looked away from her misshapen skull, resisting the urge to vomit.

"Ma'am," a voice shouted. "Ma'am, can you hear me?"

She turned and peered at the man on the other side of the door. An EMT gazed through the glass as pulsing red and blue lights bombarded Susan's blurred vision, making everything appear kaleidoscopic.

Her trip to the hospital was lost in a daze; the treatment of cuts and abrasions forgotten; the concerned faces of family and friends watching over her were nothing more than disconnected memories. It was only when Ted arrived that she allowed herself to *feel* again. She held him tightly, cried on his shoulder, asked him questions he could never answer. She needed him, needed to feel his warmth and his comforting hands on her fevered skin. She'd never needed anything so much in her entire life.

Ted never left her side.

Susan struggled with classes the following semester, unable to clear her mind of the accident and of Barron's eyes staring lifelessly into the world beyond. It haunted her nights and caused her days to run together into an endless swamp of exhaustion. She couldn't step foot into a vehicle for three months after the accident without trembling uncontrollably and hiding her eyes in the crook of her arm.

Her driver's license expired in 2002 and she never had it renewed. Her days of driving were over. Call it fear, call it PTSD, call it superstitious nonsense; whatever it was, it was final.

And fuck the Spin Doctors for being the soundtrack to her nightmare. She never liked them anyway.

Thank God for Ted. His selflessness, his calming voice, his devotion to bringing her back from the precipice of mind-numbing depression.

When Ted proposed to her in May of 2000, she jumped into his arms before he could rise from bended knee. Yes she'd marry him, love him, cherish him, until death did them part. She couldn't risk losing someone else she loved.

In seventeen years, she'd never regretted her decision. Her love ran deeper than the cold waters flowing through the aquifer.

It was indestructible.

***

Ted lifted his head and groggily looked through the broken windshield. The Barracuda was little more than twisted scrap, a junkyard discovery. One headlight stared drunkenly into the darkened forest, illuminating a small patch of wet sticker bushes. Beyond that, the forest was pitch black.

He jumped and turned to Susan as fingers of pain reached from his neck and ran down his spine. He fought back a cry and reached a bloody hand out to his wife, rubbing her cheek lightly with his fingertips.

"Susan? Susan are you okay?"

Her eyes fluttered open and her mouth twisted in a rictus of pain. She hissed through swollen lips and looked over at a very relieved Ted.

"Are you hurt?" Ted asked.

"I don't think so," she mumbled, "but I can't move my legs. They're trapped." She tried pulling them free, but they were pinned between the dash and the crumpled firewall. Ted nodded his understanding; he was in the same predicament. Adding to his confinement, the steering wheel had been pushed back, leaving only inches between it and his chest. The radio spit a grating wall of noise; the engine pinged and hissed as it cooled, sending billowing clouds of steam into the air above the wreck. Fat raindrops pattered the roof with hollow, metallic thumps.

"Oh my God, I'm sorry Susan. I should have listened to you and slowed down."

"There's no point being sorry now, what's done is done."

Todd grunted and tried freeing his pinned legs. There was some give, but not nearly enough. He banged the steering wheel with his palms and cursed under his breath.

"Stay calm, dear. Panicking isn't going to get us anywhere."

"Says the woman who's afraid to drive."

Susan shrugged and offered a thin smile.

The lone remaining headlight flickered and went out with a pop, plunging them into near complete darkness.

Ted groaned and put his head in his hands. "Goddammit," he uttered. "Shit! Fuck!"

"You've always been a man of such profound thought," Susan snickered.

"Are you seriously making jokes right now? You realize we're forty feet *below* the road?"

"I know that," she said, "but someone will see the broken guardrail and know we're here."

"That's optimistic."

"Would you like me to scream and carry on? Under the circumstances, I'd say I'm doing pretty fucking great."

"You are," he muttered. "Save your breath. No one will hear you, anyway."

"My head is throbbing," Susan moaned. She reached up and rubbed her forehead; her fingers came away covered in a thin coating of blood. "I think I might have cracked my head."

"Oh, Suzie, I'm so sorry. This is all my fault."

"I'm not blaming you," Susan said.

"I'm blaming myself. I should have pulled over. I thought we could get to the lodge before dark, but I was wrong."

They sat in silence listening to the rain's soothing drone. Ted wanted to close his eyes and let the sound take him away into merciful sleep, but his common sense rejected the idea. If he had a concussion or head injury, closing his eyes could mean they'd never open again. He cleared his throat and opened his eyes wide to stave off his sudden exhaustion.

"The Cuda is wrecked," he sulked.

"I know baby, I'm sorry, but we can always get another car."

"Not this one," he said. "This one is special."

Susan nodded. Ted had worked at restoring the Barracuda nearly as long as he and Susan had been married, buying parts when he could afford them, spending most of his free time in the garage, working on his days off, covered in grease and sweat, knuckles bruised and bleeding.

It'd been a bone of contention between them for some time.

***

Ted had been looking for a classic car to restore ever since high school. The problem was always money. Either he found well-kept or restored models whose owners had unrealistic ideas of worth, or they were in such terrible disrepair, they'd have to be rebuilt from the frame up. The Barracuda was somewhere in between.

The black interior had been untouched, and apart from torn rear seats and a busted speedometer, wouldn't require much labor. For a vehicle that had rolled off the assembly line in 1970, Ted thought this was a great selling point. The exterior was another matter. Rust on top of rust, missing taillights, dual exhaust that looked like it had been used for target practice. The front bumper and grill were missing entirely; the rear window had a nest of spider-webbed cracks; dents and dings and gouges peppered every inch of the body. The hefty 383, with four-barrel carb, hadn't turned over in a decade.

"Tell me you didn't pay a lot for this heap!" Susan moaned as she entered the garage.

"What do you consider *a lot?*" Ted asked, grinning.

"I'm thinking a pack of cigarettes and a case of Miller should have covered it." She kicked the flat rear tire and a shower of rust rained from the wheel well and onto the concrete floor. "My Lord," she sighed. "The first strong breeze and this thing is going to blow away in the wind."

"Not at all," Ted exclaimed. "This is fine, Detroit rolling steel."

"It doesn't look like it's going to be *rolling* anywhere," Susan said, "unless it's on the back of a flatbed."

Ted waved her off and circled the car with a gleam in his eye. He ran his hands over the faded and pitted paint, once called Jamaican Blue Metallic.

"No one likes a smart ass, Suzie."

"No one likes an impulse buyer, either," she retorted, "except maybe the guy who took your money and laughed all the way to the bank."

"What do you know about cars, anyway? You won't even get your license."

"That's not fair," she muttered.

She was right, it wasn't fair. After what had happened to her, Ted was surprised she'd even step foot in a car again. He walked around the Plymouth's hood and hugged her tightly, rubbing her back.

"I'm sorry, you're right, that wasn't fair. I'm just so *excited*," he said. "I've wanted a classic for as long as I can remember."

"I know, I'm sorry too."

"My father used to have a '64 Impala, cherry red with white interior. I loved that car when I was a kid and always assumed one day it would be mine. I came home from school one day and it was gone, and in its place was a brand new Buick Skyhawk. A fucking Skyhawk! From that moment I knew I wanted some old muscle, not a four-cylinder box."

"Does it make you happy?" Susan asked. She pushed him away at arm's length and looked him in the eyes.

"Well, yeah," Ted said. "It'll make me happier when it's finished."

"This isn't going to be another of your projects that sits and collects dust, is it? Like the shelves you've been meaning to hang in the back bedroom for two years."

"No, no, this is different. This will be something we'll be proud of. We can take it up to Pine Lakes every year, show it off to the old couples."

Susan laughed and looked at the car again. There were some pretty lines buried beneath the rust and dented metal. "By the time you finish it, *we'll* be the old couple."

"That's okay isn't it? At least we can grow old gracefully, and we'll have a sick ride." Ted leaned in and kissed Susan on the lips, lingering only briefly before going back to poke and prod at his purchase.

Ted didn't finish the restoration until ten years later, almost to the day. The Barracuda could have been a show car. The original blue paint had been matched as closely as possible; the chrome gleamed; the 383 growled like an angry lion. Ted drove them around town, windows open, smiling as people watched them pass, waving, gawking at the beauty he'd resurrected from the grave.

Ted had gotten the sick ride he always wanted.

***

"You never told me how much you paid for this thing," Susan said.

"What? Does it matter now? It's a total write-off," Ted replied. He shifted uncomfortably in his seat, pulling at his legs again, hoping he could free up enough wiggle room to slip his feet from beneath the crumpled dash. His left foot moved a few inches before he gave up his struggle. He needed to preserve his energy.

"Are you okay?" Susan asked.

"Yeah, I think so, I'm just trying to free my legs. Can't you?"

Susan tried again to no avail. She was trapped.

"It's getting cold," she said, shivering.

"Lucky it's not December, or we'd be nothing but icicles when they find us." Ted turned as much as he could and looked into the back seat. A black travel bag had slid onto the floor behind Susan's seat. Stretching, he grabbed the handle with his fingers and pulled it closer, unzipping the bag and pulling out Susan's hooded sweatshirt. He unfolded it and tucked it around her upper body. She smiled appreciatively.

"Thank you, babe," she said.

Ted grunted irritably; not at Susan, not at the cold, but at the circumstances. He'd been driving since he was sixteen year old; he should have never lost control of the Cuda, it was an amateur mistake.

"We have to figure out how we're getting out of here," Ted said. "Our injuries aren't life threatening, but people have died like this before. Do you remember? A few years back? They found that car off the road in the Poconos?"

"Do you think this is the best conversation to be having right now?" Susan asked.

"We have to know what we're up against here. We don't have food or water," Ted said sternly. "Do you want to die of thirst forty feet from the road?"

Susan grumbled and turned away. "I'll listen to suggestions," she said.

"At least one of us has to get out," he said. "Go for help."

"Brilliant!" Susan shouted. "Did you think of that off the top of your head? It just *came* to you?"

"You know what, Sue? You don't have to be a jerk about it."

Ted called her Susan most of the time, and Suzie when he was feeling playful or excited. Calling her Sue meant he was pissed off. He had an even more elaborate vocabulary when he was *really* pissed off.

Ted shifted in his seat and dug a hand into his pocket, feeling for his cell phone. It hadn't even crossed his mind. Ted wasn't what one would call a 'tech head.' He didn't have a cell phone until he was thirty years old, and only because Susan had bought him one and made him carry it. He didn't like being *connected.* His father had been the same way when Ted was a child. They didn't have a microwave until the mid-nineties; the same applied to their telephone, which still had a rotary dial only ten years earlier. His father thought answering machines were the most ridiculous invention ever. 'If people have something important to say,' he'd grumble, 'they can just call back.'

"Son of a bitch," Ted spat. The screen on his Samsung was shattered; the phone wouldn't even turn on. "A lot of good a cell phone does when it breaks so damn easily."

"We were in a car accident." Susan spoke slowly as if to a child. "I told you a dozen times not to keep your phone in your damn pocket. I'm surprised it wasn't broken before now."

"Fine, you were right. Okay? Can you please stop picking at me and help figure this out?" Susan nodded. Ted was right. Arguing over petty bullshit wasn't going to accomplish anything. She reached out and put her hand on Ted's arm. He was trembling. He patted her hand, apologized, and kissed her on the cheek

"Can you reach into my bag again?" she asked. "My phone is in there, it might had survived the crash."

Ted turned and rifled through the travel bag, pulling out a few packets of unsalted peanuts and a digital camera, before touching the cool plastic of her cell phone. He gave it a cursory glance to make sure it was undamaged and handed it to her. She turned the phone on and waited; it chimed musically as the screen came to life. The phone didn't have great service, but more than enough to connect a call.

Susan dialed 911 and waited. It rang three times, four times, five, but no one answered. "What the hell is wrong with this thing?" she shouted.

"What's wrong?" Ted asked.

"It's not connecting. It rings but no one answers."

"Call someone else," Ted said. "Call your parents, call my parents, call Wal-Mart, just get us the hell out of here."

"I'll call Beth," she said. Beth was one of her best friends, and likely the closest to the accident scene. She tapped Beth's number and put the phone to her ear, listening as someone picked up on the other end.

"Hello?"

"Beth," Susan shouted. "Oh, I'm so glad to hear your voice. Ted and I were in an accident. I need you to call the police. I can't get through to emergency services."

"Hello?" Beth repeated. "Is anyone there?"

"Beth? Yes I'm here! Didn't you hear me? Call the police. Tell them we're in the woods off the Old Branson Road, about fifteen miles south of the Pine Lakes Resort. Did you get that? Pine Lakes."

"Joe? If this is you screwing around, so help me God."

Joe was Beth's most recent ex-boyfriend, one very fond of kinky sex and using his hands to make a point. He'd been calling her dozens of times a day for the last two weeks, sometimes pleading, sometimes screaming and threatening. Beth was just about ready to change her number.

"It's Susan, not Joe," she shouted. "Aren't you hearing what I'm saying?"

"I can hear you breathing you sick bastard," Beth cried. "Don't call me again, I mean it!"

The line went dead.

"Beth? Beth? Goddammit! She hung up."

"Try again."

Susan re-dialed the number and listened to it ring. A computerized message let Susan know Beth's inbox was full. "Shit!"

"Give it to me," Ted said, reaching toward her. Susan put the phone in his hand and sighed loudly.

"Do you think I don't know how to use a phone?"

"I didn't say that," he replied. "Maybe it's muted or something." Ted pressed a few buttons, checked the phone's settings, looked at the signal strength, and dialed his parents' number.

No one picked up and there was no machine to leave a message.

He cursed under his breath and dialed again, this time to his friend Harold. He was forty years old, a lifelong pothead, and a die-hard video-gamer. He only left his couch to get beer or answer the door for the pizza delivery man. He hadn't worked in a decade, ever since he tore his shoulder to hell in a job-related injury. Harold wasn't faking, his shoulder was still a mess, which gave him an excuse whenever anyone asked him about his affection for sticky bud.

Harold's voicemail picked up on the third ring.

"Harry it's Ted, listen carefully. We wrecked the Cuda on Old Branson Road, about twenty minutes south of the Pine Lakes Resort. We're off the road and we're trapped in the car. We can't get through to 911, so we need you to let someone know we're here. We're not hurt, but we can't get out. Call me the second you get this. Better yet, call 911 first, *then* call me back."

Ted disconnected the call and looked at the screen. The signal was good and the battery was almost fully charged. He was confident it wouldn't take long to hear from Harold. If he and Susan could get the hell out of here before morning, they could put this entire unfortunate affair behind them. The sooner the better.

"Harry will come through," Ted said. "He's probably just taking a shit or something."

"Lovely," Susan said, grimacing.

The phone chirped in Ted's hand, signaling an incoming message.

"It didn't even ring," Ted muttered.

"It's never done that before. Maybe it *was* damaged in the crash."

Ted put the phone on 'speaker' and tapped the button to check the voicemail. A few seconds later, Harold's friendly, stoned drawl filled the car.

"Hey man," Harold's voice spoke, "I don't know if something's wrong with your phone, bro, but I think I just got a weird message from your old lady." Harold's voice went silent, almost like he was waiting for a response before realizing he was talking to an answering machine. "It was her number, but the message was garbled and full of static." Another pause. "Anyway, call me back when you get this. I'll be playing the new 'Resident Evil' game. Dude! Sick!" Harold laughed, and the message ended abruptly.

Susan shook her head and rolled her eyes. She wasn't one of Harold's biggest fans.

"Harold can barely tie his own shoes," she said. "Why the hell would he be your first choice?"

"He never leaves the house, and I know I can always count on him in a tight spot." Ted mumbled something nasty under his breath and dialed the number again. On the second ring, Harold answered.

"Dude? Is that you? What's up with the..."

The line went dead.

Ted pulled the phone away from his face and looked at it with a frown; the screen had gone dark.

"What the fuck?" he shouted. "Piece of Japanese shit!"

"Calm down," Susan said. "Give it to me." Ted handed it over and crossed his arms, agitated and acting like a petulant child. Susan nearly laughed, but figured if she did it would only upset him more. She touched the phone's screen, pressed the button to turn it on or off, even removed the battery and tried restarting the device. Nothing. It was completely dead.

"That's just great," Ted said. "Now what are we going to do?"

That's when the lights appeared.

2

"What the hell is that?" Ted asked.

"It looks like a flashlight," she replied. "Someone's out there."

"Thank God," he shouted. "Roll your window down, hurry."

Susan complied, cranking the handle as fast as she could. They couldn't risk losing the chance to let someone know where they were and what had happened. The window disappeared into the door with a thud.

"Hey, over here," Ted yelled. "We're over here!" He waited for a reply but heard none. "Do you think they hear me?"

"I don't know," she said. "Try the horn."

Ted smiled and his eyes widened. He pressed on the horn, grinning as it brayed loudly into the silent forest. The light suddenly stopped moving and focused in their direction.

"I think they see us," he said. "They know we're here."

"Then why isn't the light moving? They're just standing there."

"It's dark out here. Even with a flashlight, it's going to take time to find us."

Ted reached out and hit the horn again, but nothing happened. He pounded harder, cursing under his breath. That quickly, the horn had died. He turned the knob for the interior light, but nothing happened. "The fucking battery must have died," he grumbled.

"Wait, it's moving," Susan said, clapping her hands together happily. "See? There. It's coming closer."

Ted followed her pointing finger and watched as the light grew brighter. It disappeared behind thick brush only to reappear a few feet to the left or right seconds later. He reached out and grabbed his wife by her chin, kissing her deeply. "I knew it! I knew they'd find us, Suzie. We're going to be home in time for breakfast."

"I hear voices," Susan exclaimed. "Do you hear them?"

Ted cocked his head and listened, but heard nothing. Decades of loud music and rock concerts had given him moderate hearing loss, something that often irritated his wife and friends. In a crowd of people, Ted would need things repeated two or three times before understanding. In the cases where he still couldn't discern the voice from the noise, he'd nod anyway, often getting looks of confusion from friends who wanted more than yes and no answers.

"I can't hear anything," he said. "What are they saying?"

"I don't know, I can't make it out, but there's definitely *several* voices."

Ted started shouting again, pounding on the steering wheel, punching the roof of the car. Susan groaned and covered her ears; his voice was piercingly loud in the confines of the wrecked vehicle.

"If you keep that up, we're both going to be deaf," Susan joked.

The light was closer now; a second one flicked on a few feet to the right.

"Oh, thank God!" Ted shouted. He may have been unable to hear the voices, but the sounds of their approach were clear as day: heavy footfalls crashing through the overgrown brush, the rustling of tree limbs and snapping of dead branches. He listened to Susan's heavy breathing and smiled as relief flooded over him.

Ted closed his eyes and felt his body grow heavy. *Just for a few seconds*, he thought. *Just to catch my breath.*

The adrenaline dump left him exhausted, and before he knew it, Ted was snoring lightly as Susan watched the lights get closer and closer.

***

Ted sat up in bed, squinting and half-blind from the morning sun streaming through the windows. He covered his eyes with his forearm, yawned, and swung his bare feet onto the cool, wooden floor. Shaking his head, he went to the window and peeked into the driveway, watching sparrows dance around a worm they'd found in the yard. The Barracuda sat along the curb, gleaming, covered in beaded drops of water. The neighbor's kids kicked a soccer ball back and forth in the middle of the street. It was a quiet neighborhood, not much traffic, small-town life at its finest.

His stomach gurgled hungrily as he watched a sparrow fly off with its morning meal. "You have the right idea, my friend," he said to the empty room. He turned and gasped. Susan's side of the bed was covered in a thick, wet, crimson patch. The sheets had been turned back; several small drops of blood dappled the floor next to the nightstand.

"Susan," he shouted. "Susan, where are you?"

He ran into the hall and saw another drop of blood a few feet from the bedroom door. Panting, he gazed at the dime-sized drop, afraid to follow the trail that had been left for him. The clock chimed in the living room, breaking him from his trance. He strode down the hall with purpose, gazing into the spare bedroom and looking down the stairs for signs of Susan's passing. Ted stopped in front of the bathroom door and looked at the bloody hand print smeared on the beige paint. Another spot had stained the carpet in front of the door. He listened for a second, hearing Susan's muffled sobs inside.

Ted reached out to turn the knob, but found it locked. Susan never locked the bathroom door; most of the time she didn't even close it, whether brushing her teeth, showering, or using the toilet. She was very open with her bathroom habits, something Ted didn't get used to for years. He still couldn't a take piss in a public restroom if he had company.

The locked door was disconcerting.

"Suzie, are you okay?" Ted asked.

"I'm fine," she responded. Ted heard in her voice she was far from fine. "Just go away."

"Susan, I can't do that," he said. "You're bleeding. It's all over the bed. What's going on?"

"I said I'm fine," she shouted.

"Can you please unlock the door so I can see for myself?"

"No," she sobbed. "Go away, please. Leave me alone."

"Baby, you can either unlock the door or I'm going to break it down. I don't want to do that, but you're not giving me a choice."

He listened as Susan softly crossed the tile floor, sniffled, and unlocked the door. He didn't open it right away; he didn't want to barge in and scare her, but he was also scared for himself, unsure of what he'd find.

"Honey, I'm coming in now, okay?" He waited for a response but didn't get one. He grabbed the doorknob, tacky with drying blood, slowly opened the door, and stepped inside.

Jesus Christ, he thought as the air bled from his lungs.

Susan sat in the bathtub, partially obscured by the shower curtain. The edge of the white porcelain was streaked with dark, fresh blood. Ted crossed the room in a single bound and pulled the curtain aside as Susan raised her hands to shield her face. She wore only her stained nightgown and one lone bedroom slipper.

"Susan, what's going on? Where are you hurt"

When she looked up, his heart froze in his chest and shattered. The pain in her eyes said everything; it burrowed into his soul and shriveled it like old shoe leather. Suddenly, he understood.

"It's dead," she screamed. "Our baby is dead." Susan wailed until her voice faded to a raspy squeal; tears poured from her face and streams of snot dangled from her nostrils. She wrapped her left hand in her thick, brown hair and tugged weakly; her right hand rested on her belly, caressing the flesh where there'd once been life.

Ted cried uncontrollably, unaware he'd begun. He looked at her stomach and groaned. For hours they'd sit together in bed, waiting patiently for the tiny life inside her to reach out its hand and make contact, to kick and thrash around, anticipating its escape into the bright and beautiful world beyond.

Susan's screams were little more than a dull buzzing in the back of his brain. This couldn't be happening. Not to them. Ted reached out absently, needing to touch her, feel her warmth, know she was still alive. His world was turned upside-down with those two simple, but all-powerful words. *It's dead.*

Ted hated referring to their baby as *it*, but they'd decided to keep the sex of the child a secret. What would it matter now? Would they still name their dead child just to have something written on its tombstone?

What the fuck do people do? Ted thought. *How can such questions exist in a sane world?*

When Susan felt her husband's fingers brush the flesh of her stomach, she gasped and hissed like she'd been burned. She grabbed his hand painfully and flung it away.

"Susan, let me help you," Ted croaked.

"Help me?" she cried. "Can you stop our baby from leaking out of me? Can you do that?"

"You know I can't," he said. "We need to get you to the hospital and make sure you're okay."

"Of course I'm not okay," she screeched. She swung an open hand and smacked Ted across the cheek with a loud slap. She screamed and slapped him again and again, over and over until her hand stung. Ted's cheeks were bright red and swollen; Susan's blood stained his flesh. "I'm broken," she blurted. "My womb isn't even fit enough for life."

"Stop talking that way," Ted scolded.

"What do you know? You didn't carry this baby for five months, you didn't feel it inside of you every second of every day." She rubbed her belly with both hands and whined miserably. "There's nothing," she said. "Nothing at all."

Ted grabbed her chin harshly and turned her head so she was facing him. "That doesn't mean I didn't love it too," he shouted.

"You know NOTHING!" she raged. "You couldn't possibly understand…"

Ted smacked her across the face and grabbed her by the shoulder, shaking her back and forth. "Susan, please," he begged. "Stop and take a breath. I'm not here to fight you. I love you, you know that right? This isn't your fault, it's *no one's* fault. It happens all the time, you know it does. We were dealt a shitty hand, that's all. You can't blame yourself."

She wanted to hit him again, wanted to punch him in the face until blood streamed from his nose, wanted to gouge out his eyes with her fingernails and tear at his flesh. Instead, she hugged him. She clutched onto him like a drowning woman, squeezing him, bellowing into his ear with rage, and anger, and undying grief. She cried on his shoulder until the well ran dry, and Ted cried with her.

It was the hardest day of their lives. It tested their faith in the world and their faith in each other. Months passed when it looked certain they'd never survive this tragedy. Ted saw how she moped around the house, vacantly staring into corners. He was afraid he'd lost her for good. They walked on egg shells and passed with few words. They ate dinner in silence, and often spent entire days apart, grieving in their own way. Susan preferred doing so privately.

It was a year before things began returning to normal. Susan had become more like her old self; she laughed again; she left the house; they made love. Ted kindled that spark, slowly and carefully, giving her the space she needed and being there for her when that space became too much. They reached a balance, a place where life was once again worth living.

Still, when the sun went down and the world filled with shadows, Ted would find her staring across the yard, lost in thought, far away. She'd smile thinly and grab his hand, but Ted knew she was still hurting. They both were.

They never talked about trying again, not because they didn't want children, but because Susan was terrified of having the same result. She couldn't go through that loss again or it would consume her.

Their love for each other would have to be enough.

**

Ted's eyes shot open and he sat up stiffly.

"Did you say something?" he asked.

"I *said* they're gone. Were you sleeping?"

"I must have dozed off," he said. "What's gone?"

"Them," she pointed, "out there. The lights just vanished."

He rubbed his eyes and gazed through Susan's open window. "Gone? Where the hell did they go?"

"Maybe if you'd stayed awake, you would've seen where they went," she said. "How the hell can you sleep at a time like this?"

"I just closed my eyes for a second," he said.

"It was more like ten fucking minutes." Ted winced at her tone and looked away. She immediately regretted snapping at him. "I'm sorry," she said. "That was uncalled for."

Ted brushed it off and cleared his throat. "Tell me what happened."

"They just disappeared," she whispered. Susan had a habit of whispering anything she deemed secretive. It didn't matter if they were alone in a locked room, if she thought a comment would make her sound silly, or crazy, she'd whisper it, as if by doing so would negate the effect. "They were there, they were getting closer, and then they just winked off."

"That doesn't make any sense," he grumbled.

"I didn't say it made sense," Susan retorted, "I'm telling you what happened. They were there one minute, and then *poof*!"

"*Poof*? You don't say?"

"Oh, piss on you Ted," she hissed. "Don't make fun of me."

"No," Ted giggled, "*poof* is fine." He hung his head and chuckled.

"Asshole," she muttered.

"What do you want me to say?" he asked. "Maybe they couldn't find us, or they're going to call for help."

"Or maybe they won't be back at all."

"You're really being a Debbie Downer, you know that?"

"A fucking Debbie Downer? Are you kidding me? We're trapped in a wrecked car, in the woods, in the rain, at night, and no one knows we're here. If my legs weren't pinned beneath the dash, I'd be doing fucking cartwheels."

"Now you're just being a bitch."

"I'm being a what? I'm being a *bitch*?"

"Listen, I'm sorry, okay? I expected to be sitting in our cabin with our feet up and a chilled bottle of wine next to the bed."

"I'm sorry too," Susan said. "I don't want to fight with you."

"Tell me one more time," Ted said, turning toward his wife.

"There's nothing to tell. One minute they were getting closer, and then they were gone. I heard their voices, Ted, and when the lights disappeared, the voices went with them. Like they'd never been there."

"But I heard them crunching through the brush."

"So did I," she nodded.

"Maybe it's some rednecks fucking with us."

"For God's sake," Susan exclaimed. "Are you serious? You have a hell of a way of soothing my nerves."

"I'm just thinking out loud."

"Well stop it!"

They sat in silence, listening to the rain beat on the roof. Ted's right leg was beginning to go numb. He knew if they didn't get out of this car by morning, the chances of walking away unscathed dwindled rapidly. The dash was cutting off blood flow below the knees. He shook his foot and couldn't feel his toes.

"I think we should try to get some sleep," he said. "We're not going to figure this out if we're exhausted."

Susan nodded and patted his thigh. "It's a little after three," she said, glancing at her watch. "The sun should be up in a few hours."

"Set your alarm," he said. "We should be up by six or seven."

Susan pressed a few buttons and set the alarm on her wristwatch. She couldn't wait for daylight. It may still be raining and overcast, but even gray light was better than none.

"Maybe it was some luminescent gas or something," she said. "You know? Like swamp gas? People are always reporting lights in the swamp."

"We're not in the swamp," Ted said. "Just get some rest. No point wracking your brain over it."

Susan closed her eyes and fell asleep at once. The drive, the crash, the adrenaline. She didn't realize how tired she was.

Ted listened to her quiet snores as he continued trying to free his leg from the crumpled steel beneath the dash. He twisted his ankle painfully and heard his jeans tear on a jagged piece of metal. Instantly, he was able to move his leg. Not much, but enough to give him hope and get the blood flowing again. He clenched his fists as the numbness turned to pins and needles, the blood-deprived nerves screaming as they woke.

Ted smiled through the pain. It meant he was alive. One step closer to getting the hell out of here.

***

Ted dreamed of their first weekend at Pine Lakes.

They'd only been dating for a short time, but Susan agreed to go along. She wasn't big on nature and was even less thrilled with the idea of leaving modern amenities behind. Her parents weren't campers and Susan had become a product of her time. That first weekend changed everything. The quiet rippling of the water on the lake, the soft sigh of the leaves in the trees, air so clean she felt as if she was experiencing it for the first time.

The sun felt brighter, warmer; food tasted richer; the sex was absolutely primal.

The resort wasn't the first time they'd made love, but it *was* the first time one of them didn't have to get up and sneak past sleeping parents. They stayed in bed that first day until after noon, naked, basking in the freedom of seeing and feeling one another in a whole new way. Susan didn't want to leave. Pine Lakes had worked its magic, a magic that hadn't faded in twenty years.

Ted was still envisioning that first vacation with his wife when he felt himself being shaken by a persistent hand. He wanted to retreat into the safety and warmth of his memory, but the shreds of his dream tore apart like smoke in the wind. He opened his eyes sleepily and yawned. His head pounded. It was the same feeling he had after a night of heavy drinking with friends, but this wasn't a hangover, this was his battered body's way of telling him to shit or get off the pot.

"Get up," Susan said, shaking him steadily. "Come on, get your ass up, we slept through the alarm."

"Slept through it?" Ted muttered. "It's still pitch black out here."

"Yes, Captain Obvious, I see that." She held her arm up so Ted could see the display on her wristwatch: 8:14 a.m.

"After eight? That can't be right." He rubbed his eyes and peered into the forest. Thick fog had settled in the valley, a swirling white wall that enveloped the Barracuda and danced around the black trunks of tall pine trees.

A distant wail cut through the mist and froze the blood in Ted's veins. He held his breath, waiting for the sound to be repeated.

"What in God's name was that?" he asked.

"That's the third time I heard it," Susan said. Her voice trembled. "Why isn't it light, Ted? Why? It's after eight. The sky should be bright, the birds should be chirping."

"I don't know," he said. "Your watch is obviously wrong."

"Why do you have to rationalize everything?" Susan shouted. "Something strange is going on and you know it."

"All I know for sure is that I have to piss like a racehorse," he groaned.

"Could you please not minimize this?"

"I'm not minimizing anything," he said. "We saw a few lights and heard a dog howling. It's not time to call *The Enquirer*."

"A howling dog? *That's* what you think it was? I've never heard a dog sound like that in my life."

"A wild dog."

"You're ridiculous. It wasn't a dog."

The shriek came again, and even Ted had to admit it wasn't a dog. He'd never heard something quite like it. It began like the deep hum of a distant foghorn and quickly rose in pitch, becoming a blood-curdling scream that tapered off to nothing. Through the mist, Ted was positive he heard faint laughter, but he kept it to himself. He gripped the steering wheel and held on tight. Susan blew a whistling breath through her teeth, eyes darting from shadow to shadow.

"There," she whispered. Susan pointed through the broken windshield at a faint point of light twenty yards away. It grew brighter as they watched it rise from the forest floor, weaving through the branches, casting a dim glow on the rotting bark of a dying elm tree. The strange light created a dim halo of bluish-white light that illuminated patches of the surrounding trees. Susan gasped as several pairs of glowing orange eyes opened and watched them from the canopy. The eyes were moving, blinking. She covered her mouth with both hands and whined deep in her throat, watching as the sets of eyes were joined by others.

"Jesus Christ," Ted said. "What the hell is that?"

The same strange moaning howl broke the silence yet again, this time much closer. The ball of light reacted to the sound, first growing in intensity and then fading as the scream ebbed to nothing. The sets of glowing eyes watched them, getting lower as they descended through the trees. Susan started crying and yanking at her legs in an attempt to free herself. Ted reached out and grabbed her arm and Susan responded by slapping at his hand fearfully. She whirled on him and raised a hand to ward off her attacker, pulling her punch at the last second. Ted shook his head side-to-side and raised his index finger in front of his lips. Susan choked back a sob and closed her eyes, trying to gain comfort from Ted's touch.

The glowing eyes were coming closer, surrounding the wrecked car as the ball of light was joined by another. Susan closed her eyes and muttered, refusing to believe what she seeing. She and Ted heard the soft crunch of dead leaves as the shapes approached. A branch snapped loudly ten feet in front of the car and Susan gasped, grabbing Ted's hand painfully. Her palm was slicked with sweat, her skin hot.

Ted watched as one of the shapes stopped at the Cuda's crushed bumper and sniffed at the pool of anti-freeze that had leaked from the ruined engine. Loud, wet snuffling came from outside Susan's door as two large, glowing eyes peered in at them through the passenger window. The balls of light dimmed as the strange, warbling moan began again. A second moan joined the first, creating a haunting harmony like two ships calling to one another in a fog bank. The lights brightened at the call's apex and dimmed as the cry faded.

Ted's mind raced, flooded with stimuli it couldn't process. One of the shadows uttered a short yip and bounded into the forest as another growled deeply, brushing against the car with a thumping hiss.

"What are they?" Susan cried. "Oh my God, what are they, Ted?"

"I don't know," he whispered. "Just stay quiet."

She buried her face in her arm and wiped snot on the soft fabric of the sweatshirt. Her body thrummed with terrified energy as the shapes surrounded the car in an ever-tightening circle like sharks around an injured seal. Suddenly, the fog came alive with blue light and Ted squeezed his eyes shut against the glare. The *things* surrounding the vehicle cried out in irritation as their cover of darkness vanished. The haunting bray echoed across the forest floor as the woods glowed with an ethereal light. Ted listened as the creatures scrambled in the dead leaves, crunching away into the forest as they screamed their displeasure at being interrupted.

Ted opened his eyes as the light slowly dimmed. He watched transfixed as the two balls of light descended to the forest floor. He gasped and held a hand over his mouth as he saw the newest arrivals crowding the woods. Through the fog were dozens of figures, human shapes, silhouettes of all sizes, standing in groups and separately by the gnarled trunks of old growth. They didn't approach, they simply *watched*.

The balls of light winked out, plunging the forest into darkness once again. Susan lifted her head and squinted into the gloom, wiping tears from her eyes and exhaling a shaky breath. The forest had gone back to its unnatural blackness. Susan hadn't seen the human figures, and for that, Ted was thankful. He had an empty feeling in the pit of his stomach; for nearly twenty years, he had protected Susan as much as he could from what life had to throw at them, but this was entirely different. How could he protect her from something he didn't understand?

Ted pried his hand from hers, shaking out the pain that crept into his fingers from Susan's grip.

What the hell is going on?

"What were they?" Susan asked. "What in God's name just happened?"

"I don't have a clue," Ted replied, "but now we know we're not alone."

3

Four months after the miscarriage, Ted and Susan stood outside the large display window of the Elmview Mall's only pet store. The plan had started as dinner and a movie, but Susan had gotten sidetracked by a Yorkie in the window and couldn't stop watching as it rolled around playfully in scraps of cut newspaper. The puppy stared up at her, barked, licked the glass when she placed her palm against it, wagging its tail frantically and stepping in its water bowl without notice. He put on a show for smiling spectators without without even realizing it, hamming it up as they passed.

"He's gorgeous," Susan said, tapping the window glass as the Yorkie yipped at her.

"Certainly knows how to get attention," Ted laughed.

"Maybe we should take him home," she said.

"Just what we need," Ted laughed, "cold puddles of piss to dodge in the dark."

"Dogs are smart," she said. "They learn fast."

"You're serious?"

"Sure, why not?"

"Suzie, when the hell do we have time to house train a puppy?"

"I have all the time in the world," she said. She turned and Ted withered beneath her glare. He knew this wasn't going to wind up being the fun day out he'd hoped for.

"I'm always at work," he said, "when would I even see him?"

"I'm just saying. I'm home all day, by myself, it would be nice to have something to keep me company. Something to take care of."

"Do you think that's what we need right now? Dogs are a lot of work."

"You think I don't know that?" she hissed. A passing couple looked at her with raised eyebrows, snickering at one another. "Look, the perfect couple," she shouted. "They never argue because their minds are too empty to have opinions."

"Okay, let's dial it down," Ted said. "We don't need to cause a scene in the middle of the mall. Let's just get dinner and we can go home early, have a glass of wine, relax."

"That's your answer, isn't it? Just stay numb all the time and not have to deal with *anything*."

"I'm not going to fight with you Susan," Ted huffed. "If you want to go, let's go."

Susan turned back to the puppy as it curled up in its bed and looked up at her with sad eyes. Even he felt the moment slipping away. She tapped the window with her fingernail, but the puppy closed its eyes and turned away. She watched his tail wag twice and go still. Just another living creature she'd disappointed.

"I want to go home," she said.

"Suzie," Ted comforted, "if you want to talk about getting a puppy, we can." He tried to hug her, but she pulled away.

"What's the point? I'd probably just kill the fucking thing."

"Sue, let's not do this now, huh?"

"Do what?" she shouted. "I see how you look at me. Like I'm a strange new bug on the windshield. I had one job to do, and I failed."

"You didn't fail at anything," he said.

"Didn't I? It's like a door slammed in my face, and you and my parents were on the other side wondering what I'd done wrong?"

"No one thinks that, for Christ's sake, Susan, don't you think we've all suffered?" He looked around, feeling eyes on them. Judging them.

"I gave you a gift and fed it to the wolves," she cried. "I can't do this, I need to leave."

Ted tried touching her, consoling her, telling her he didn't blame her for anything. Then it hit him: today would have been their child's due date. Instead, it was a birthday that had gone unrecorded, a date to be forgotten and avoided rather than celebrated.

They left the pet store behind; Susan glanced back one last time and saw the Yorkie jump to life as a little girl squealed in delight, begging daddy to give the little guy a happy home. Tears streamed down Susan's face as she staggered drunkenly to a bench and collapsed, her entire body shaking as she wept openly. She forgot where she was. The mall melted away as she receded into the dark shroud of her own misery. She didn't feel Ted's soothing hands, didn't hear his pained assurances or urgings to get her home. All she heard was the drone of her inadequacy and the hollow thud of her dreams falling to the ground and being trampled by heavy feet.

Susan had no concept of passing time. She felt Ted grab her arm and lead her away from the Christmas muzak that tinkled from the mall's overhead speakers. Through the blur of her tears, she saw people pass, strangers watching her through masks of false concern. She buried her face in Ted's shoulder and let him carry her away. She lost herself in his warmth, in his scent, in his familiarity.

What felt like seconds later, Ted's strong arms lowered her to the bed and removed her shoes. She was all cried out. Exhausted. He kissed her tenderly between the eyes and pulled the blanket up to her chin. She reached out and held his hand, offering a smile so slight it was almost indiscernible.

"I know baby," he said. "I know."

Ted closed the bedroom door, flicked off the light, and crawled into bed next to her without a word. The sun set on another day.

When she awoke, the bedroom was ablaze with early morning sun. She felt pressure on her chest and opened her eyes to a tiny, fuzzy face looking back at her. Before she could sit up, the Yorkie puppy leapt forward and jammed its tongue in her eye, covering her face in kisses with the smallest tongue she'd ever seen. She reached out to push him away as he latched onto her shirt sleeve and tugged playfully. A second later, he was back to wildly licking her cheek and ear, pouncing on her chest, nibbling at her hair with sharp little puppy teeth.

"Get away, get away," she shouted gleefully. The child inside her awoke with a roar. Her heart swelled as the Yorkie's tail flitted back and forth in a blur, vibrating more than wagging. The puppy rolled over on the blanket and wiggled around on its back, miniature legs pumping in the air. "I know you," Susan squealed.

"He wanted to come home," Ted said from the doorway.

Startled, she sat up in bed as the puppy barked shrilly. Ted entered the room and sat on the edge of the bed as the puppy jumped up on his back, trying to sink its teeth into the brim of his baseball cap. When he couldn't reach, he settled with nibbling on the skin of Ted's arm instead.

"You went back to the pet store," she said, smiling. "Ted, you didn't have to."

"I saw how you looked at him. Besides, I wasn't going to let that little girl have him."

"I thought she would take him home for sure." Susan reached out a hand and let the puppy nibble on her fingers. She was in love with him immediately.

"If she was there, I was prepared for a fight," Ted said.

"Her father was a big man," Susan laughed.

"Not him. *Her.* I'm not above knocking a little girl on her ass."

Susan laughed warmly and swatted his arm.

"You're going to smack a little girl around?"

"In a heartbeat. If she was there, she was going down." They laughed together as the puppy watched them, its head cocked to the side. "So what are you going to name him?"

"Ringo," she said without hesitation. Ringo was her favorite Beatle, a fact Ted teased her about frequently.

"Not Sir Paul?"

Susan shook her head as the puppy flopped down on the bedspread. It watched them with bright eyes that slowly closed, sighed contentedly, and curled up in the blanket.

"Definitely Ringo," she said. Her bottom lip quivered as she looked at Ted. A part of her she thought was missing or damaged beyond repair clicked back into place, heavily tarnished but intact. "Thank you," she said. "For everything."

Ted smiled and caressed the smooth skin of her cheek. She rested her head in his hand and sighed.

"I'm going to make breakfast," he said. "Why don't you keep Ringo company and I'll bring it in when I'm done."

She scratched Ringo's head as Ted crossed the room. He turned around in the doorway and smiled; he always thought she was the most beautiful when she was just waking up; her eyes were still half closed, her hair a nest of knots and tangles.

"We're going to be okay," she said.

"We're going to be just fine," he assured her.

Ted turned and shut the door behind him. Ringo sprang up and barked twice, his tail twitching. He walked to the edge of the bed, looked at Susan, and pissed on the mattress. A second later he returned to his warm spot on the bed and curled up next to Susan's leg. She shook her head and smiled. Ted was right, a puppy was a lot of work, but she was ready for the challenge.

***

"I hope Ringo's okay," Susan said quietly. They'd remained perfectly still and silent since the lights faded and the forest went back to sleep.

"I'm sure he's fine," Ted said. "Lauren is checking in on him twice a day." Lauren was their neighbor. One of the sane ones.

"I know, but I worry." She looked at her watch and pressed a button. Her face lit with a soft blue glow, and in the gloom Ted saw her brow wrinkle with confusion.

"What time is it?"

"According to this, it's a little after noon."

"More like midnight," he muttered. "We have to get out of these woods, Suzie. Something's not right here."

"Not right? You've just won the prize for understatement of the year."

"Well, the good news is that soon our parents will wonder why we didn't check in," Ted said.

"Not mine," she replied. "Their flight for Pensacola leaves soon. I'm sure they're busy with last-minute preparations. You know how my father is."

Ted mumbled something under his breath and nodded slowly. He'd forgotten his in-laws were beginning a week of food and fun in sunny Florida. "What do you think those things are?" he asked, changing the subject.

Susan shook her head and patted her thigh nervously. "I don't have the slightest clue. A dog pack?"

"All dog's eyes glow like that? Did they climb the trees with flashlights too?"

"Ted, you asked a question, and I answered. If I knew what was going on, you'd be the first to know."

"Tonight on Unsolved Mysteries," Ted said in his best Robert Stack impersonation.

"Your Stack sounds like Telly Savalas."

"You're a harsh critic."

Susan giggled and reached for his hand in the dark just as a light appeared deep in the forest. She squeezed tightly and shivered as goosebumps crawled over her flesh. Her laughter died in her throat.

"Ted?"

"I see it," he whispered.

The ball of light was near the ground, moving east to west, disappearing behind the trees and reappearing seconds later. Although its arrival had always been heralded by the strange siren and the appearance of the creatures, this time it was alone, casting a dim glow in the tangled brush. Ted felt Susan's hand tremble, and he squeezed it reassuringly. The balls of light didn't give him the same, all-consuming feeling of dread the other creatures did, but still, they were wholly unnatural.

A branch snapped outside Susan's window with a loud crack. She turned just in time to see a pair of glowing eyes approaching the car. A haunting howl broke the silence as it turned and crunched back into the forest.

"I think they're *afraid* of the light," Susan said.

The forest came alive with a chorus of howls, wails, and yips, like a distant pack of coyotes on the hunt. The ball of light grew brighter, and the sounds ceased, leaving only echoes behind. Something heavy slammed into the front of the wrecked car and Susan screamed as the Cuda rocked on its springs. It collided with the vehicle a second time and Ted felt the car move back a few feet. The remaining headlight smashed with an explosive tinkling of glass. What the hell was large enough to move a three thousand pound vehicle through the soft ground of the forest floor on flattened tires?

"Make it stop, make it stop, make it…"

Susan's terrified rambling was cut short by a loud squeal of static from the Cuda's dead radio. Ted flinched as if he'd been struck, reaching out and turning the volume knob. The crackly warble of faraway signals tripped over one another, creating a muddled, obnoxious series of voices and musical passages. Susan covered her ears and moaned.

A snippet of 'Seize The Day' by Avenged Sevenfold.

A snippet of 'Stairway To Heaven' by Led Zeppelin.

An announcer calling plays on a Red Sox game.

A verse of Uriah Heep's 'The Wizard' followed by Deep Purple's 'Perfect Strangers.'

A commercial for Wal-Mart and Anderson Windows.

"Turn it off," Susan shouted.

"I can't, it won't go off," Ted replied.

A passage from 'The Devil Went Down To Georgia.'

The chorus of 'Turn It On Again' by Genesis.

'Hotel California.' 'Hell Is For Children.' 'Highway To Hell.'

Ted grimaced at the theme and pounded on the stereo, but couldn't make the grating, persistent noise go away. He never hated classic rock until that moment. He looked through the broken windshield at the small point of light hovering a hundred yards away. If anything had crept up to the car, they'd never hear it, never know it was there. The radio drowned out all other sound.

Suddenly, the constant barrage of noise settled, and a voice spoke through a wall of static. A deep, chilling, monotone voice.

"Zero, two, one, five, one, nine, eight, one," the voice droned. "Zero, six, zero, five, two, zero, one, seven."

"What the fuck is that?" Susan cried.

The series of numbers repeated, then a third time before a loud crack of static ended the transmission.

"I feel like I'm in an episode of *Lost*," Ted said, laughing nervously.

"Zero, eight, one, four, one, nine, eight, one," the voice drawled. "Zero, six, zero, five, two, zero, one, seven." Again the series of numbers repeated twice more before the radio went silent.

The distant ball of light flickered and disappeared. The cracked display on the stereo went black. Thunder rumbled, and the sky opened; fat drops of rain hammered the car like handfuls of thrown ball bearings. Susan held her head in her hands and cried steadily, her body hitching with painful sobs.

"What were those numbers?" she moaned. "What the hell did they mean?"

Ted didn't reply. Just like the balls of light, just like the creatures that stalked them and the *thing* that hit the car, the radio numbers were a mystery. It sounded like gibberish. The string of digits repeated over and over in his head until they bled together. Why were they so familiar?

Ted sucked in a breath and held it. "Oh. Oh shit."

"What? Oh shit *what?*" Susan shouted over the rain.

"The numbers. I know what they are."

"What? Tell me goddammit!"

"Zero, two, one, five, one, nine, eight, one," he repeated. "February 15, 1981. My birthday."

"Your birthday? I don't understand."

"The second set is today's date."

"Who fucking cares, Ted? We have to get out of here, now!"

"August 14, 1981," he said. "Your birthday and today's date."

"You're not making sense," she shouted. "What is that supposed to mean?"

"I'm not sure," he said. "I guess it could be anything. A coincidence?"

Susan went back to crying, staring out the passenger window into nothing. "Then forget about it and help me," she said, tugging on her legs. "We're leaving. Somehow."

Ted nodded and agreed to help. Susan was right. Escaping this wretched place was now their top priority.

***

"Why do you watch this crap?" Susan asked.

Ted sat on the couch with Ringo curled up next to him. Instead of spending the day in the garage working on the Barracuda, he opted for a quiet, lazy day with popcorn and Netflix. He watched little television these days, but when he did, he binged. Today was all about *Twin Peaks* and the mystery surrounding Laura Palmer. He was barely ten years old when the show wrapped production and his parents weren't much into the *spooky* stuff as his mother was wont to say. Going back to that town was like getting a second chance to be a kid again.

"This is not crap, my dear," Ted said, wiping butter from his fingers. "This is genre-defining television."

"Genre-defining crap," she laughed.

Susan plopped on the couch next to him and dug her fingers into his bowl of Jiffy Pop. She sipped from his bottle of Yuengling Lager and belched loudly. Ringo looked up at her sleepily and buried his head beneath the blanket.

"You, ma'am, are no lady," Ted said.

"If you wanted a lady, you wouldn't have married me."

"Smart *and* beautiful," he quipped.

"What's this about anyway?" she asked.

"Who killed Laura Palmer?"

"So it's a murder-mystery?"

"It's not that simple. See that guy?" he pointed. "That's special agent Dale Cooper. He came to the town of Twin Peaks to investigate the murder of a popular high school student."

"I know him! That's the guy from *Desperate Housewives.*"

"And you call my shows crap?" Susan tossed a piece of popcorn at him playfully and Ringo miraculously woke from his slumber to make it disappear. "Oh there, that's the Log Lady."

"The what now?"

"The Log Lady. She gets psychic visions from the log she carries with her."

Susan laughed at the absurdity of it, thinking Ted was pulling her leg. "Oh God, you're serious?"

"Absolutely. She plays a big part in the investigation."

"She has talking wood?"

"I'll have talking wood too if you show me *your* twin peaks."

"Oh my *God*," she laughed. "You think that's clever don't you?"

"I do," he said, cramming a handful of popcorn in his mouth.

"You're a barbarian," she giggled. "Oh, I know that guy," she pointed.

"That's Laura Palmer's father," Ted said.

"He doesn't have a talking, psychic log?"

"Not that I know of," Ted laughed. "You want to watch with me?"

"Sure, why the hell not? I can use some mindless entertainment."

They sat on the couch for twelve hours, only pausing briefly for snacks and walking Ringo in the yard. When they finished, they noticed it was after three in the morning and they'd downed two six packs of beer. They turned off the television, took Ringo out to do his business, and put him in his pen. Susan didn't like having to lock Ringo up over night, but the dog was as stubborn as they come. Even a year later, he still lifted his leg on the furniture when he thought no one was looking. Caging him had been the catalyst for several arguments between them, but Ted got his way in the end.

They slipped into bed, tired and buzzing from the alcohol. Ringo circled in his bed a few times and plopped down with a sigh. Ted had relented, allowing Ringo to sleep in the room with them since he couldn't sleep in bed. It was a compromise he was willing to make.

"So when can we watch more?" Susan asked as she nestled beneath the covers.

"Next time I'm off, if you want. I guess you don't think it's stupid anymore?" he said.

"It's okay," she conceded.

Ted listened to Susan rustle around beneath the covers and closed his eyes. He felt her warm hands on his chest and his eyes popped open. "What are you up to?"

"What was that you said about my twin peaks?" She straddled him and kissed him lightly on the lips. "Something about your wood?" She reached down between them and rubbed his crotch through the thin fabric of his pajama bottoms. "Oh, yep, there it is."

"I see," Ted said. "Now you're coming to the dark side."

"Be quiet and kiss my face," she said, grabbing his cheeks and licking his lips playfully.

They made love until the sky brightened and slept until noon. By then Ringo was tap dancing on the plastic mat beneath his pen.

All in all, it was a good day.

Hopefully, the beginning of many.

***

Ted was so focused on freeing Susan's legs from under the dash, he didn't realize the numbness in his own legs had subsided, replaced with pins and needles as blood flowed into his toes. He wiggled his feet and groaned as pain shot from his ankles to his knees. He didn't think anything was broken.

"Suzie," he said, "I think I can get out."

"Well then get out," she shouted. "What are you waiting for?"

"Calm down, baby," he soothed. "This miserable experience is almost over. We'll be eating breakfast tomorrow morning and laughing about this."

"I don't know about laughing," Susan said, "but I'll certainly have a smile on my face."

Ted wriggled around and grunted with exertion as he tugged on his left leg, feeling it pop free from the wreckage beneath the dash. He rubbed life back into his thigh as he worked on freeing the other leg. There was movement, but it still felt tightly wedged against the firewall. When the leg suddenly pulled free, Ted gasped and started laughing as he worked the kinks out of his ankles and knees.

"I got it!" he exclaimed. "I never thought I'd be so happy to feel pain."

"Get your happy ass over here and get me out," Susan said. "The sooner the better."

Ted pushed on his door but it wouldn't budge; the impact had twisted the Cuda's body significantly. Instead, Ted elbowed the fractured window and felt it give as rainwater trickled in from outside. One more heavy blow and the window buckled and fell to the ground. The muffled thunder and steady rain suddenly felt closer, more alive. Water dribbled through the opening, soaking his clothes and chilling him instantly. For a summer night it was downright frigid; his breath escaped in white clouds as he struggled to crawl through the tight hole.

Ted tumbled to the damp leaves of the forest floor, lying still as rain spattered his face. He rubbed his hands over his legs to make sure they were in one piece, wincing only once at a deep gash in his right calf. The blood had dried on his jeans in a large, tacky patch.

"What's going on?" Susan called from inside. "Are you okay?"

"I'm great," he yelled, "better than great to be honest."

He stood next to the car and stretched, his back crackling. There was just enough light to see the mangled wreck. He exhaled deeply and shook his head. They were lucky to be alive, but the Cuda would never hit the open road again; ten years of his life sitting crushed and broken in the muddy ground. If not for the fact that he'd been freed from his steel prison, he'd likely be weeping over the hunk of battered metal.

"Get me out of here," Susan called. "I have to pee, seriously."

Ted chuckled and rounded the car as the rain plastered his shirt to his skin. The trunk of the vehicle had popped open in the crash and dumped the contents onto the forest floor like discarded trash. He made a mental note to check for the flashlights and rain gear as soon as he freed Susan from the wreck.

Prepared for a fight, Ted tugged on the passenger door handle and fell back into the mud as it opened without resistance. Susan reached her arms outside and flailed her hands at him, feeling the rain drip from her skin.

"Get up, get up," she said. "I'm going to piss my pants if you don't get me out of here."

"Your knight in shining armor is on his way," Ted joked.

"Where is he? All I see is you playing in the mud."

He laughed and stood, pushing the door open further as Susan slid around in her seat. Her right leg was already free; she waggled her ankle and hissed at the soreness that had crept into her joint.

"I feel like I've been sitting here for years," she said.

"We're almost out of here, babe. One more tug and we'll be on our way."

"Less talking, more tugging." Ted felt around in the dark interior of the car and made sure Susan wasn't injured. He grazed her breast, and she slapped his hand away playfully. "Now is not the time for twin peaks," she groaned.

"Is that what you think of me?" Ted laughed. "That I'd take advantage of a woman in distress?"

Susan watched the dark forest behind him, waiting for the slightest sign of movement. The only sound was of the rain and the chill breeze rustling through the trees. What if the entire thing was hallucinatory? What if this miserable experience could be chalked up to fear and trauma? For their sake, she was perfectly fine to have imagined the things going bump in the night.

"Okay," Ted sighed. "There's only one way to do this, and I don't know if it will hurt, but we don't have many options."

"I hold my breath and you pull as hard as you can?"

"Exactly!"

Susan did just that as Ted wrapped his strong arms around her waist and planted his feet firmly in the mud. Before he had a chance to pull, a branch snapped behind him and he froze. It was hard to tell where it had come from, but it was close.

"Jesus Christ," Susan muttered.

A loud, wet snarl grumbled from nearby and Ted's blood ran cold. The rain had given the creature an advantage, allowing it to sneak up on him without being heard until it was too late. Ted turned and squinted into the darkness, knowing it was too late to escape the jaws of whatever lurked in the brush just beyond his field of vision.

Without further hesitation, Ted slammed the passenger door with a loud thunk and scrambled in the slick mud. He rounded the front of the car and slipped onto his side, falling into the slimy leaves with a grunt as the wind exploded from his lungs. He heard the wet patter of approaching feet buried beneath Susan's shrill screams as he waited to come face to face with whatever stalked them. Ted saw its silhouette lumbering ever closer; heard its wet breathing and smelled the awful, sour stink wafting off it in waves. Its eyes opened, large yellow globes watching his every move.

Ted slid backward in the muck, using the Cuda's twisted bumper as a handhold. The rain had made it too slick for it to be an effective grip. He slid a few inches further as the beast hovered over his chest, exhaling reeking bursts of rotting meat. Ted gaped at its size. It stood on four legs the size of traffic cones, its shoulders easily three feet across as it hunched over him. It reminded him of one of those damn wolves from *Game of Thrones*, those massive bastards the size of ponies. If it was going to sink its teeth into him, at least it would be a quick death.

Ted listened as Susan screamed his name from inside the car; the Cuda rocked with her exertion as she tried to free herself.

"Suzie, stay in the car," he bellowed. The creature growled deeply, sounding like garbled, sinister laughter. "Don't come out here. Please, stay in the car," he cried.

Giant teeth wrapped around his shoe like a bear trap, tugging harshly. Ted shouted into the rainy sky and swung his arms frantically, trying to hit the beast with his closed fists, but it was out of his reach. He gripped the front of the car with both hands as he was violently shaken.

His hands slipped on the wet bumper as the beast dragged him several feet through the wet leaves. He looked up at the passenger window and saw Susan's terror-stricken face plastered to the glass. He saw her at prom in a gorgeous plum-colored dress, her hair spilling over her shoulders, her smile shy and guarded. As the beast's hot muzzle nudged his arm, he held onto the first time he and Susan had touched, the first soft caress in the dim light of the school auditorium. He reached out to her as she put her hand to the window, crying his name with heartbreaking clarity.

The monster clamped harder on his thin sneaker and began pulling him away from the wreck. Susan's cries faded as the Cuda was swallowed in darkness. Ted dug his hands into the soggy ground, tearing the skin from his fingers as he grabbed blindly at sharp rocks. He reached out and grabbed the slick, gnarled bark of a tree, only to have his fingernails ripped painfully from their beds. He screamed, he cried, he cursed his captor and invoked the name of God, but in the end he was only pulled faster and faster into the forest, his nose full of the scents of wet earth and musky rot.

He heard a final cry from Susan just as he blacked out.

At least he wouldn't suffer.

4

Susan sat alone in the wrecked car, shaking uncontrollably. Her head pounded from crying and her sinuses were clogged. Snot ran from her nose, but she was too terrified to wipe it away. She watched her husband get dragged into the woods, kicking and screaming and calling her name, and she was powerless to help. Once his cries dwindled away, she was left utterly alone with only her imagination to fill in the blanks. Anyone who said an imagination was a wonderful thing was full of shit.

For several minutes, she screamed Ted's name until her voice was nothing more than a raspy cackle. Her throat was sore, her eyes burned, her heart was broken. The steady rain hammering on the roof of the car wasn't nearly enough to drown out her own thoughts. For a while, she tried to free her other leg from under the dashboard, but gave up after a few futile attempts. Freedom be damned. Did she want to escape this nightmare without Ted at her side? She hadn't known anything else since she was seventeen years old.

Susan leaned back in her seat as her cries ebbed to soft sobs. She was utterly exhausted. The pain in her bladder faded. Fat drops of rain landed on Ted's vacant seat and created a small puddle where he'd been sitting only minutes earlier. Lightning lit the surrounding forest in a series of bright strobes as Susan's eyes grew heavy. She welcomed sleep, relished the idea of just slipping away.

When she heard whispering, her eyes shot open, and she sat up, gripping the dash and staring through the broken windshield. The whispers came from every direction at once, louder than the rain and the constant thunder rolling across the sky. That's when she noticed them standing around the broken Cuda, a circle of human silhouettes of varying sizes and shapes. They approached the car and their whispers grew louder, but still she couldn't make out any words in the din.

The shapes were featureless. Even in the brightest flashes of light, they were nothing more than blurry shadows. No clothes. No faces. Her overtaxed brain no longer thought in terms of reality and fiction. The whispers became a steady drone; the drone became a chorus of melodic vocalizations. She watched them tighten the circle around the car, expecting them to start singing campfire songs, holding hands and swaying to some cosmic rhythm. One of the figures stood only two feet from her window, close enough for her to make out its fingers and toes. Her assumption had been correct; the visitor had no face, just a blank wall of flesh on a perfectly oval-shaped head. No hair, no ears, nothing.

Susan couldn't move. She didn't *want* to move. The interior of the car grew warm, and the windows fogged over, blocking her vision of the approaching shadows. It was a pleasant heat, a Sunday afternoon nestled beneath the covers with Ted. She was once again bulldozed by thoughts of living without him. The fear of what watched her from outside the car was replaced by the fear of being alone. Still the musical whispers grew in volume as the rain intensified, lulling her deeper and deeper into her own personal darkness, to a place where this was nothing more than a vivid dream.

Her eyes grew heavy and her head dipped, her chin resting on her chest. Susan's skin tingled from the strange heat as she drifted away. When the forest came alive with the wolves' angry howls, she barely noticed. She only wondered if one of those monsters was the one that had dragged Ted kicking and screaming into the forest. Was it still hungry? Was its muzzle still dripping with his fresh blood?

Sleeeeep, a voice hissed.

Susan could no longer fight. Sleep claimed her.

***

Susan sat on the couch surrounded by crumpled tissues. Ringo laid nearby, snoring contentedly. It was getting darker outside and still Ted hadn't come home. She was beginning to think he might not return. She'd said some pretty awful things, but goddammit, so did he. Susan wasn't going to shoulder the blame, not this time. She pulled another tissue from the box and blew her nose loudly, making Ringo jump up, startled, growling at the corners of the room.

"It's only me you stupid dog," she said. Ringo licked her hand and plopped back down, satisfied that he'd protected her from whatever made those harsh snorts.

The day had started out fine. Ted tinkered in the garage, attaching the new grill to the Cuda. He'd picked it up on eBay for a song and had been looking forward to the weekend for a chance to install it, the last piece he needed for the car's front end. Susan made them a light breakfast and figured she'd have a chance to catch up on laundry, maybe finally get to open the new Bentley Little novel she'd been dying to read.

As she sat down, Ted stormed in from the garage, his face dark and angry. She'd seen him this way a hundred times, especially when working on the car. If something didn't go exactly as planned, Ted took it as a personal affront. Susan figured the stress of that damn car had likely taken ten years off his life by now. He didn't say a word as he passed through the room and into the kitchen where he grabbed a can of beer from the refrigerator. He slurped it loudly, grumbling under his breath, slamming the refrigerator door with a rattle.

Susan joined him in the kitchen, preparing something cute and witty to break him from his anger, but the words caught in her throat when he looked up with glaring eyes. He wasn't in the mood for cute and witty, so instead she simply raised her eyebrows in a silent query.

"Were you in the garage?" he asked. "Like yesterday or today?"

"Yeah, I put a box out there yesterday for the clothing drive. Why?"

"Did you bump into the car? Maybe scrape the box against it?"

"No, not that I know. Will you just tell me what's bugging you?"

"What's bugging me is a fucking scratch on the driver's door," he said angrily. "That paint job cost me a fortune."

"Well it wasn't me," she shouted. "I didn't go anywhere near the damn car. I dropped the box by the door and came back inside."

"Someone sure as shit scratched it," he said, "and it wasn't me. I guess that only leaves you."

"For Christ's sake, Ted, it could have happened at any time. You don't have to come in here throwing around accusations."

"I'm not accusing you, Susan, I'm *telling* you. It had to be you. Did you bring that dumb dog with you? Maybe he jumped up and scratched it. It's not like you ever watch what he's doing."

"That's not fair," she yelled. "When do you ever watch him? He's your dog too."

"I bought him for you, or did you forget that? I told you he'd be a hassle, and you didn't want to listen."

"You bought him for us. Don't put the responsibility all on me."

As if called, Ringo trotted into the kitchen and stared up at them quizzically. His tail wagged sporadically, unsure if the shouting meant it was time to play or time to hide. He jumped up on Susan's leg but she brushed him aside. He tried his luck with Ted, instead, which turned out to be a mistake.

Ted kicked at the terrier and connected squarely with his hindquarters, sending him sliding across the waxed linoleum with a shrill yip. Scared, Ringo looked up at him, ears laid back, tail tucked between his legs. He scampered from the kitchen and hid beneath the dining room table.

"You asshole," she screamed. "You're going to take your anger out on the dog? Like he has any idea why you're upset."

"Maybe it'll keep him the fuck away from me and away from my car. Either keep an eye on your damn dog or I'll drop him off at the animal shelter."

"Like hell you will. I'll drop *you* off at the shelter first."

"That's just like you," he said as he downed the rest of his beer. "The dog always comes first, right? Fuck your husband, side with the dog."

"The dog doesn't treat me like a child."

"No, he gives you unconditional love, right? Just what you need, a project. Something that will love you no matter what."

"That's what you're supposed to be doing, but apparently you've forgotten that."

"I haven't forgotten, but you don't make it easy, do you?"

"Easy? I let you siphon our money into that goddamn car, and I get to listen to you ramble on about parts, about the time it's going to take to attach a new bumper or a new rearview mirror. I don't complain when you spend entire days out there buffing out the fucking paint job for the hundredth time. I don't bitch at you when I put dinner on the table and you blow it off because you have to put on a new taillight. You pay more attention to the car than you do us, and I smile and let you have your hobby."

"Us? Us? You and that damn mutt? Is this the kind of parent you would've been? Overbearing, smothering it and taking sides any time I had something to say."

"You son of a bitch," she hissed. "How dare you?" She grabbed the empty beer can from the counter and threw it at him, hitting him in the forehead. "You hateful bastard."

Ted shrugged and kicked the can across the floor. He hit a nerve, one he knew he shouldn't have. It was beneath him, and yet at that moment he couldn't contain it. "Suzie, I'm sorry, I didn't mean…"

"*Fuck* you and what you meant," she screamed. "You said exactly what you meant to say, all over a scratch in your precious car."

Ted hung his head, his face red from anger and embarrassment. It was a low blow. He took a step forward and extended his arms, preparing to hug her, to apologize for being such a monster, but she stepped away, crying from barely contained rage.

"Suzie…"

"Don't fucking *Suzie* me, you son of a bitch. Don't touch me. I don't even want to see your face right now."

Ted went from being sorry to being defensive in the blink of an eye. He pushed past her and opened the door to the garage. "Then I'm going out," he said. "I'll be back when I'm back. *If* I come back."

"Go," Susan said. "Maybe if you do come back, I won't fucking be here."

Ted looked at her and stormed through the door, slamming it behind him hard enough to knock a decorative rooster from the kitchen wall.

That was eight hours ago. Eight hours of conflicting emotions as she sat on the couch contemplating her options. She'd never thought Ted was capable of such unabashed hostility. What kind of father would he have been? Would he have taken his anger out on their child like he took it out on her and Ringo? Susan had no idea if she scratched his precious car, but she didn't deserve his unbridled fury and thoughtless accusations.

A 24 marathon played on television, but she paid very little attention. Keifer Sutherland went on killing as Susan emptied a box of tissues. Ringo nudged her hand now and then to let her know he had her back. She stroked his shoulders absently, lost in her own misery.

After midnight, Ted stumbled in from the garage, obviously intoxicated. He drunkenly tried to apologize, even attempting to pet Ringo's scruffy little head, but Susan wasn't ready to hear it. Ringo kept his distance, still feeling the sting of where Ted had kicked him across the floor. He staggered to bed and Susan slept on the couch with the dog curled up behind her legs. She and Ted didn't share a bed for over a week, and even then there was a boundary, a demarcation line of pillows between them.

It wasn't a bump in the road, it was a huge fucking chasm that had the potential to tear them apart.

A month passed before they spoke to one another about anything more important than a grocery list. Two months before the pillows disappeared. They eventually slipped back into their routine, going from forced civility to something approaching normalcy. She wasn't about to let him off the hook, but she was willing to give him another chance to either mend the bridge or destroy it for good.

She'd seen a side of Ted she never knew existed, and she didn't like it one bit.

***

Susan woke with a gasp, a scream bubbling from between her lips, as a figure squeezed through the window and jumped into the back seat. A second later, a massive, snarling head appeared and jammed its dripping muzzle through the missing window; teeth the size of railroad spikes tore at the steering wheel and ripped the headrest from the seat before continuing the violent attack. The giant wolf-like monstrosity tried desperately to force its massive shoulders through the opening, eyes blazing as it bent the steering wheel between powerful jaws.

Susan shrank against her door as teeth snapped only inches from her face. The hot wind from the beast's wild panting blew the hair from her forehead and bathed her in the rancid stink of its last meal. Ted grabbed the travel bag from the rear floor and beat at the creature's face, doing nothing but pissing it off even more. The wolf grabbed the bag and tore it apart, flinging the unwanted contents aside. Hot strings of saliva splattered the inside of the car as the beast roared in irritation; the Cuda rocked and bounced as it tried to gain entry, covering everything in a coating of warm slime.

Ted pulled his legs back and kicked as hard as he could, connecting squarely with the wolf's jaw. It bayed piercingly and backed away from the car; the monster was dazed, its broken jaw dangling uselessly. Their attacker ran into the vehicle over and over again, crushing the door further into the passenger compartment. In the flickering light, Susan saw its shaggy black muzzle dripping with blood from fresh wounds, eyes glowing from within with hellish light. It continued slamming into the twisted metal, opening large cuts and gashes in an already battered face. One pointed ear dangled from the side of the thing's head from a single scrap of flesh.

"What do we do?" Susan shrieked.

"Nothing," Ted panted. "It'll kill itself, just keep away."

They watched as the giant slammed into the car over and over again. A jagged piece of steel pierced its right eye with a wet, squishy pop; the orb deflated and ran in a sticky clot over its muzzle, but the unnatural glow remained, emanating from deep within its skull.

"It's tearing itself apart," Susan moaned.

"Exactly!" Ted laughed shrilly, maniacally, a man on the edge.

The creature slammed into the door again and howled; an audible crack sounded out as its skull split wide open. Stepping away, shaking its giant head stupidly, the monster fell into the mud. After a few shallow breaths, its struggles ceased. In the short flashes of light, Susan saw gray lumps of brain leaking from its mangled skull and dripping into the rotting leaves.

"Suzie," Ted screamed, "Suzie, tell me you're okay."

"I'm okay, I'm okay. How did you get away? I thought you were dead," she wailed. "I thought I was never going to see you again."

"You're not going to get that lucky," he said. "I'm not going anywhere." He leaned between the front seats and Susan grabbed his face and kissed him, tasting blood on her lips.

"You're bleeding," she said. "Your head is bleeding." She looked at his torn fingers, seeing the cracked and torn remains of several of his fingernails dangling from scraps of flesh.

"It's nothing, I'm okay. A little bruised, but I'll live."

"How did you get away? I thought it was going to kill you." She rubbed his face lovingly, afraid if she took her hands away he'd disappear like a distant mirage.

"It just left me there," he said, "dropped me in a clearing and ran off into the woods. I had no idea where I was, but I wasn't alone."

"What? There are people out here?"

"They were all dead, Suzie," he shivered. "There were bodies everywhere, piled on top of each other like firewood. I could smell them; the sweat and fear and death. Skulls hung from the trees like Christmas decorations," he sobbed. "Men, women, animals, stacked up like a fucking totem." Ted's chest hitched; his ordeal was beginning to sink in. He'd almost become one of them, one of the butchered dead.

"I thought I lost you," Susan cried. "I thought you were gone."

"There was a cave," he continued, "about thirty feet away. Just a ragged hole carved into the side of the mountain. The rocks were blackened and cracked by the heat; it was like a blast furnace. The entrance to Hell itself."

It was hard for Susan to watch Ted's face wrinkle with the unbelievable memory. Surely he'd seen *something*, but what? What he was saying was impossible.

"There were voices," he continued. "Voices coming from *inside* the cave, hundreds of them, thousands, the sound of a packed arena. They were screaming, calling for help. My God, it was the most terrifying thing I've ever heard, and I couldn't do a damn thing, not even if I wanted to. The heat was so *intense*, Suzie. I felt like I was standing in the caldera of a volcano. I just wanted to get away from there, away from the incessant screaming and stink of rotting corpses."

"Ted, please, calm down. You're okay now," Susan soothed.

"Okay? I'll never be okay again, not after what I saw, what I *heard*." Ted wiped tears from his cheeks and inhaled deeply. "I saw my chance to run and I took it. I had no idea where that fucking *thing* was, or if it was watching me from the forest, but I didn't hesitate. Anything was better than staying there, helpless."

Susan nodded, grabbed his hand, and kissed his fingers. She noticed the hair on his arm had been singed; she could feel heat rising from his flesh in waves.

"Baby, please," she pleaded. "You're safe, that's what matters. You're here now."

"All those voices," he cried. "What's going on here, Suzie?"

Susan cried with him as steam rose from the corpse outside the window. She wanted to tell him about her experience, about the faceless figures that had surrounded the car, how their disembodied voices made her feel safe. Now was not the time, not after what had happened to him. Although impossible to believe, Ted carried evidence with him: his hot skin, his hair curled up into tiny, white curlicues on his arms, his nails torn from his bleeding fingers.

"Please," Ted muttered, "we have to get the hell out of here."

"I've never wanted anything more," she replied, wiping tears from her cheeks.

Ted jumped into the front seat, peered outside, and took a deep breath.

"No time like the present."

***

Ted crawled through the window and carefully stepped around the wolf's cooling body. It gave off a wet, meaty stink, like bloated roadkill along the highway. He covered his nose, crept around the vehicle, and opened Susan's door. He grabbed her around the waist and pulled; she uttered a quick gasp as the jagged metal tore through her jeans and sliced her calf.

"Are you okay? Is it working?"

"One more time," she said. "and I think you got it. Don't worry about hurting me, just get me out of here."

Ted dug his feet in and yanked; her leg pulled from beneath the dash with little resistance, spilling them both to the soggy ground. She gave him a quick, crushing hug and kissed his forehead before standing on wobbly legs. She rubbed her knees and ankles, working out the kinks in her joints, before staggering to the rear of the car, out of sight.

"Susan, what the hell are you doing?"

"Give me a second," she said. "I have to pee." Ted listened as she slid her zipper down and marked the leaves behind the wreck. She sighed with relief as the pressure in her bladder subsided. She'd never been so happy to go to the bathroom; one of life's little moments she'd never take for granted again. She finished and slopped through the mud and wet leaves to join Ted at the driver's door, where he collected a few of the contents from the ruined travel bag and piled them on the roof of the car.

She reached inside, grabbed her sweatshirt, and pulled it on over her wet clothes, taking what meager warmth it had to offer.

"I have slickers and a couple flashlights in the trunk," he said. "As long as we didn't lose them in the crash."

Ted dug through the trunk and produced two yellow rain jackets and a heavy MagLite; the other flashlights were missing, likely scattered somewhere on the mountain behind them. They donned the slickers and stood beside the car, scanning the area; the MagLite cut a path through the dense fog, allowing them a clear glimpse of their surroundings for the first time. The forest here was thick, swampy, almost primordial.

The car had come to rest over forty feet from the road; a sheer, granite wall climbed up and disappeared in the darkness. There wasn't a chance they'd get back to the road this way; the incline would be like climbing a wall of ice. Small rivers of muddy water cut paths down the hillside, forming a large pool at the bottom that sucked at their shoes.

"North is that way," Ted pointed. "If we keep following the mountain, we'll eventually wind up at the resort."

"Eventually? How far is it?"

"About five miles I'd guess. The road winds up the mountain, but this is a more direct route."

"That means we have to stay in the woods," she groaned.

"I'm sorry, there's no other way."

Susan crossed her arms and hugged herself to keep warm. By her watch, the sun should have been directly overhead, but instead they were mired in endless gloom creeping in from all direction. As Ted picked his way through the thick brush, she turned and looked at the wrecked Barracuda, suddenly sorry to leave it behind; it had given them refuge up to this point, now they were left completely in the open with nowhere to hide.

"I can't wait to get out of these wet clothes," Ted said.

"We're lucky to be alive, that will have to suffice for now."

He nodded, his face clouding over, remembering his short but traumatic time on the corpse-strewn ground beside the cave. He was lucky to be alive, but at what cost? Could he truly ever forget what he'd seen and heard? No amount of therapy would erase that. He knew he'd never be able to tell anyone what he'd witnessed here; not his parents, not his closest friends. They'd locked him in a padded cell and would make him wear a muzzle like a rabid dog. How would he live knowing this place exists?

"Do you remember that camping trip we went on with Barb and Mike? About five years ago?" Susan asked.

"That's what you're thinking about right now? Really?"

"Until now, that was the most miserable experience I've ever had in the woods. I guess there's really no comparison."

"I remember," Ted said. "It rained the whole time and you were pissed because you wanted to go fishing and you'd forgotten your rod at home."

Susan chuckled and nodded. "I didn't think I was being unreasonable. What else was there to do besides listen to Barb and Mike bicker all weekend?"

"I nearly forgot that," he said. "Barb accused him of cheating on her and tore down the tent. Those two were a mess."

"All couples are a mess at some point," she said. "*We* were a mess."

"That was a little different, Suzie."

Susan huffed her agreement. "What ever happened to those two?"

"Turns out Mike *was* cheating on her," he said. "He took the dog, a few hundred bucks, and the clothes on his back. He moved down to Philly with his mistress."

"Seriously?"

"Yep. I thought I told you?"

"No, I'd remember that," she replied. "Suits them right for ruining our damn trip."

Ted laughed behind his arm, trying to muffle the sound. They were free of the car but they weren't out of the woods yet. One of those wolf-like creatures howled deep in the forest to let them know they weren't alone.

"That sound goes right through me," Susan said. Ted nodded his agreement. Suddenly, the stories he'd heard about these woods seemed more than plausible. They were spot on.

"I guess the tall tales might have some truth after all," he said.

"Don't you dare, I can't hear any of that right now."

"I'm serious. My father was full of local legends, folklore, stories about Satan worship and ritual sacrifice. He told me there were secrets buried in these woods and I just listened and laughed. I wonder if he knew more than what he told me. Under the circumstances, I'm willing to bet he does. You better believe when we get out of here I'm going to ask him."

"He's going to think you're crazy, Ted. I'm starting to think we're *both* crazy."

"You didn't see that fucking hole in the ground," he said.

"No, I didn't, but you hit your head pretty hard. You said so yourself."

"So what? Do you think I imagined it? Can you explain why the fucking hair is burned off my arms?" Susan shook her head and turned away. "What I saw was real and what I felt was real, and that's all there is to it." Ted retreated into himself, unable and unwilling to discuss it further.

How could Susan know what had happened after he was dragged away? She didn't have an explanation, not for what Ted experienced, and not for what she'd seen. They'd had the misfortune of getting trapped in the middle of something that defied reality. Places of power supposedly existed all around them: the Pyramids, Stonehenge, mystic ley lines connecting points of significance, yet without any real pattern or explanation. Even the impossible wasn't truly impossible.

The forest floor continued on a slight incline, leaving the swampy ground behind them. Their shoes squished quietly in the mud as Ted tried to navigate around the thick tangles of growth. Patches of the forest stood out in contrast; large circular clearings where nothing grew, draped in thick luminous fog made white in the glare of the flashlight.

"The British call them torches you know?" Susan said.

"What?"

"Flashlights. They call them torches. Seems much more appropriate, doesn't it?"

Ted grunted.

"I'm just trying to make conversation, Ted. I'm scared too."

"I know, I'm sorry. I'm just trying to get us out of here before *they* come back. Whatever *they* are."

Thunder greeted them as they crossed a swift but shallow stream.

"You know, when I was kid I was terrified of the dark," she said.

"Really? You never told me that."

"Really," she replied. "My mother had night lights all over my bedroom. I made her keep the light on in my closet, too. I was petrified. Every time I climbed out of bed to use the bathroom I was certain something would grab my feet from under the bed."

"What caused it?"

"Nothing, at least not anything I remember. I just hated not knowing what was in the shadows. I pictured the most awful shit, the nastiest monsters. One day I slept without the night lights, and a week later I turned off the closet light and never needed it again. It happened just like that."

"That's strange," Ted said. "But you're not afraid anymore?"

"After tonight, I may need to turn the closet light on again for a while." She wiped rain from her face and focused on the bright beam of light ahead. "Weren't you afraid of anything as a kid?"

Ted thought about it for a moment and chuckled. "The Fraggles."

"What?"

"The Fraggles. Don't you remember *Fraggle Rock?* Those things creeped me out, running around and eating those poor Doozers' houses."

"You're a nut," Susan laughed.

"And that damn talking trash heap! Who makes these shows?"

"For me it was Oscar the Grouch," Susan said. "Just a dirty, angry, miserable monster living in a garbage can. My parents took me to New York City when I was seven, and I saw a homeless man pushing a shopping cart. I pointed at him and shouted 'look mommy, Oscar the Grouch.' She grabbed my hand and pulled me away as fast as she could. The man frowned and flipped me the bird," she laughed. "He had a fly in his beard. I thought it was hysterical at the time."

"You were young," Ted said. "You didn't know any better."

"It wasn't until years later I saw a program on television about New York City's homeless problem. I swear I saw the same guy, wearing the same stained overcoat and pushing the same battered shopping cart. I cried. My mother didn't understand why, but something just clicked. These people weren't dirty and living out of busted luggage because they chose to. At one time they were people just like us who maybe made one bad decision, one wrong choice, and they ended up in the street. It frightened me. I was scared I'd wind up like that some day, carrying around a torn teddy bear and picking scraps out of a dumpster."

"You were a very sweet, and very emotional little girl," Ted said.

"I guess I was," she said. "Part of me still thinks about that little girl and wonders if I've changed that much."

The trunk of a massive pine tree split open and fell to the forest floor with a shattering crunch. Susan held her hands protectively over her head and scampered back, bumping into Ted and knocking the flashlight to the ground. He quickly retrieved it, wiped water and muck from its lens, and shined it into the darkness. The tree blocked their path, forcing them to find a way around.

"Come on, this way," Ted said, grabbing her hand and pulling her along behind. "I think we're wearing out our welcome."

They fled through the forest without feeling their feet touch the ground. Sets of eyes appeared one-by-one in the dense brush to her right, keeping pace as they continued their ascent out of the valley. The creatures bayed and barked excitedly as they closed the gap; the forest was alive with the sound of their pursuit. The time for silently stalking their prey had come to an end.

The dense growth thinned and suddenly opened into a wide clearing. A squat, one room cabin stood twenty yards away, backed up against the hillside. A fragrant, white plume of wood smoke drifted into the sky from a short stone chimney. A cracked path led up to the cabin's porch where an ancient swing gently rocked on rusted chains. Susan had never been so happy to see something so wickedly creepy. She scanned the forest's edge, prepared to see Hansel and Gretel emerge from the woods on the other side of the clearing.

"Holy shit," Ted laughed, "would you look at that?"

"Go, go," Susan shouted, out of breath. "We can admire the view later."

They climbed the half-dozen rickety steps and stood on the porch as the wind whistled through the eaves. The windows had been covered in scraps of old newspaper, making it impossible to see inside, but a soft light flickered around the edges, letting them know someone must be in there. Ted rapped loudly on the heavy wooden door and waited for a response. Susan gulped the air like a fish out of water; she felt dizzy and disconnected. Her legs ached, her lungs burned. She hadn't had this much physical activity since high school gym class, now nearly twenty years in her past.

"Come on, come on, answer," Ted shouted, pounding on the door again.

The creatures had given up their chase. They stood at the tree line in a semicircle, panting and grunting, but no longer approaching. They were content just watching, and to Susan that was even worse. She felt like a rabbit trapped in a snare, like those monsters had pushed them in this direction purposely.

As Susan heard the lock click on the cabin door, she held her breath, unaware if they'd found their salvation or another step on the road to madness.

5

THE ROOM WAS STIFLING.

The old woman who had answered the door had gone back to a small wooden chair in front of the fireplace. There were several others arranged in a circle around a handmade coffee table. She picked up a steaming cup of tea and sipped noisily as a thin trickle of liquid ran over her chin and dripped into her lap. She brushed it away absently and smiled up with a mouthful of yellow, crooked teeth. Susan felt safe in her company, like a weekend trip to grandma's house.

"Ma'am," Ted panted, "we don't want to scare you, but there are *things* out there. They've been chasing us for miles."

"Don't you worry yourself over them," she cackled. "They know better than to bother with me."

"We need to use your phone," Susan added. "We were in a car accident and we need to get out of here."

The old woman spread her arms and snickered. "Does it look like I have a telephone, young lady? They don't run lines down here. No electricity, no running water."

Susan felt hope of rescue slipping away. She looked around the cabin and saw the old woman was telling the truth. There wasn't a single appliance: no blender, no coffee maker, no refrigerator, no television. *How can someone live this way??*

"I know what you're thinking, missy," the woman said. "I'm from a simpler time. I have no need for new-fangled gadgets."

"But we need help," Ted groaned. "What do you do if you get in trouble?"

"Trouble?" she asked. "No trouble here." She sipped her tea again and placed it on the table. "Can I get you two some tea? I just made it."

"No thank you," Susan said. "Tea isn't going to get us out of here."

"No, of course not," the woman laughed, "but it'll warm your bones. Why don't you both take a seat, keep an old woman company for a spell?"

Ted had no desire to stay here longer than he had to, but warm tea and a comfortable chair sounded inviting. He and Susan exchanged a glance, Susan shrugged, and they stepped into the circle in front of the fireplace. The fire crackled and spit; warmth seeped into their bones.

"Take off your shoes," the woman demanded. "Put them by the fire, they'll be dry in no time."

"Ma'am, we really can't stay. We need to get up to the resort, find a phone. Our families are going to start wondering where we are."

She waved her hand and brushed off Ted's comments. "Are you in a hurry to get back out there? The rain isn't going to slow down any time soon. It's *always* raining here, and obviously you've caught the attention of the *hounds*."

"The hounds?" Susan asked. She sat in a straight-back chair across from the woman; Ted sat next to his wife protectively. Something was off about the old woman and he couldn't put his finger on it. "You mean the wolves?"

"One name is as good as another," she said. "Once they catch your scent, they're relentless. Nothing more than a nuisance if you ask me."

"Nuisance?" Ted shouted. "They nearly killed us!"

"Oh, I don't doubt that," she laughed. Susan and Ted shared a nervous glance as the old woman toddled to an ancient wood stove and poured two mugs of steaming water. She placed them on the table and fell back into her chair. "Drink that," she ordered. "It'll calm your nerves."

Susan sniffed at the aromatic steam and wrapped her hands around the warm mug, feeling her skin tingle from the heat. Ted eyed his mug warily and pushed it away.

"Do you think I'm trying to poison you, lad?"

"No ma'am," he huffed. "I just don't want any."

"Ted, drink it," Susan said. "It's wonderful," she sighed. Heat flooded her body. The woman nodded, pleased.

"It's not often I get company," she said. "Tell me what's wrong. How did you get here?"

"We went off the road," Susan offered. "Our cell phone doesn't work and we're being chased by those monsters, the hounds. Lights in the sky, whispering voices. What is this place?"

The woman nodded as if it was a story she was familiar with. She showed little interest, sipping at her tea and plucking at her old dress with crooked, arthritic fingers.

"If I had a nickel for every time a young couple wound up in these woods, I'd be a very rich old woman."

"You mean this happens a lot?" Susan asked.

"Sure," the woman replied, "all the time. That road is dangerous. There are dozens of cars out there going back decades. Even a bus or two if I recall."

"A bus?" Ted asked.

"Yessir, an old school bus. Came off the road about thirty years ago. A whole bus of little ones. It's harder when they're so young, you know? A lot of broken dreams in this forest."

Ted found he was suddenly interested in the old woman's stories. Her voice was soothing. He grabbed his mug, sipped, and placed it back on the table. He couldn't remember anything tasting so sweet.

"One of those things grabbed me," Ted said, "and dragged me into the woods." His face twisted from the memory.

"Then you're one of the lucky ones," the woman said. "Not many get away from the hounds."

"It took me somewhere, a cave. A burning cave."

The woman raised her eyebrows. "That would have been the end of you. Take my word for it."

"But what *is* it?" Ted asked. "I heard voices." He coughed and cleared his throat to keep from crying.

"These woods have been a place of power for centuries," the woman answered. "A thin line exists here, one between this world and others. Those hounds and the figures you've seen in the forest don't belong here. They're trapped."

"Trapped?" Susan asked. "I don't understand."

"No, I don't imagine you will. I don't even understand everything and I've been here since your granddaddy's parents were still in the womb."

"Can we go back a minute?" Susan asked. "What exactly do you mean about a *thin line*?"

"Just what I said," she responded. She would offer nothing more in the form of an answer. She sipped her tea and watched them closely. "There's a war going on here, and you two crashed right in the middle of it."

Ted's mind felt fuzzy. Between the heat and the strange brew the woman had concocted, he was beginning to grow tired; like he'd eaten a large meal and needed to curl up on the couch and nap away the afternoon. *Afternoon? Morning? Night? What time is it anyway?*

Susan felt the effects as well. She struggled to raise the mug to her lips, spilling some down the front of her rain slicker. She looked over at Ted and saw he was having the same problem; his head nodded and his eyes had grown glassy. The woman watched them, smiling, sipping at her tea frequently.

"Go ahead," she said. "Finish your drinks. You'll feel so much better if you do."

"What did you put in here?" Susan slurred. "You drugged us."

"I did nothing of the sort," she said. "Just drink. When you're done, you're going to thank me."

Susan listened as Ted began snoring lightly. The woman stood, walked to Ted, and removed his shoes and raincoat, placing them by the fire. She grabbed a log from a small wooden crate and tossed it into the flames. Susan had a million questions, but her lips wouldn't form words. She mumbled incoherently as the woman removed her slicker and hung it next to Ted's. She took their mugs and put them in a wash basin, looking over her shoulder and humming a tune under her breath. Rain lashed the cabin; their pursuers, the *hounds*, bayed in the distance. Sad, mournful cries.

"Why are you doing this?" Susan managed.

"Just close your eyes. Everything will be better when you wake. The tea will throw off your scent," she added. "Those hounds won't bother you again, for a while at least."

The woman covered them with thick blankets and returned to the wash basin; the mugs clinked together musically as she rinsed them and placed them on the counter. Susan's blanket was itchy, but she couldn't scratch, couldn't move at all. Everything was fuzzy; she heard what was happening around her but couldn't react. They were at the woman's mercy.

Susan felt as if she was floating, like she was under some powerful anesthetic.

Maybe just a quick nap, she thought.

"That's more like it," the woman soothed. "No sense fighting it."

You can hear my thoughts?

The woman laughed, put the clean mugs aside, and took her seat next to the fire.

"Rest, my darling. Nothing good comes out of exhaustion. You'll need all your strength to get out of here. All your strength and all your will."

***

Susan was shaken harshly. She moaned in her throat and snuggled beneath the blanket; she wasn't ready to leave her warm place, not yet. Ted could wait.

"Suzie, come on," Ted said. "You have to wake up."

"I don't want to," she mumbled. "Another five minutes."

"This isn't like sleeping in on a Saturday morning," he scolded. "You to get up! Now!"

She stretched her arms over her head and yawned. She felt disconnected, like she'd been sleeping for ages. She wanted to curl up beneath the blanket and stay there.

"Damn it, Susan, you have to get up!"

Ted pulled the blanket from her and tossed it aside. A cloud of dust drifted into the air; gray light shined in from gaps in the newspaper covering the windows. It was light outside. Overcast, but light. Susan sat up and looked around the cabin.

"How long was I sleeping?" she asked.

"I don't know," Ted replied, "I've only been awake a few minutes."

"Where's the old woman?"

"Gone," he stated. "Nowhere to be found. I even looked outside."

"You went out?"

"I had no choice. I needed to find out for myself." Ted walked to the washbasin and brought over one of the mugs. "And look at this." He held out the mug to Susan, and she wrinkled her brow.

"That's impossible," she blurted.

The mug was covered in thick, gray dust, as if it'd been there forever. She wiped a finger over the surface of the mug and looked at the dingy, coating of grime covering her skin. She stood on wobbly legs and scanned the small room.

The hearth was cold and dead, the rough stone coated in soot. A layer of dust covered everything. Thick cobwebs hung from the corners of the room, fluttering in the breeze generated from their passing. The empty husks of flies and other insects dotted the webs and the dirty, wooden slats of the floor.

"I don't understand," Susan said. "It wasn't like this last night."

"Last night? More like last year. Last century."

"That's ridiculous. It's surely only been a few hours."

"Then you explain it," Ted shouted. "You think this happened overnight?"

"I can't explain it. It doesn't make any sense."

"What do you remember?" Ted asked.

"Not much. The fire, the heat, the tea."

"The tea she fucking *drugged*," he yelled.

"She was in my head," Susan said. "She could hear my thoughts."

"Now who's being ridiculous?"

"I'm serious. She answered me like I was talking out loud. It was so bizarre."

"That's one way to put it," Ted grumbled. "At least it's light out."

Susan looked at her watch and frowned; the digital display had gone dead. Ted poked around in the ashes in the fireplace and grunted. Just hours ago, the cabin was like an oven; now the air was chilly and damp. Ted kicked at a small wicker basket and it toppled over, spilling its contents onto the floor with a clatter.

"What the hell is this?" he asked, puzzled.

Dozens of cell phones lie scattered on the floor, some of them well over a decade old. Susan studied them and reached into the pile, trying to power them on to no avail. They were all as dead as this forgotten cabin. She tried one after another, tossing them to the floor with an irritated sigh.

"How strange," Susan whispered.

"Strange? This is some serial-killer shit," he replied.

"*We're* not dead. Confused, but not dead."

"Then why did she drug us?"

"I don't know Ted, but if she wanted us dead, we wouldn't be having this conversation."

Ted paced the room, trying to gather his thoughts. His aches and pains had been eased by the soothing heat of the flame. "Where'd she go? You saw her, she must have been ninety years old. She didn't just grab a coat and go for a hike."

"Some older folks are perfectly capable, Ted."

"For Christ's sake Susan, would you stop fooling yourself," Ted exploded.

"We're not going to figure it out if you're just going to keep yelling at me."

"I don't mean to shout," Ted said, calming himself. "I'm just scared. Giant fucking dogs, caves full of voices, lights in the sky. Now this," he pointed at the pile of phones and kicked them aside. "What did she say? This is a place of power? What the hell does that even mean?"

"A thin line," Susan uttered.

"Means nothing! The crazy ramblings of an old woman, that's all. She doesn't have a working phone, but apparently she collects the damn things. Look where she *lives*," he said, his voice escalating. "How does she get food? How does she survive out here?"

"I'm sure there's an explanation," Susan said.

"Sure there is," Ted mocked. "She's batshit crazy! She drugged us and ran off so we didn't bury her out in the yard."

"Okay, enough with that," Susan said. "We're fine, she's gone, and we still have to get to the resort and call for help."

"I'm not fine," Ted stammered. "I feel like I'm losing my mind."

Susan wrapped her arms around him and hugged tightly. She looked up and kissed him on the lips. Deeply. Passionately.

"What was that for?" he asked.

"Did that feel like you're losing your mind?"

Ted grinned and his features softened. "That's the most sane thing I've felt since we got here."

"Then focus on that," she grinned. "Focus on getting up to Pine Lakes and calling for help. Focus on our warm bed and all the wonderful things we'll do there."

"You drive a hard bargain," Ted laughed.

Susan patted his cheek lovingly and stepped back. "Let's grab the slickers and get out of here. We have to be close to the resort by now."

Ted nodded silently and removed their rain gear from the hooks by the fireplace. It was no longer raining, but it couldn't hurt being prepared. He scanned the cabin one last time, sighed deeply, and opened the cabin's only door. They walked slowly to the center of the clearing, arms around each other's waists, and looked back at the rotting cabin surrounded by gnarled, overgrown shrubs. The air was cool and still. Nothing moved. Not a breath of wind rustled the tall trees surrounding them.

"Can we get the hell out here, please?" Susan asked.

"I've never been so ready in my life," Ted replied.

They crunched through the forest with purpose, as low, gray clouds scudded overhead. Susan took some comfort in being able to see the sky. Gray or not, it was there. The utter blackness of the night before had thankfully retreated, revealing that everything was still where it belonged. The world was still here.

She and Ted were still here.

***

"Do you remember the first song we ever danced to?" Ted asked out of the blue.

"The first song? Yeah, that one by Journey. 'When You Love A Woman.' Why the hell are you thinking about that?"

"I don't know," he chuckled. "I was just thinking of how nervous I was. I wasn't exactly Fred Astaire on the dance floor."

"You did fine. Although I remember feeling your sweaty palms through my dress."

"Your date was dancing with Jenny Pullman," Ted recalled. "She had more men pass through her legs than a subway turnstile."

"I forgot about her," Susan exclaimed. "She dyed her hair bright blond and her eyebrows were jet black. She looked like a Halloween mask."

"*My* date, from what I heard, left early and hooked up with someone on the football team. Likely the *entire* football team."

"Why were you with her?"

"She had a reputation for putting out," Ted laughed. "I was seventeen. Promiscuity and teenage angst go together like chocolate and peanut butter."

"You're an animal," Susan laughed. "If it wasn't for terrible prom dates, we may have never met."

Ted nodded and grabbed her hand. "I used to love those High School dances. Not because I was trying to get laid, well, not all the time, but just the atmosphere. A room full of sweaty teenagers trying to make out in the dark. Loud music. Friends. Do we ever have friends as close as we did in High School?"

"I was twelve when I went to my first dance," Susan said. "The boys stood on one side and the girls on the other, scared as hell to cross that line in the middle of the floor. My first dance ever was with Billy Masters. I'll never forget it."

"You had a crush on this Billy?"

"No, not at all," she laughed. "We danced to a Bon Jovi song. We were at arm's length, afraid to touch each other. You know what I mean? The Frankenstein dance?" Ted nodded and laughed. "The room was quiet, and the chorus was just kicking in and Billy farted."

"He *what?*" Ted laughed loudly and held his stomach.

"He farted," she repeated. "It was loud. I'm talking train wreck loud. He ran out of the auditorium like tigers were chasing him."

"That is the best story ever," Ted said, still laughing. "What did you do?"

"I sat down with my friends and wouldn't talk about it. If it wasn't dark in there, I'm sure they would have seen my face was beet red."

"Hilarious," he shouted.

"It is now," Susan said. "It wasn't then. Twelve years old and traumatized."

Ted laughed louder and harder. It was refreshing. In all of this craziness, he was still capable of laughter.

"Okay," Ted said, rubbing his waistline, "now I have to pee."

"So go pee," she said. "I'm glad you can laugh at my expense," she teased.

Ted winked and walked twenty feet into the brush. As he urinated into the layer of dead leaves, he watched a squirrel slowly crunch across the carpet of pine needles. It was the first animal, the first *normal* animal he'd seen since the accident. It stopped, sniffed the air, and looked at Ted, its nose wiggling.

"What are you looking at buddy?" Ted called. "Peeping Tom."

The squirrel turned to leave, leaping into the air to latch onto a nearby tree, when a hand shot up from the mud and leaves and grabbed it in mid-flight. The squirrel chattered and squeaked as the filthy hand crushed it between strong fingers. Ted heard its tiny bones cracking in the hand's grip; blood shot from the squirrel's mouth as a head popped above the forest floor, caked in wet earth and pine needles. It was a young boy, maybe eight years old; it was hard to tell with his face and hair coated in dark filth. He looked at Ted and smiled; mud tumbled from his mouth, his teeth were caked in thick sludge.

Ted backed away slowly, fumbling with his zipper.

"Hi," the boy exclaimed. He put the dead squirrel to his lips and bit its head off in one clean crunch. "Tastes like chicken," he said.

"Nonono," Ted whispered. "Not happening."

"Do you know where the bus is, mister? My mom's going to kill me if I'm not home in time for dinner."

Ted backed away, step-by-step, afraid to take his eyes off the child as he smeared the squirrel's blood on his lips. Other hands broke the ground's surface, like a scene from one of Romero's zombie flicks. Ted found he couldn't make his mouth work, couldn't manage to call out to Susan and warm her. His vocal chords were paralyzed.

Ted broke through the brush, still staring into the forest when Susan called out to him.

"Who are you talking to?"

"N-n-no one," he stuttered. "I wasn't the one talking."

"What? I'm sure I heard voices."

Ted pointed into the forest with a trembling hand.

"What?" Susan shouted. "What is it?"

Susan walked past him, to the edge of the clearing. She stopped and put a hand over her mouth.

The ground was a churning sea of clutching hands and bobbing heads. The little boy Ted had seen was still munching happily on the raw squirrel meat; a little girl with filthy pigtails had a mouthful of earthworms; a second boy grabbed at the bark of a tree, trying to pull himself from the wet ground. Wrinkled, pale fingers continued breaching the surface of the forest floor as Susan watched in abject horror. She counted a dozen heads, all belonging to children under the age of ten. She remembered what the old woman had said, a bus full of kids that had gone missing after tumbling down the mountain.

Susan was meeting them for the first time.

"Those poor kids," she muttered.

"Poor kids?" Ted shrieked. "He's eating a fucking squirrel he killed with his own hands."

"Hey lady," a little girl shouted. "Over here. Come play with us." Her eyes were white; her nose was missing completely, leaving a ragged hole in her face packed with mud and waxy, gray, wriggling worms.

"Suzie, we have to go," Ted cried.

"It's so sad."

"Fuck sad," he screamed. "We have to get out of here."

The boy gripping the tree had pulled himself from the earth. Susan gasped, noticing that nothing existed below his waist but the tangled remains of his intestines. She choked, gagging as her mouth was suddenly filled with the sour tang of bile.

"For God's sake, Suzie, run!" Ted shouted.

They tore blindly through the forest as the shrill voices taunted them. The woods burst to life with wet crunching and the soft thumps of muddy earth being tossed aside by groping hands. Susan looked over her shoulder, afraid they were being pursued. She tripped on an exposed rock and fell to the ground with a thud, sliding in the wet leaves. She cracked her head on a tree root and felt the warm blood run down over her face. Ted charged ahead, unaware his wife was in trouble.

"Ted!" Susan screamed. "Ted, help me!"

He stopped and turned, seeing Susan lying on the ground, breathing heavily and bleeding profusely from a scalp wound. As Susan struggled to stand, the ground *tasted* her warm blood. Hands shot up through the earth on either side and clutched at her flesh, scratching her skin with jagged, black fingernails. One pale hand grabbed her hair and pulled viciously; another squeezed her breast painfully. Susan was beyond words. She screamed into the sky; blubbering, unintelligible, terrified wails.

"Susan, get away from them," Ted hollered.

"I can't," she moaned. "Ted HELP ME!"

A fish-belly hand burst from the muck and wrapped around Susan's face. Her horrified shouts grew muffled as she thrashed wildly on the sodden ground. Pale, wrinkled fingers probed inside her mouth and pushed into her nostrils, tasting of mold and soggy, rotten vegetation. Her tears cut lines through the filth on her face.

Ted fell to his knees at her side and pried the groping fingers from her face. The hands pawed his thighs and crotch as he knocked them away with his closed fist. Just the touch of the clammy, frigid flesh was enough to send horrified tremors up his spine.

"Get them OFF!" Susan wailed

Ted stood and kicked at the hands, stomping on them, hearing brittle bones snap beneath his shoe. Muffled cries of rage bubbled up through the ground as the soft mud heaved with their frantic movements.

"They're going to pull me under," Susan cried. Already, her right leg had been dragged beneath the surface, disappearing as if in quicksand.

"The hell they are," he panted, continuing his assault. "Get the fuck off," he bellowed.

"Get the fuck off," a voice mocked from beneath the mud.

Ted crushed another hand beneath his shoe, noticing a tree branch five feet to his right. The end was jagged and broken. A perfect weapon. He rushed to grab the heavy spear and came back to Susan's side.

"Whatever you do, don't get in the way," he warned her.

Ted raised the branch above his head and jammed it into the soft ground. Immediately, he felt the tip deflect off something hard as a pained squeal sounded beneath him. He had no time to celebrate.

There were at least a dozen of them below. Time and time again, Ted jammed the branch into the mud; each time he was greeted with a satisfying cry of pain. As the hands retreated beneath the surface, Susan rolled away from the branch, stood, and ran behind Ted who'd begun sweating profusely from exertion. He couldn't stop.

Three minutes of skewering the ground with his new weapon was all it took. The cries faded away; the earth settled. The end of the stick was coated in thick, crimson slime. Flaps of skin and hair clung to the splinters. Susan babbled and looked at the ground, waiting for other hands to reach up through the earth and pull her down to where they lived.

"They're only children," she sobbed.

"They aren't children anymore," Ted panted. "This place has gotten to them, ruined them. I don't know how, but I know *that*."

"Just kids," she whined. "Just little boys and girls whose parents will never know what happened to their babies."

"I know baby, I know, but we can't dwell on that. I need you to be with me. I can't do this by myself."

Susan shook her head slowly and wouldn't look at her husband. She was slipping away, into that dark place her mind had retreated to after the miscarriage. She'd gotten so much better over the years since, but still she'd disconnect now and then, unable to deal with the reality of what had happened. Ted couldn't afford to lose her now. They had to keep moving. He had to be her rock; he couldn't let fear control him, or else Susan would fall into despair permanently.

"Baby, we *have to go*," Ted pleaded. "We can't let it get dark again, we just can't."

"Sitting at home, waiting by the telephone, praying when it rings there's good news on the other end."

Ted planted his branch in the ground and grabbed Susan by the shoulders, shaking her hard. Her head snapped back and forth lifelessly.

"Susan, you have to snap out of it," Ted shouted. "Look at me."

She shook her head and mumbled sadly.

"Look at me!" Ted screamed. Susan lifted her head and stared into his eyes. "Susan, listen." Ted paused. He had to choose his words carefully, or he risked losing her for good. "What happened is not your fault. It's no one's fault. You can't blame yourself for something that's out of your control."

He wasn't sure if she was hearing him. She watched him silently, lips quivering, tears leaking down her face.

"We've made it this far," Ted continued. "We didn't even know if we'd make it through those first months, do you remember?"

Susan nodded imperceptibly, but at least it was something.

"We did it *together*. Always together. We worked through our pain and we made it. No one expected it to be easy, but dammit, we did it. Our love is the glue that holds us together, and it's stronger than anything this world can throw our way."

Susan's lip twitched in what may have been an attempt at a smile. Her tears slowed.

"Don't you realize we survived something other couples haven't? We're strongest together. Nothing will ever change that."

When Susan nodded, she was more herself, more alert. She was seeing him, hearing him. His words slowly sank in, shining a light through the waves of darkness threatening to consume her.

Susan threw her arms around him and hugged tightly. She knew he wouldn't let her drown; no matter how much she felt like slipping beneath the waters of tragedy. It was in Ted's nature to protect her, with his life if necessary.

"I love you so much," she cried. "You'll never know how much."

"I know," he whispered in her ear. "I've always known." He ran his hand over her damp hair and wiped away her tears with his thumbs. Her color returned and her trembling ceased. She felt safe in Ted's arms.

"Thank you," she said.

"For what?"

"For never giving up on me."

Ted kissed her forehead and beamed. "Not a chance."

Ted pulled the branch from the ground and wiped the bloody tip in a pile of dead leaves. Susan grimaced and turned away, peering into the woods for the slightest movement. She looked back at the disturbed ground and squinted. Already it felt like a bad dream.

Susan gasped. Her fear reawakened as a dozen small figures appeared in the distance, shrouded in fog. Dirty, tattered clothing clung to their bodies. Their eyes were full of sadness.

"Ted," Susan whispered.

"I see them," he replied.

One little girl stepped forward as Susan tensed to run. Instead of running after them, the girl stopped and raised her hand in a quick wave. The gesture hurt Susan's heart. How many lives had this forest claimed? How many little girls who'd never see their sweet sixteen, or little boys who'd never grow up to be doctors or lawyers. How many parents' lives were shattered when the laughter stopped and the silence filled their once-happy homes?

How many sleepless nights waiting for a phone call or a knock at the door?

Susan put it out of her mind and returned the wave. She couldn't help herself. The scattered line of children slowly dissolved into the fog as if they'd never been there. In the few moments of struggle, they hadn't noticed the sky slowly darkening.

"Let's get out of here," she said. "I don't think I can handle any more surprises."

Ted grunted and clutched his branch tightly. Everything felt like a dream within a dream; time was beginning to fray around the edges.

"The resort has to be close," he said. "If we hurry, we might get there before dark."

Susan nodded and grabbed Ted's hand. "Is any of this real?"

"I've been asking myself the same thing," he replied.

6

As they crested the ridge, they stopped and looked into the gloom. Campfires dotted the darkness, casting circles of glowing orange light. It *had* to be the resort; there was nothing else out here. They continued forward, hopping over the rusted guardrail onto the macadam surface of the road. They hadn't noticed it had begun drizzling again; the thick canopy had kept them dry, thus far.

The section of road was unfamiliar. Dense forest crept in on either side; the road was pocked with deep potholes and the yellow centerline was faded and nearly nonexistent. Ted and Susan were glad to have their feet back on solid ground, gracious to be standing beneath an open sky. They untied the raincoats from around their waists and put them over their clothing before the rain intensified.

"I don't remember this stretch of road," Ted mused.

"You're the navigator," she replied. "If you don't recognize it, I certainly won't."

A warped, rusted sign appeared in the gloom, tilting at an angle over the road. A few white letters were still legible beneath years of rust and grime.

"It's a sign for the resort," Susan said happily. "We're close."

Ted scratched his head. None of this seemed familiar.

"Maybe it's an access road?" Susan said. A half-dozen fires flickered nearby, scattered along the sides of the street. "Part of the resort?" Susan asked. "A part we haven't seen?"

Ted shrugged and said nothing. He couldn't help feeling they were still lost. The road was cracked and crumbling and hadn't seen traffic in a decade. Sections were spray-painted with names, vulgarities, and crude sketches of genitalia. Typical signs of disuse and abandonment.

"It's getting darker," Susan said. "Maybe we better stop for the night."

Ted groaned, suddenly realizing he'd forgotten the flashlight back at the cabin. "What's a few more miles? At least we're finally getting somewhere."

"*Somewhere.*"

Their shoes slapped the wet road as they carried on. Everything was bathed in the dim light of eternal dusk. After ten minutes of walking, the shadowy shapes of buildings began popping up along the sides of the road. On the broken sidewalk, a fire burned fiercely in a battered steel drum. No one was around, but the ground was littered with trash, cigarette butts, and four filthy sleeping bags.

"Someone was camping *here*?" Susan asked, shocked.

"It certainly looks like it." He nudged one of the sleeping bags with his foot, revealing an empty bottle of wine and a crumpled pack of Winston cigarettes.

The door of the nearest building - identified as Carlo's Drug Store by a faded sign in the cracked window - burst open, and a man charged out onto the sidewalk.

"You get away from there," he grumbled. "That's mine."

"Yes sir, we're not bothering your stuff," Ted said startled, backing away.

"*Sir*," he cackled. "Aren't you a fancy one?"

"We don't want any trouble. We're just passing through."

"Passing through, are you? You sure about that?"

"Yes, I'm sure." Ted didn't understand the man's question.

"That doesn't mean you stop and poke around in someone else's belongings."

"No, of course not. I apologize, sir. We didn't know anyone was living here."

"Oh, with the *sir* again. I could get used to this," he chuckled.

"We'll just be on our way," Susan said, hiding behind her husband.

"Ah, there's a pretty one here too," the man said. "Kathy, come out here and see what washed up."

A skinny woman, with an unruly mop of black hair, joined them on the sidewalk and eyed them curiously. She may have been attractive once, but the years had not been kind. Her hands and face were traced with thick wrinkles; her dress was two sizes too big, revealing the pale knob of her exposed shoulder.

"Well, look here. I wasn't expecting company," Kathy said. She ran her hands through her tangled hair and pressed the wrinkles from her dress with her hands.

"No one cares what you look like, woman," the man chided.

"Uh, nice to meet you," Susan said.

"She *is* a pretty one," Kathy purred.

"My name's Jack," the man said, offering a thick, grimy hand. Ted shook it politely and quickly let go.

"I'm Ted, and this is my wife Susan."

"Well Ted and Susan, what brings you to our neck of the woods?" Jack asked.

"We had an accident," Susan explained. "We were on our way to the resort and wrecked the car down in the woods. We're just looking for a phone."

"Down in the woods?" Kathy asked. "You're lucky you're walking at all."

"A lot has happened since then," Ted muttered.

"You don't say," Jack said. "Why don't you stay a while, tell us all about it?"

"No, really, we have to get to a phone and call our families."

"No phones here," Jack said with a wave of his cruddy hand. "Not in a long time. You can probably call from the resort, but you don't want to make the trip in the dark. This road is a bastard if you're not careful where you're walking."

Ted sighed and hung his head. In a world where everyone carried a cell phone with them everywhere, they'd managed to find the one stretch of road where that rule didn't apply. "What is this place?" Ted asked. "I've been up here dozens of times and I don't recognize it at all."

"No, I guess you wouldn't," Jack said. "They closed this section off decades ago. Killed the town and took its name."

"What do you mean?" Susan asked, stepping forward.

"That old resort popped up overnight," Jack informed. "No warning, nothing. One day they tore up the mountain and the next there were lines of people for miles just waiting to get in. Listen, I'm willing to tell stories all night, but I'm not going to do it out here in this damned rain. You're welcome to come inside."

"Inside? The drug store?" Susan asked.

"Ain't been a drug store for as long as I can remember," Kathy added.

A loud snarl came from across the darkened street. Ted squinted into the darkness and raised the branch in his hand, ready to strike out the second a target presented itself. A mangy Black Lab sauntered into the fire's glow and looked at Ted quizzically. He heard Jack laughing behind him.

"Don't worry about that old mutt," he laughed. "He's slow and half blind."

The dog walked up and nudged Susan's hand. She giggled and patted the old girl on the head. It licked her hand and walked back into the shadows.

"You're welcome inside if you'd like," Kathy said. "We ain't got much in the way of appetizers, but we can afford to feed you before you get on your way."

"No, really, we don't want to impose," Ted said.

"Impose shit." Jack laughed. "We could use the company and you look like you could use a warm meal."

The sky rumbled overhead and lightning slashed across the sky. Susan looked at Ted questioningly and shrugged. *Why not?*

"Okay, you twisted my arm," Ted laughed.

"Excellent!" Jack exclaimed. "Come on in and take a seat and we'll see what we have cooking."

They followed Kathy through the front door as an old bell jingled overhead.

"We haven't had the heart to take it down," Kathy explained. "It's kind of nice once you get used to it."

Susan smiled and entered the room.

***

The inside of the drugstore was dimly lit by several ancient Coleman lanterns. The furniture was a haphazard collection of cast-offs, and the wall decorations were a mismatched hodgepodge of tacky knickknacks. The metal shelving units had been pushed to the sides of the room, blocking the windows. It looked to Susan like something she'd seen in a post-apocalyptic TV series, like The *Walking Dead* or *Revolution* or one of the other dozen science fiction shows Ted binge watched on Netflix.

Kathy served macaroni and cheese with sliced hotdogs in large plastic bowls. She watched them as they ate as if waiting for word on her gourmet menu. Jack scarfed his meal hungrily with a plastic spoon, drizzling melted cheese into his thick, full beard. He belched loudly and placed his bowl on a worn coffee table.

"Kathy, you did it up good," he said.

"Oh, you," she said bashfully.

"So you crashed your car," Jack said, changing the subject.

"Yes," Susan replied, putting her bowl aside. She wiped her mouth on a paper towel and looked at Ted. "We were on our way to the resort when it started raining and we hydroplaned and went over the mountain."

"Car's totally wrecked," Ted added. "I spent ten years of my life rebuilding her and only twenty seconds to rip her apart again."

"Yeah, that's a tough one," Jack said, "but you're alive and both look unharmed."

"We're fine," Susan said. "Physically at least."

"What do you mean?" Jack asked.

"Ah, nothing," Susan said. "It's been a very long night."

Jack raised an eyebrow. He knew he wasn't getting the entire story, but his imagination filled in the blanks. He'd been in those woods before. Long time ago.

"Well you're here now," Kathy interrupted. "That's what matters."

Ted nodded and finished his macaroni. "Thank you for letting us in, and for feeding us. I didn't realize how hungry I was."

"It's no bother," Kathy said. She grabbed the empty bowls and disappeared through a shadowy door at the back of the room.

"What were you saying about the resort, Jack?" Ted asked. "Killed the town and took its name?"

"Yep, that's what I said," he grunted. "One day we were doing just fine and the next our lives were uprooted and torn apart. As soon as that place opened, the decline began. We had a school, a post office, a bunch of mom and pop shops. All gone now."

"I don't understand," Susan said. "I would think the resort would help local business."

"They put in a new road," Jack said, "and bypassed the town entirely. They have a gift shop up there. They have their mail picked up and their food delivered. We were like the oxpecker on a rhino's back, hanging on for scraps. Didn't take long for folks to pack up shop and put their homes on the market. Only thing is, everyone had forgotten we were still here. Those houses stood empty for years; most still do. A fire wiped out a good chunk of the town about five years back - our house included - and me and Kathy wound up here."

"Why didn't you leave?" Susan asked.

"Leave? Thought never even crossed our minds. Most of us have been here as long as we can remember. It's part of us and we're part of it."

"It's so sad," Susan sighed.

"We get by," Jack said. "The town of Pine Lakes might not exist anymore, but her people do."

"This *town* was named Pine Lakes?" Ted asked.

"Sure was. The resort took its name from the town and then put it out of business."

"How many of you stayed?" Susan asked.

"Oh, hard to say," Jack contemplated. "Few hundred I guess. A group of twenty or so have set up house in the old post office. Another forty at the High School. We're spread out all over this mountain." Jack lit a cigarette and offered the pack to Ted and Susan. They both took one and thanked him.

"How do you get your supplies?" Susan asked. "These cigarettes? Your food?"

"Living off what's still here," Jack said, filling the room with a cloud of smoke. "We picked through the supermarket and the convenience store. Had a sporting goods store and a few clothing stores, too. We make do with what we have."

"You're going to run out eventually," Susan said.

"Suzie, that's enough," Ted warned.

"No, no, it's okay," Jack said. "I don't mind. She's right. We've been lucky so far, but it's not going to last forever."

"And yet you're feeding us and letting us smoke your cigarettes,"

Susan said. "You didn't have to do that."

"We know what it's like to be in trouble," Jack replied. "You needed help, so we helped."

Ted inhaled deeply and blew out a plume of white smoke. It was stale, but had never tasted so good.

Kathy entered the room and took her seat next to Jack. "What are we talking about?"

"That damned resort," Jack blurted.

Kathy wrinkled her face distastefully. "Nothing much to say. Ruined our nice little town."

Thunder rattled the glass in the windows, making Kathy cringe.

"She hates the storms," Jack informed. "Always has. Lately they've been getting worse. I don't remember when we last saw the sun."

"I can't keep any of my flowers alive," Kathy stated. "Not enough sun. They shrivel up and die, just like we will someday."

"Okay Kathy, we have guests. Why not put away that depressing shit for another day?"

"It's fine," Susan said. "I can't imagine how you must feel."

"No, you can't," Jack said. "You'll leave this place and we'll still be here."

"You really should think about leaving," Susan said.

"No," Kathy interrupted. "We couldn't leave if we wanted to. Those first few months after they diverted the road, some of us tried, but we were chased right back here."

"What? Chased by who?" Ted asked.

"The people at the resort," Jack said. "The *guards*. They don't like our kind creeping around their million dollar campground."

"Guards?" Susan asked. "I've never seen a guard."

"No, I bet you haven't. They don't want to be seen. They hide in the trees and patrol the perimeter with their attack dogs. They keep us as far away as possible." Jack stubbed out his cigarette on the floor and kicked it away with a booted foot.

"Attack dogs?" Susan laughed. "You're joking! It isn't a military base."

"What the hell would you know about it?" Jack shouted. "Your kind are allowed there."

"Our kind?"

"Okay, that's enough," Ted said, patting Susan on the arm. "We're sorry for intruding. We'll just be on our way."

"Nonsense," Jack said. "I apologize. It's a touchy subject." He looked over at Kathy and shook his head. "We don't mean any harm."

"We're not used to people coming through here," Kathy added. "We get a little *enthusiastic* when we see new faces."

Ted thought it was a strange choice of words. Enthusiastic?

"We don't need to drag this out," Jack said. "It's over and done. Let's say we sit back and enjoy each other's company while we can."

Susan sat back in the chair and eyed Jack warily. Armed guards? Were these people crazy? Were the guards and dogs metaphors for something else? She suddenly remembered the things in the woods and wasn't so sure.

"Why don't you grab the cards, Kathy?" Jack said. "You two up for a little gin rummy?"

"Hey, why not?" Ted asked. "Not much on television." He eyed the dusty console TV a few feet away and laughed. Kathy laughed along, but it didn't reach her eyes. They didn't see the shadow fall over

Kathy's face, or the large knife she'd secreted away in the arm of her dress.

"Gin it is!"

***

"Damn, you're good at this," Kathy exclaimed.

Susan shrugged and laughed. She hadn't played in years.

"My father taught me," she said. "When I was young, dad generally came home late. We'd eat dinner, and afterward he'd play cards with me. Gin, War, Hearts, Spades, you name it. I think he fancied himself some sort of card shark," she laughed. "Taught me everything I know."

"That's sweet," Kathy said. "You're close to your daddy then?"

"Oh yeah, daddy's little girl. I don't do much of anything without him knowing about it."

"That's the truth," Ted grumbled. "All our dirty laundry on display for the in-laws to see."

"Oh, stop," Susan said. "It's not like that."

Jack laughed and shuffled the deck. "Only married folks and siblings bicker back and forth like that." Jack looked at Kathy and winked.

"My kin are mostly gone," Kathy said. "My sisters, my parents, gone. Just dust in the wind, like that old song said."

"I'm sorry," Susan said. "I didn't mean to bring any of that up."

"No worries. Been so long I barely remember their faces." Kathy's eyes went far away as she picked at the hem of her sleeve. "Strange the way that happens, when you forget the sound of your own mother's voice."

"They've been gone a long time?" Susan asked.

"Feels like a hundred years," she replied.

As Jack began dealing the cards, the nearest lantern sputtered and went out, plunging the room into darkness.

"Goddammit," he blurted. "We're out of kerosene."

"Don't we have more in the back?" Kathy asked.

"Nope, used it all up." Jack placed the deck on the table and stood. "I have to go to the post office and see if they have any."

"The post office?" Ted asked.

"Yessir, that's where we store most of the kero."

Jack walked to the door and opened it onto the rain spattered pavement. He looked up and down the empty street and came back to the table, his heavy hands planted on his hips in irritation.

"So what now?" Ted asked.

"I have to make a run to the post office, grab a few cans. If you're up for the walk, I could sure use the help," he said. Ted had no intention of doing anything of the sort, but after the hospitality Jack and Kathy had shown them, it would be rude not to offer assistance. It couldn't be that far, and he still had his raincoat.

"Sure, I'll come along," Ted answered. Susan looked at him, worried. She wasn't keen on spending quality time with Kathy and her sad tales. Jack caught her eyes and smiled.

"It's fine, dear," he said. "Twenty minutes and we're back in business. Kathy can keep you company."

"Sure, I guess so," Susan said. "Just hurry back."

"Two shakes of a lamb's tail," Jack said.

Susan giggled.

"Never heard that one before?" Jack asked. "It goes way back. We're a little behind the times out here."

"Don't worry, I'll take good care of your woman," Kathy said.

Ted nodded and pulled the slicker over his clothes. He raised the hood and kissed Susan on the cheek. "We'll be back in a bit, don't worry."

Susan shrugged. She didn't like it one bit, but how could Ted say no? These strangers were nice enough to invite them into their home and feed them. It was the least Ted could do to return the favor. When this was over, she planned on a hot shower, a steaming cup of coffee, and staying in bed for a month. How could they ever explain any of this to their friends or family without getting looks of pure disbelief?

"Let's get going then," Jack said. "The sooner we're gone, the sooner we'll return."

Ted offered a quick wave and followed Jack into the downpour.

"We got some time to kill," Kathy said. "What would you like to talk about?"

***

The rain soured Ted's mood instantly. Just when he thought they'd left soggy socks behind, he was gearing up for more of the same. At least when they returned, he'd have somewhere warm and dry to lay his head. Maybe he'd even have a chance to catch a few hours of sleep without the constant threat of wild animals and old women who hoarded cell phones like a Precious Moments collection.

"Your girl seems nice," Jack shouted over the rain.

"She's a keeper," Ted replied. "She put up with my shit after all these years."

Jack laughed and wiped rain from his face. "Been together long then?"

"We started dating in High School."

"Long time," Ted stated. "Still got that passion, huh?"

"Yeah," Ted laughed. "I guess we do."

"Me and Kathy got that," he said. "Oh, and that girl knows how to fuck, if you know what I mean."

"Uh, yeah, that's pretty plainly stated," he replied uncomfortably.

Jack roared with laughter. It was clear to Ted that years of self-imposed exile had changed their ability to interact socially. He scratched his forehead and kept his thoughts to himself.

"That woman bends in ways you wouldn't imagine," Jack said. "And when she gets a hold of your tool, forget it! She'll tug on it like a hungry dog."

Ted choked back laughter and wondered what stories Kathy was filling Susan's head with. If she was anything like her husband, Ted was sure Susan would be getting quite the education right about now.

"Maybe later on, you take her for a spin," Jack said. "She's always up for trying new things."

"Oh, no, uh, no really. I don't think Susan would like that very much."

"So she's a prude then? Well, your loss."

"No, not a prude," Ted explained. "Conventional."

"To hell with convention," Jack barked. "Does she suck your cock or what?"

Ted looked at him, stunned, slowing his pace. "Jack, not to be disrespectful, but I'm not going to discuss that with you."

"Sure, sure, I understand. Not everyone's as open as me and my Kathy."

No one is as open as you and Kathy, Ted thought. *Thankfully.*

"How far is the post office?" Ted asked. Being alone with Jack suddenly felt like being part of a gag reel. The sooner they finished their trek across town, the better.

"Few blocks," Jack said. "Town's not very big."

Conversation died. Ted didn't know if he offended Jack, but it wasn't high on his list of priorities. Whatever he and Susan did behind closed doors was private. He'd shared in locker room talk with his buddies, but Jack was a complete stranger and old enough to be his father. He wasn't about to divulge he and his wife's sex life to a man who lived in an abandoned building.

"You two have kids?" Jack asked.

"No," Ted replied quickly. "Haven't had the time."

"Time's all we got out here," Jack chuckled. "Kathy and I have seven," he said. "All girls if you believe that."

"I'm sure that keeps you busy," Ted said.

"Our oldest has ten years on you. She looks after the little ones. I swear I can't look at Kathy without her getting pregnant."

"I didn't see them back at your place."

"No, hell no. They don't live with us. I fucking hate kids," he laughed.

Ted bit his lip.

"Kathy got pregnant the first time when she was seventeen. Fucked her once in the shed behind the house and *bang*, another mouth to feed."

"Uh, wow," Ted groaned. "That's tough."

"Tough? It was tough when daddy found out. He didn't approve one bit."

"Her father didn't?"

"*Our* father," he grumbled. "Daddy didn't think what we were doing was right, so he made her keep it. That kid was never going to win any beauty contests, that's for sure," Jack bellowed. "Ugly as a shaved Pitbull."

"Wait, what? You have the same father?"

"Ain't you paying attention? Kathy's my little sister. Who better to understand you than your own blood, am I right?"

Ted was stunned by the sudden clarity. Of course they wouldn't leave this place behind; Jack and Kathy were brother and sister, siblings who'd had a brood of children conceived out of incest. It made his stomach churn. The macaroni and cheese laid in his gut like a hot ball of wax.

"She started growing them little titties when she was eight."

"Okay, Jack, I don't need to know any of this. This is your thing, doesn't have to be mine. I'm not judging anyone."

"Judging us?" Jack said, stopping short. "Who are you to judge us? You drive around in your new cars and wear your hundred dollar shirts, and you're going to judge us."

"No, Jack, I said I'm *not* judging you. Whatever you choose to do with your life is none of my business."

"You're damn right it's none of your business," Jack scolded. "We're simple people. We don't need all that distraction you surround yourselves with. We have each other and that's *all* we need. Everything else just rots your brain."

"Of course," Ted agreed. "You're right."

"All we need is the love of a good woman and children to carry on our legacy."

"Sure, sure," Ted nodded. "I hear you Jack."

"I should think so, I'm right here."

"Maybe we should head back," Ted said. "Susan's going to start worrying about me."

"Your woman is in safe hands. Kathy fed you and kept you out of the cold, least you can do is get her some kero for the lamps."

"Okay," Ted said. "We get the kerosene and we get right back."

"Well hasn't that been the plan all along?" Jack laughed. "Sometimes I think you city folk don't have the brains God gave you."

Jack turned and continued along the rain soaked street and Ted followed at a safe distance. They passed darkened buildings on either side: a market, a dress shop, a jewelry store, a restaurant. Each one had been boarded up and was coated in grime; in some, orange light flickered through the cracks between planks that had been nailed over the windows. This had been a place where people worked, had children - *normal* children - and lived out their lives. Ted wondered if all of Pine Lakes' residents had similar stories to Jack's. God, he hoped not.

They passed a tall, white church on their right. A burn barrel blazed at the top of the front steps and a small group of people stood huddled around it. Jack raised a hand and several people waved in return. A woman dressed in rags, grabbed a small child and pushed him behind her. Whether for the child's safety, or for Ted's was uncertain. A bulletin board hung on the church's front wall. Faded, plastic letters read: Repent! And ye shall be saved!

Looking around, Ted wondered if anyone actually believed that.

Ted thought he heard quiet singing behind the sturdy doors, but couldn't be sure over the crashing thunder. The group dispersed and entered the church. Soft light spilled into the rain in a yellow arc. They closed the door behind them without even a glance over their shoulders.

Not a very friendly bunch.

"Used to be St. Joseph's," Jack said. "Doesn't really have a name anymore. We call it The Refuge."

"The Refuge?" Ted asked. "Refuge from what?"

Jack's only reply was a deep, rumbling laugh. He turned down a wide side street, crossing beneath a dark traffic light that swung in the wind.

"Post office is right over here," Jack pointed. "Next to the booby bar."

"The what?"

"The booby bar. What? You think we don't have any entertainment in this backwater town? I have a mind to stop in and fill my flask while we're here."

"You've got to be kidding me?"

"I kid you not. Man has desires, you know. Even a man such as yourself must like to look at a naked woman now and again."

Ted was becoming more and more certain that coming with Jack was a mistake, but there was no way to back out now, barring just turning around and running back to Susan. Were these people dangerous?

"You coming or what?" Jack asked.

Ted followed.

***

"Can I get you anything else from the kitchen?" Kathy asked.

"No, I'm fine, thank you."

Kathy returned to her seat and stared out into the rain. She'd opened the front door to get some air in the room, but it did little for the smell permeating the old store: faint chemicals, wet wood, and the oily stink of unwashed bodies. The moist air blowing through the open door carried the smell of wood smoke and the less pleasant tang of spoiled trash. Ted had only been gone for five minutes and already Susan was wondering when they'd return. There was something seriously *off* about this place.

"Do you and your husband have children? They must be wondering where you are by now."

"Oh," Susan said. "No, we don't have any kids."

"Young couple, I just figured you'd be working on that great American family," Kathy said. "White picket fence, swing set in the yard."

Susan visibly deflated. Not *this* conversation again. "We were trying," she said, "but I lost the baby."

"Oh, honey, I'm sorry. I didn't mean to bring it up."

"No, it's okay. I think I'm finally able to deal with it, most of the time anyway."

"It's that nasty air drifting in from the city," Kathy explained. "All that pollution. It gets up inside you and starts to fester."

"It just wasn't our time," Susan said.

"Is that what you've been telling yourself?" Kathy laughed. "Mark my words, it's the air and the chemicals in the food. It muddies the waters."

"Maybe that's part of it, I don't know. I never really sat down and thought about why."

"It was God's way of saying you ain't cut out to be a mother."

"What?" Susan gasped.

"God has a way of correcting mistakes," she continued.

"You're saying my baby was a mistake?" Susan asked, exasperated.

"No, honey, relax." Kathy leaned forward and patted Susan's knee. "I'm not saying anything. God made that decision. It was He who decided your baby was a mistake."

"That's ridiculous," Susan shouted.

"I don't make the rules, I just abide by them. I can dump out kids like a stray cat. I haven't offended God. I live a simple life."

"You're insane," Susan yelled. She stood and walked a few steps away as if Kathy was contagious. "We didn't do anything wrong. It just happened. It happens to a lot of couples!"

"Couples drenched in sin," Kathy stated. "Your little snapper is drowning in the filth of a society hellbent on destroying itself."

"That's disgusting," Susan moaned.

"Yes it is," Kathy replied. She stood up quickly and Susan saw the glint of metal sticking from beneath the cuff of Kathy's sleeve.

"What is that?" she asked. "What are you going to do?"

"I'm going to help you," she said. "Help *purify* you."

"Purify me?" Susan backed up and bumped into one of the steel shelves. Assorted bric-à-brac rattled and fell to the floor. "You stay away from me."

"There's no reason to behave that way," Kathy said. "Just a few cuts and you'll be one of us."

"You're crazy!" Susan shrieked. "Get the fuck away from me."

"Now you're trying my patience," Kathy scolded. "We've been nothing but kind to you and this is how you repay us?"

Susan glanced at the open door but Kathy was on her before she could move a muscle. She pressed her body against Susan's, their faces only inches apart. Susan smelled the fetid reek of Kathy's rotting teeth and choked back a sour belch. She felt pressure between her legs and looked to see the knife Kathy had been concealing. Eight inches of gleaming steel. Kathy pushed the pointed tip into Susan's jeans and traced lines around the swell of her vagina. Susan wanted to vomit.

"You don't want to move right now," Kathy whispered. "Not unless you want this blade up your cooze."

"You're sick," Susan hissed. "Let me go, right now!"

"Let you go? Where do you think you are little girl? You don't get to tell me what to do. This is *my* world. You're still breathing only because I've allowed it, but you keep talking out of turn and I might just slip." The point of the blade poked through the fabric of Susan's jeans and cut a small gash in her leg. She whimpered and attempted to melt through the wall as blood trickled down her leg, tickling the tender flesh of her thigh.

"Please," Susan pleaded. "You don't have to do anything crazy. Just let me go. You'll never see me again."

"You say *crazy* one more time and I'm going to bury this blade so far inside you that you'll taste blood in the back of your mouth."

A single tear escaped Susan's left eye and streaked over her cheek.

Kathy wiped it away with her rough, gnarled hand and licked it from her fingertip. Susan shuddered and tried to pull away but Kathy pushed even closer. Her breathing had become more frantic. She was enjoying this.

"Are you getting wet down there?" Kathy rasped. "I certainly am. Your crying only helps."

Susan sniffed, took a deep breath, and tried to get herself under control.

"Oh, even your breath is sweet," Kathy cooed. "We're going to have some fun, you and I."

Kathy put her hand between Susan's leg and cupped her vagina with a trembling hand, applying pressure in just the right way. Susan cried out, disgusted that her body reacted to the woman's touch. It made her feel dirty.

"Stop," Susan said. "Please stop."

"You stay stop and I say go," Kathy giggled. "You just hold still for a minute and we'll get this party started."

Kathy fumbled with the button on Susan's pants, grumbling and talking to herself. Susan's skin crawled as a thin line of drool escaped from Kathy's mouth and ran over her chin. Without a word, Kathy removed the knife from Susan's crotch and placed it on the coffee table. With two hands, she had Susan's button open in seconds. She stood up, smiled, and saw the look on Susan's face a moment too late.

Susan swung her arm as hard as she could, connecting with Kathy's jaw with a loud pop. The shock of the impact sent a bolt of pain up Susan's arm. Kathy staggered back, tripped over the leg of the table, and fell to the floor with a garbled shriek. She recovered quickly, reaching up for the knife as Susan kicked out, striking a glancing blow on the woman's elbow. Susan reached down and picked up the blade, brandishing it in front of her. The spasming flicker of lightning made the entire struggle appear like it was happening in slow motion.

"Oh, you stupid whore," Kathy screamed. "You're going to regret that."

"No, *you're* going to regret it," Susan shouted. "If you get off that floor I'm going to cut you, I swear I will."

Kathy cackled and pulled herself into a sitting position. "You don't know what you've done, you stupid bitch. You just signed your fucking death warrant."

"I'm the one holding the knife," Susan said, smiling. "Who's the stupid bitch now?"

Susan backed toward the door, opening a gap between them.

"When Jack gets back, he's going peel the skin from your face," Kathy hissed. "Do you hear me?"

"I'm not going to be here when he gets back," Susan said. "I'm going to find them first. God help anyone that gets in my way."

"Oh, the little girl's got a pig sticker and all of a sudden she's going to be a hero. You went and fucked with the wrong family."

"No one has to get hurt," Susan said. "You just let me go, I'll find my husband, and we'll never have to see each other again. That's fair, don't you think?"

"I don't think it's fair at all. The second you grabbed a hold of that knife, fair went out the window."

"You were holding it on *me*!" Susan screamed. "You cut my fucking leg."

"When Jack comes back, you'll think that little scratch was nothing more than a lover's kiss," Kathy said. "He'd going to gut you like a fish and feed your uterus to the dog!"

"You're *vile*," Susan moaned. "What's wrong with you people?"

"*You* people," Kathy said. "You think you're so much better than us?"

"We don't do stuff like this to each other. There's a civilized world out there that you know nothing about."

"A civilized world?" Kathy scoffed. "War, famine, murder. That's a civilized world? Teenage girls strangling their babies because they wouldn't stop crying. Is that what you consider civilized?"

"I'm not having this conversation with you," Susan said. "We're done here. You can get your kicks some other way. I'm not going to be part of it."

"Oh, you're already part of it." Kathy said, wiping blood from her bottom lip. She planted her hands on the floor and stood, brushing dirt from her dress. "The little ones will eat good tonight."

"The… what? What are you talking about?"

Kathy cackled and took a step forward.

"Stay back, goddammit, I'm not fucking around." She slashed the knife through the air with a whistle and Kathy jumped back. Susan scrunched her shoulders as thunder erupted outside, but she didn't take her eyes off Kathy.

"You think you have it figured out, I bet," Kathy said. "You think you're just going to walk out of here and go back to your life as if nothing happened. *This* is your life now."

"That's not true," Susan cried. "I'm nothing like you."

"You eat, you piss, you shit, you fuck. You're exactly like us."

Somewhere in the distance, a church bell tolled sadly. The sonorous tones ebbed and flowed over the town, carried by the wind.

"What is that?" Susan asked.

"The bell on old St. Joe's church," Kathy replied. "Not much of a church goer, are you? I figured as much."

"I know it's a fucking bell," Susan yelled.

"Church is letting out, you stupid cow. And when it does, all hell breaks loose."

The bell's cry distracted her for just a second; one second too long to notice the shadow cross the floor. Susan gasped and spun on her heel, coming face to face with a giant of a woman. Her fat lips were spread over rotten teeth, her eyes darker than a winter sky. Without time to react, Susan took the full brunt of the woman's punch. She felt her nose shatter beneath the blow. Her feet left the ground as the knife was jarred from her hand. She hit the floor in a puff of dust, banging her head on the wood hard enough to see stars. The giant loomed over her, daring her to move. Susan didn't have the energy to lift her head as blood poured from her broken nose and pattered on the floor.

"This is my oldest daughter, Tess," Kathy said happily. "Good thing you got here just in time."

Tess nodded at her mother and smiled. A messy mop of hair covered portions of her face as she looked down at Susan, shoulders heaving as she inhaled huge lungfuls of stale air. A ridge of flesh jutted from above her eyes, like pictures Susan had seen of Cro-Magnon man. The skin on her massive forearms was deeply scarred from an old burn. A thick, white line crossed her throat, running from one ear to the other. Her clothes were covered in patches of filth, muck, food, and what appeared to be dried blood.

"Tess doesn't talk," Kathy said, "but she doesn't need to. She gets her point across with those lovely hands of hers."

Tess stomped across the floor with feet like canoes. She stood over Susan, dripping cold water onto her skin.

Redneck water torture, Susan thought, braying laughter.

"What the fuck's so funny?" Kathy shouted angrily.

"You. All of this. You're monsters and you don't even see it."

"Maybe we are," Kathy mused, "but we're *your* monsters now."

Tess bent down, grabbed Susan's shoulders, and slammed her head into the floor with a loud thud.

Susan chased the sound of the tolling bell as she slipped into unconsciousness.

***

Jack's booby bar was exactly what Ted had pictured in his mind: a rundown dump with photos of nude women locked behind glass cases. A large, dark sign above the door read 'Neal's Pub.' Maybe in better times the establishment had been reputable, but looking at it now, Ted only grimaced distastefully.

Men stood out front, their clothes soaked from the rain. Their conversation ceased as Jack and Ted approached. A boy of about ten jumped up and down in front of the building's only window, trying to catch a glimpse of the wonders beyond. He turned and studied Ted with eyes that pointed in opposite directions. He had a cleft palette that twisted his mouth into a painful-looking grin. His feet were bare.

"What brings you out tonight, Jack?" one of the men asked, tossing a cigarette into the street.

"Needed kero. Figured I'd stop for a drink and a grope."

"Who's your friend?"

"This is Ted. He's just passing through, aren't you Ted?"

"Uh, yes, passing through. Nice to meet you," Ted said, offering his hand.

The other man shook his head and lifted his arm, showing off a stump covered in twisted flesh. His mouth was smiling, but his eyes were blank. Another man laughed, lips flapping wetly over toothless gums.

"How're the girls tonight?" Jack asked.

"Doing okay," the one-handed man replied. "Julie got smacked around again."

Jack laughed and put his hands over his sizable stomach. "What happened this time?"

"She's still getting a little *toothy* with her blowjobs," the man laughed. "She's been warned how many times?"

"Too many," Jack grumbled. "Next time we're going to have to take her teeth. Can't have that kind of thing going on or the guys will stop coming."

"Ain't no one coming if she keeps it up."

The group erupted in hearty laughter and applause. The one-handed man fancied himself a comedian.

"Come on Ted," Jack said, "let's get out of the rain and see what's on the menu."

Ted shook his head side to side but followed anyway. Jack scared him. This entire town scared him. Better to keep the peace than piss him off again.

The room was dimly lit by several well-placed lanterns, but the back of the space was still cloaked in shadow. Ted wrinkled his nose at the mixture of smells: stale booze, cigarette smoke, spoiled food, sweat, and sex. Lots of sex. The floor was covered in sawdust and peanut shells and bodily fluids much more disgusting than just congealed vomit. A long, L-shaped bar was filled with men of all ages, from seventy, to a boy barely old enough to grow a beard. A gray boom box sat on the edge of the bar. The shell was cracked and the tape deck played an old Creedence cassette. A stack of D-cell batteries sat nearby; obviously another stockpile they'd pocketed from one of the local stores. How else would one play their Creedence tapes without electricity?

"Daddy!" a woman said cheerily.

The woman in question would never be pretty, no matter how much make-up she caked on her pockmarked face. Her dirty blond hair had been cut crudely, likely with a dull pair of scissors; she was completely nude, and her left breast was scarred and missing a nipple. She wrapped her thin arms around Jack and kissed him passionately on the mouth. Ted looked away, horrified.

"Who's this?" she asked, motioning to Ted.

"No one you need to worry about," Jack said. "He's a happily married man."

"Oh, the married ones are the most fun," she cooed.

"Never you mind. Just get back out there and do your thing. The customers don't come here to see you yapping."

The woman patted Ted's chest, winked, and walked away.

"One of my girls," Jack explained. "Three of my daughters work here. Have to make a living somehow."

"They're paid to work here?" Ted asked.

"Not with money. We don't have any need for that. It's all in trade."

Ted didn't want to think about what exactly they were trading. His stomach was already twisted in knots just being here. Jack not only condoned his daughters' behavior, but he was their biggest fan. The way Jack watched his daughter's naked body wind through the assembled patrons made Ted sick, not to mention the passionate kiss they'd shared just moments before.

"She'll do anything you want," Jack said, leaning toward Ted. "We taught her well."

"No thanks, really. Susan's all I need."

"Your loss."

They continued through the darkened room and Jack took a seat at the bar. He patted the stool next to him and ordered two shots he called the 'house special.' Ted sat next to him and scanned the back bar. There were dozens of bottles without labels containing a variety of different colored liquors. The bartender grabbed one with a thick, clear fluid and poured it into two dirty shot glasses. Jack slid one over and smiled wryly.

"That's going to put hair on your chest."

"I shouldn't be drinking," Ted said.

"It's only a shot. Drink it." Jack left little room for interpretation. It wasn't a request, it was an order.

Ted raised the glass to his nose and sniffed at the pungent concoction.

"Down the hatch," he said, raising his glass to Jack. He downed the shot in one swallow and groaned. It burned all the way down, igniting a flame in his gut.

"Smooth, ain't it?" Jack smiled.

"Sure," Ted coughed. "Smooth."

"Another round," Jack called.

Ted turned and watched as a woman walked to the end of a handmade catwalk. She was greeted with applause from most, but several jeers boomed from the back of the room.

"That's Julie," Jack informed. "Hell of a body, but she can't please the men to save her life. She ain't one of mine, no sir."

Ted could *see* that clearly; she didn't belong here. Her skin was unmarred, and long auburn hair hung down to her full breasts. She did her best to hide her most private areas from the leering crowd. She smiled shamefully, exhibiting a set of straight, white teeth; teeth Jack said he was going to remove if she didn't learn how to please the patrons without biting.

"Grind it!" a raspy voice shouted from the shadows.

"Yeah, show us the fur," another called.

"She's new," Jack said. "Only been here a short time. Came into town and decided she liked it so much, she just couldn't leave."

Ted doubted that. Doubted it very much. She was gorgeous. Too classy to be spending time being ridiculed in a sleazy strip joint off the grid. Something was very wrong with this picture.

As "Fortunate Son" blared from the tinny speakers of the ancient tape deck, Julie gyrated and spun around a grimy pole, only looking into the audience when her name was called. She squinted through clouds of stinging smoke, bumping her backside to the beat of the music. Ted's eyes and hers connected for just a second, and her pain flooded over him in a series of waves.

She's a prisoner, Ted thought, suddenly weakened by the realization. *She's trapped here, just like they intend on trapping me and Suzie here.*

"Enjoying the show?" Jack asked, sliding another shot in Ted's direction. Ted downed it, grimaced, and nodded.

"She's beautiful," Ted said. He watched as Julie stoically went through the motions, trying to hold on to her last remaining scraps of dignity. A loose plan formed in his mind; a plan to get Julie out of this dump, to get them all out. Ted suffered from something Susan called *injured bird syndrome*, the need to help those who appeared damaged and in need of rescue. She wasn't wrong. Seeing someone suffer just wasn't in his nature.

And there was no question Julie was suffering.

"Show us your goddamn bush," a man shouted. A glass mug flew through the shadows and hit Julie in the knee. By the look in her eyes that one hurt. Once she recovered, she turned to the crowd and offered what the man wanted. Ted looked away as scattered cheers filled the room. He wasn't interested in seeing any more of Julie than he already had, especially that all-consuming hurt in her eyes.

"She's still learning the ropes," Jack growled, crunching on a mouthful of stale corn chips. "Maybe you'd like a turn with her," he winked. "In private."

A light flicked on in Ted's head. "Yeah, I sure would," he said. "How about another drink?"

"Now that's more like it," Jack shouted. "Get this man a drink!"

The third shot went down like wildfire, but Ted was beginning to grow accustomed to the taste. He looked into the crowd and saw a man near the catwalk unzip his fly and dangle his penis next to the stage.

These people are cavemen, Ted thought.

"Give it a tug," the man with the exposed privates shouted. "It's not going to tug itself."

Ted looked away. If Julie did what she was told was not his concern. His stomach rolled.

"When does she get off?" Ted asked.

"Ten minutes or so," Jack replied. "You're raring to go, ain't you?"

"Is it that obvious?" Ted played along.

Jack laughed and slapped him on the shoulder. "It'll be our little secret."

Over the course of several more songs, Ted ran through his options. If this was going to work, it needed to happen quickly and quietly. He knew he needed a little liquid courage to pull this off, but too much was going to make him slow and stupid. Already his head was swimming from the effects of the alcohol.

"You have private rooms in the back I assume?" Ted asked.

"Sure we do," Jack said. "Or you can take care of your business right here. Ain't no one bashful in this group," he laughed.

"I think I'd prefer to be alone," he said. "I'm not much of an exhibitionist."

"Any way you want it."

The song ended and Jack waved Julie over to the bar. A few of the drunks pawed at her as she made her way through them, grabbing at her breasts and ass. She smiled and did her best to dodge their groping fingers. When she got to the bar, she sat on an empty stool and crossed her legs. This close, Ted saw she was absolutely stunning, but also completely horrified at what she'd been forced to do. She couldn't make eye contact with either of them.

"Julie, this is my new friend, Ted." Jack said. "You're going to give him anything he wants."

"Yes, Jack," she mumbled.

"That's a good girl. Take him back to room three. Anything he wants; everything he wants."

"Yes, Jack."

"You bite his cock and we're going to have a discussion about your future here at the club."

Ted felt a soft hand take hold of his arm and lead him to the shadowy corridor at the end of the bar. There were closed doors on either side, six in total. The door to room three was open; a smell like bleach and sweat wafted into the hallway. All around him Ted heard the muffled grunts of others partaking in the bar's dancers. His stomach churned thinking of what awful things must have taken place here.

Julie led him into the room, lit by a single lantern hanging from the ceiling. One straight-backed chair sat in the middle of the floor, surrounded by cigarette butts and several bottles. One of them was full to the brim with yellow liquid that Ted assumed was piss.

"Let me get that out of the way," Julie said, grabbing the bottle and putting it in the corner of the room. "Some of the guys are into water sports."

"Huh?"

"They like to be peed on," she replied. "It's not always easy to pee on command, so we store some for special occasions. I'll do it if you want to me to, but I'd rather you didn't."

"No, oh my God, of course not."

Julie grabbed a thin sheet of plastic from a pile on the floor and draped it over the chair. "Jack wants us to keep the place clean," she said. "Have to use the plastic or he gets irritated."

"Jack owns the place?" Ted asked.

"Jack owns everything," Julie said, "and everyone."

Once she covered the chair, she motioned Ted to sit. She knelt between his legs and undid the button on his pants. He grabbed her hand and shook his head slowly. "No," he said. "Sit in my lap, facing me."

"No foreplay? I'm fine with that."

Julie sat in his lap and started grinding back and forth on his thighs. He put his hands on her shoulders and pulled her closer. "Don't," he said. "Listen to me and listen carefully."

She stopped, her eyes full of fear. "Am I doing something wrong? Please, I'll fix it, don't tell Jack or..."

"No," Ted interrupted. "You're not doing anything wrong. Just listen."

Julie put a finger up to her lips and made a display of looking to either side of the room. "Whatever you want," she said, acting on his cue.

Ted nodded, understanding. They were being watched. He pulled her closer, feeling her nipples press against his chest through his shirt. He wrapped a hand in her thick hair and pulled her face to within inches of his. Ted hadn't been this close to another woman in over twenty years.

"Listen," he whispered in her ear. "We're getting out of here."

She pushed him away, looked in his eyes, and began crying silently. It broke Ted's heart to feel that kind of pain radiate from another human being so profoundly.

"Do you know what you're up against?" she asked.

"I have a pretty good idea," he said, "but it doesn't change anything."

Julie leaned in and kissed him on the cheek lightly. "You get me out of here and I'll do anything you want, I swear."

"I'm married," Ted laughed, displaying his wedding band. "Happily married."

"Of course you are. All the good ones are taken." She blew a hot, trembling breath against his neck. "So what do we do?"

"Is there a back door to this shit hole?"

"Yeah, through the kitchen," she said. "Jack usually has one of his goons there so the girls don't try to slip out."

"We'll cross that bridge if we have to," Ted said. "Can you run naked?"

"I've done worse things naked."

Ted nodded sympathetically. "Then that's what we do. Quick as we can."

"That's the plan?"

"Do you have a better one?"

Julie shook her head and frowned.

"On three, you run for the door. I'll follow you."

Julie nodded.

"We're only going to get one chance to pull this off," Ted said.

"Then we better make it a good one."

7

TED DIDN'T HAVE TIME TO THINK OR REACT; WHEN HE SAW THE slovenly bodyguard standing at the door, his body took over. He punched the man in the face in one fluid motion, stepping out of the way as he collapsed to the floor in a heap. Blood dripped on the tile from his broken nose.

"My God," Julie said. "You knocked him out cold."

"I've never punched anyone in my life," he said, suddenly feeling like a superhero.

Julie reached out and twisted the latch on the door. It opened silently into a rear alley clogged with garbage and broken furniture. Rats scurried away from the commotion as Ted and Julie splashed onto the wet asphalt. Behind them came the muffled shouts of Jack's men; Ted turned and watched them tumble from a hidden door in the wall.

The sick bastards had a network of passages behind the walls of the private rooms where they could watch the festivities. Ted watched one man button his jeans frantically, tucking his erection into a pair of filthy jeans. He frowned and slammed the kitchen door behind him. To his right sat a large metal dumpster overflowing with soggy garbage bags.

"It has wheels," Ted exclaimed. "Help me push."

Julie joined Ted at the side of the dumpster and braced her bare shoulder against the cold steel. They were both pleasantly surprised when the dumpster rolled freely; five feet and the heavy container blocked the bar's only rear entrance.

"Jack, they're running!" a voice shouted. "They're running out the back."

Heavy blows slammed the other side of the door, but the dumpster didn't budge. Ted figured it gave them a short, but very welcome head start.

Jack's weathered face appeared at the single window, eyes blazing, spittle glistening in the thick fur around his mouth. He gripped the chicken wire and pushed but it stayed fast. Ted was momentarily paralyzed by the all-consuming rage in the man's eyes.

"You're a dead man," Jack spit. "You and the whore."

They didn't stay long enough for conversation. They ran to the edge of the alley where it opened out onto the main street and stopped briefly to get their bearings. Tall, vacant buildings surrounded them on either side. Julie hopped up and down on bare feet to keep herself warm as she waited for Ted to make the next move.

"I have to get my wife," Ted panted. "She's at Jack's."

"Oh, no," Julie cried. "That's the first place they're going to look."

"I know that, but I'm not leaving Susan to fend for herself. She's with Jack's wife, sister, whatever the fuck she is!"

"That way," Julie pointed. "I think it's that way."

They ran up the center of the street, hearing the commotion a block away; Jack's bar had emptied out onto the sidewalk and his clientele were gathering in front of the building. Ted couldn't see them, but there was no mistaking the raucous sound of a lynch mob.

"We're too exposed," Ted whispered. "We have to get off the road."

"What about there?" Julie asked, pointing. A narrow, weedy path ran along the side of the first building in a ramshackle row of houses. "Maybe we can cut through the yards."

"Do people live there?"

"I don't know," she whined. "I haven't been outside of the club more than two or three times, but I remember that alley; it leads down to the woods."

"It's worth the risk, I guess," Ted said.

Ted led them through the tight passage as Julie tip-toed carefully around scattered fragments of glass. The further they went, the darker it became. Behind them, angry shouts echoed into the night as the throng quickly spread out and searched for their prisoner. At the end of the tight path, Ted pushed on a rotten, wooden gate, and they entered an overgrown yard covered in trash.

"You really know how to show a lady a good time," Julie said.

Ted laughed nervously and scanned the area behind the houses. Halfway down the block he noticed firelight flickering in one of the yards, but the space appeared empty.

"If we follow this, it'll take us to Jack's?" Ted asked.

Julie nodded. "I think so. I haven't been outside in so long." She scrunched her toes in the grass and sighed. "God, I almost forgot what this felt like."

Ted frowned, nodded, and started wading through the waist-high growth. The wet grass felt good on his sweaty arms, but the rain had begun falling more steadily, quickly turning the sensation into more of an annoyance as they carried on. They approached the fire cautiously, scanning the dark, ready for a fight if necessary. Julie bent and picked up the broken neck of a beer bottle. Any weapon was better than none. She held it in front of her defensively, gritting her teeth.

Ted stopped and gasped.

They'd stumbled on someone's dinner.

"What the fuck?" Ted cried.

A human ribcage sizzled on a large branch like a pig on a spit. Several other choice cuts sat nearby, steaming, filling the air with the pleasant aroma of cooking meat. Ted bent over and vomited, his stomach cramping painfully.

"It's true," Julie moaned. "It's all true."

"What's true?" Ted asked, wiping his mouth.

"They're cannibals!" Julie exclaimed. "I've heard stories, but I never saw it with my own eyes."

"Is this enough proof for you?" Ted shouted, suddenly regretting it. "I'm sorry."

"No, I am," Ted said, patting her shoulder. "You didn't know."

Ted gagged. His mouth watered from the smell of the cooking meat while his mind fought against the reality. His head swam from the alcohol and his skin felt greasy and hot.

"Come on," Julie said shyly. "Jack's isn't far."

As they crept through the shadows, they heard angry shouts from the street out front. Jack's men were combing the entire area, banging on doors, kicking over garbage cans. It was obvious they'd done this before; they were prepared, organized, conducting a professional grid search. It was only a matter of time before someone noticed the trail of crushed grass they'd left behind. Ted glanced at the rear of one of the houses and saw pale faces pushed up against the cloudy glass, watching them with wide, blank stares.

"There," Julie panted. "That's Jack's."

She was right. Ted recognized the two-story building where they'd shared a meal with Jack and Kathy. He gagged again and covered his mouth with his arm. *What was in that bowl? What in God's name did they feed us?*

As they stood hunched behind the porch of the last house, a hollow bell chimed in the distance. It was a constant, booming, warble that rattled Ted's teeth in his skull. He'd never heard something so ominous in his life.

"What is that?" he whispered.

"The church bell," Julie replied. "That's where they gather."

"Gather for *what?*" he whined.

"Most of the time, to pray and beg forgiveness for their sins."

"Most of the time?"

"When it keeps ringing, it only means one thing."

Ted opened his eyes wide and held his breath.

"It's a hunting party."

***

When Susan opened her eyes, she saw only shades of gray. It took a moment for her vision to clear. Her head was on fire from the blow to the face and she found it difficult to breathe through her swollen nose. She tasted the coppery tang of blood in her mouth. She quickly realized the ringing in her ears was real; that damn church bell was still clanging incessantly, drilling into her brain.

"Well, look who's awake," Kathy cooed. "I thought that knock to the head was going to put you out for good."

"Fuck you!" Susan spit. Her voice was so thick she barely recognized it.

"Is that any way to treat your host?"

Susan struggled and noticed her arms and legs were both bound with thick hanks of rope. She was tied to a long metal table covered in a sticky, yellow film.

"Why are you doing this?" Susan asked.

"We have to, honey," Kathy said. "This is just our way of life out here. Eat or be eaten."

Susan didn't like the sound of that one bit.

"Sounds like your old man got himself in a bit of trouble," Kathy said, cupping a hand around her ear comically. "Bell don't ring this long unless there's something big going down."

Susan writhed on the table as the rope bit into her flesh. Her hands slipped around in the slimy goop as Kathy leaned over her with a dripping paint brush. Susan looked down and saw she was only wearing her bra and panties. It made her sick imagining what the woman had done to her when she was unconscious. Kathy dipped the brush in a cruddy wash bucket and ran it over Susan's arm. She sucked a painful breath through her fractured nose and suddenly recognized the odor; the salty tang of butter.

"What are you doing?" she shrieked.

Kathy only laughed and continued slathering Susan's flesh.

Butter! The crazy bitch was basting her!

"You're NUTS!" Susan screamed, writhing around as much as her bonds would allow.

Her head rocked to the side as a heavy fist slammed into her cheek. She looked up groggily and saw Tess standing next to the table, smiling stupidly through a mouthful of brown teeth.

"What did I tell you about using that word?" Kathy asked. "We ain't crazy, we just do things a bit differently."

"Differently?" Susan laughed. "You're covering me in butter you fucking monster!"

Tess hit her again, hard enough for Susan's vision to cloud over. She pushed her tongue against the side of her mouth and felt one of her molars wiggle in the socket painfully.

"Be careful Tess," Kathy warned. "You know the meat gets sour if you rough them up."

Tess nodded and backed away, wringing her massive hands. For her, the beating was the best part.

The fight had gone out of Susan. Her head throbbed, her tense muscles burned. She felt her bladder let go as Kathy angrily tossed the brush in the bucket.

"Well that's just great," she said. "The nerve of some people."

Tess made a rumbling noise that may have been laughter.

"Ted," Susan moaned.

"Don't you worry your pretty little head about your old man," Kathy said. "I'm sure Jack's taking *good* care of him. Hell, he might have even gotten him laid by now," she laughed. "Jack's very giving when it comes to the girls."

Susan had no idea what she was talking about. She couldn't follow the conversation. It was just jumbled nonsense. The rain, the thunder, that goddamn bell.

Kathy grabbed one of Susan's breasts harshly and giggled. "I'm going to enjoy eating these," she said. Susan groaned and cried out weakly. This was not the vacation she'd hoped for.

"Once Jack gets back with your man, we can get this party started," Kathy said.

"Why?" Susan cried. "Why would you do this?"

"Oh, you poor thing," Kathy said. She ran a hand over Susan's hair and brushed it back from her forehead. "You really don't know anything about how the real world works. We're not the oddities, dear, you are."

"We don't eat people," she whined.

"Just because you don't serve them up for dinner doesn't mean you're not a bunch of hungry vultures. You fight each other for the biggest houses, the fastest cars, the fanciest furniture to put on your finely manicured lawns. You stab each other in the back for the big promotions, throw your friends under the bus just to get ahead. You advertise yourselves like the whores you are, always chasing the illusion of a lost golden era. The American Dream. You're hiding behind white, picket fences, convincing each other that you're building walls to protect what you've worked so hard for, when in reality all you're doing is hoarding what you've stolen from the weak and less fortunate. The sewers run under your feet, just like ours, and they carry the same shit. You're just inclined to think your shit smells better than ours.

Let me tell you something, honey," Kathy whispered, leaning in closer. "We all have bodies buried somewhere. Yours may be wearing Rolex watches, but they stink just the same."

"It's not true," Susan said. "Not like this. This isn't... natural."

"Natural? Who are you to decide what's natural? That's exactly what I mean. You think you're better than us just because you eat your dinner from fine china plates with fancy, expensive silverware. We're still eating, aren't we? Survival isn't based on finery, but your willingness to get your hands dirty."

The room rattled as thunder crashed overhead.

Kathy grabbed the brush from the bucket and spread a thin layer of butter across Susan's midsection, dabbing it playfully in her navel. Susan had the sinking suspicion that her story would end here, spread out on the table like Christmas dinner, but all she could think of was her last words to Ted.

Did she tell him she loved him?

She recalled something her mother had told her on she and Ted's wedding day. It was sunny and warm, and by some miracle, everything had gone exactly as planned. Minutes before walking down the aisle, her mother had pulled her aside and hugged her as only a mother can.

I'm so happy for you, her mother had gushed. *You look so beautiful.*

Mom, stop it, I'm going to ruin my makeup.

If you remember anything I've ever told you, remember this. Never go to bed angry and never leave a room without saying 'I love you.'

It had stayed with her. Sound advice from the one person who meant the most to her.

Did I tell Ted I loved him?

"I love you," she whispered.

"That's very nice, dear," Kathy cooed, "but it's too late for sweet talk."

Tess slapped her hard across the cheek, and once again Susan slipped away.

***

Ted and Julie crept to the side of the drug store, hiding in the shadows. The patrons of the strip joint had gotten closer; no building, no trash can, no tree or bush went unnoticed. If nothing else, the mob was thorough. He couldn't tell how close they were, it was simply too damn dark. The bright bursts of lightning only hurt his ability to adjust to the darkness; his eyes burned with afterimages.

"Do we just go in?" Julie asked.

"I don't see another way. When I left her, she was alone with Kathy. How much trouble can one woman be?"

"You'd be surprised. One night at the bar, one of Jack's dancers was getting a little frisky, kissing him, groping him. Kathy usually joined in the fun, but that night she was in rare form, and she wasn't having any of it. She broke a bottle over the bar and opened the girl's stomach in one motion. She bled out on the floor holding an armful of her own intestines."

"You're fucking kidding me!"

"Unfortunately not. She's as crazy as the rest of them."

He couldn't wait any longer. Ted darted across the gap between the house and the drug store, pressing himself against the wet brick, hugging the wall tightly. Julie followed, holding her breasts with her arm as she jogged to meet him.

Ted suddenly felt like Charlton Heston, running from the apes and pulling Nova behind him in all her scantily clad glory. He wanted to laugh, but he was afraid if he started he'd never be able to stop.

"I'm going in first," Ted whispered. "You don't have to come with me if you don't want. This is my responsibility."

"Are you crazy? You got me out of that damn bar. I owe you my life. If this goes wrong, at least I didn't die in a cage."

Ted smiled and nodded. "Okay then. Here we go."

He crept around the edge of the building, scanning the sidewalk in front for any sign of movement. The barrel still burned fiercely, painting the drugstore in flickering orange light. His muscles were tensed, ready to spring into action at the slightest sign of company. He wished that damn bell would stop ringing; between that, the wind, the thunder, and the steadily falling rain, it made it nearly impossible to hear anyone approaching.

Ted slid across the front of the building to the open door and peered into the dimly lit interior.

The room was empty.

He entered and slowly crept forward, testing the floor for loose boards. If he wasn't careful now, his entire plan would amount to nothing.

Where the hell is she?

Julie tapped him on the shoulder to get his attention and pointed at the doorway at the back of the room where lantern light glowed dimly. Ted had no idea what they were walking into. How did he know Jack hadn't beaten him here? Was he waiting in the shadows, ready to strangle them both with his massive hands?

He walked to the door and cautiously peeked into the darkened room, waiting for his eyes to adjust. The room was empty of furniture; towers of cardboard boxes were stacked against both walls. There was a smell Ted couldn't immediately identify, one that reminded him of holidays at his grandmother's house. Holding his breath, he crossed the threshold.

It was then the gleaming metal table came into view, and his wife's motionless body tied to it. He walked forward cautiously, expecting a trap or an ambush. The thought hadn't even fully formed in his mind when Kathy stepped out of the shadows and stopped before him. Julie moaned and turned to run, but instead came face-to-face with the wall of flesh that was Tess. The giant woman grabbed Julie by her shoulders and flung her into the room. She slid across the floor as her weapon tumbled from her hand and skated into a dark corner. She looked up at Ted apologetically.

"Look who came for dinner," Kathy cackled. "I knew you'd be back."

"Let her go, Kathy. We didn't do anything to you."

"Didn't do anything? You're running around with one of Jack's best whores. You stole from us."

"We don't want to stay here; we're not your fucking prisoners."

"It's cute you think you have a choice." Kathy walked closer, near enough for Ted to smell the sour sweat pouring off her. "We're going to start by carving up your pretty little wife."

"No!" he shrieked. "Don't you dare touch her."

"Relax," Kathy said. "There'll be plenty to go around."

Ted was pushed forward roughly; Tess walked in behind him and shut the door. His first glimpse of the towering form sent shivers up his spine.

"My daughter," Kathy said proudly.

Julie backed away, sliding on her bare rump across the floor and watching the mammoth intently. They were trapped.

Something inside Ted snapped. Without thinking, he rushed forward, tackling Kathy and knocking her into a stack of boxes. She fell to the floor with a scream, batting at him with her fists. Ted dug his thumbs into the woman's throat, intent on strangling the life from her, but before he could lock his hands, Tess grabbed him by the arm and tossed him across the floor. While she was distracted, Julie crept behind her and pounced on Tess's back, riding her like the world's ugliest horse, tearing at her face with her fingernails. Tess wailed and reached behind her, trying to yank Julie from her back. Julie tore at her hair, poked at her eyes, punched her in the neck, anything to get an advantage.

"No you don't!" Kathy shouted. "No you fucking don't!"

"You crazy bitch," Ted raged. He crawled over to Kathy and punched her square in the face, feeling her jaw crack beneath his fist. He straddled the woman's stomach and punched her over and over again as she writhed beneath him.

"Kill her!" Julie screeched. "Kill the bitch!"

Ted didn't need instructions; over and over again, his fists pummeled Kathy's fear-stricken face. Blood sprayed and spattered his shirt as her nose snapped like a dry twig. One of her eyes had already begun swelling shut; she spit teeth out like sunflower seeds.

"You crazy bitch, crazy bitch, crazy fucking bitch," he screamed. It became a mantra, timing his blows with his words as he battered her face to hamburger. He heard Julie struggling behind him, but couldn't stop until he knew Kathy wasn't going to get up. Tess wailed as Julie dug a finger into her eye socket and turned it to jelly. Her deflated eye ran down her cheek and plopped wetly to the floor. She backed up and slammed them both into the wall with crushing force. Julie's breath exploded from her lungs and she saw stars swimming before her eyes, but she held on with the rest of her waning energy.

"Just keep her away," Ted shouted. "Don't let her get the upper hand."

"Don't you think I'm trying?" Julie wailed.

Ted wrapped his hands around Kathy's throat and applied as much pressure as he could muster. With a crackle, Kathy's windpipe collapsed as she choked and gasped for air. Her one good eye vibrated in her head as she struck Ted's back weakly. Pain exploded in his ribs as Tess kicked out with one massive foot. He flew across the floor, coming to rest at the base of the table. He glanced at Susan and clutched at his bruised ribs, watching as Tess jumped and spun frantically, trying to throw Julie from her shoulders.

"No you don't you filthy monster," Ted shouted. It hurt to talk. He was afraid she'd broken his ribs. He looked at Kathy and watched her twitch out her final breaths, suffocating in her own blood. It was nothing less than what she deserved.

Ted braced himself on the metal table and his fingers grazed the wooden handle of a large butcher knife. He grabbed it and smiled. Obviously they'd underestimated his tenacity, or they wouldn't have let weapons just lying around within his reach. He ran forward, timed his attack, and plunged the blade into Tess's flesh just beneath one wildly swaying breast. Ted felt the blade sink deep, squealing across the woman's ribs. Tess screamed unintelligibly and thrashed with renewed vigor, swinging one meaty arm and nearly taking off Ted's head. He dodged at the last second, only receiving a glancing blow across his bicep.

He pulled the knife from her chest and swung it in an arc, tearing a huge gash in Tess's arm. Her blood flowed freely, dripping to the floor and staining her clothing.

"Ted, you have to hurry this up," Julie panted. "I can't hang on much longer."

"Just one more minute, Julie. Please. One more minute."

Tess spun and reached for the door, suddenly realizing the tables had been turned. She gripped the knob just as Ted speared her again. He buried the knife up to the handle just above her waist. Tess bellowed, babbling what may have been some form of crude speech. He pulled the knife from her as warm blood flooded over his wrist. Tess staggered and crashed against the door as Julie lost her grip and tumbled to the floor in a heap. The deformed monster turned and eyed Ted fearfully, clutching her fists and preparing one final charge. Before she could, he swung the blade high and dragged it across her face. A large flap of flesh dangled from her cheek; her nose opened and exposed the dark, wet cavern of her sinuses.

"NO!" Tess blubbered. "NO!" It was the only word Ted understood.

"Yes," he replied calmly. "You did this to yourself. You and your fucked up family."

He swung the blade again and opened a zipper in Tess's neck. A hot shower of blood fanned into the air, splashing Ted's face and raining onto his shirt. Julie slid away, leaving a trail of Tess's blood in her wake.

The behemoth fell to her knees, shaking the entire room. She reached for Ted as he backed away, blood running from her neck wound in a torrent. Ted smiled as as she quickly bled out. She fell on her face with a hollow thud as blood pooled around her. Her body shuddered once and grew still.

"Ted," Julie shouted, "behind you."

Ted gasped as fingers reached around his ankle. He looked down to see Kathy pulling herself across the floor. Her mouth moved, but no words came out. *Why won't you fucking die?* Ted thought.

"Cat got your tongue?" Ted asked.

The hate in Kathy's eye chilled his blood.

He shook her clutching fingers from his leg and stomped on her hand, shattering the thin bones in her wrist.

"You asked for this," Ted said. "You got exactly what was coming to you."

He held the knife above his head and plunged it down, skewering Kathy's face with a crunch.

The room stank of blood and shit, but was mercifully silent. Ted collapsed against the wall, chest heaving. He smiled at Julie and closed his eyes. "That could have gone better."

"Are they dead?" Julie asked, standing and brushing dirt from her sweaty skin.

Ted nodded. "Our biggest problem is what's going on outside. They're going to be here any minute, and I don't want to be around when they kick the door open."

Ted tucked the knife into his waistband and crossed the room in two large steps. He looked at Susan, his throat constricting, his eyes burning with tears. Her exposed skin was covered in a layer of grease Ted identified as butter.

"Oh my God," he whined. "They were going to cook her, just like those bodies in the yard! They were actually going to eat her."

Julie nodded. Nothing here surprised her anymore.

"Suzie? Honey, are you okay?" Ted patted her swollen cheek lightly. He wished Kathy and Tess were still alive so he could kill them again. He tugged at the rope binding her to the table, and had her free within seconds, but it wasn't nearly as easy bringing her back to consciousness. Whoever had been beating on her had done a hell of a job.

"Just carry her," Julie said. "We can't wait around any longer."

She was right, their time had run out. Any minute, the drugstore would be packed with them, and there was only one way that was going to end.

Ted lifted Susan's motionless body from the table and nearly dropped her. It was like trying to carry a greased watermelon; she kept slipping through his fingers. He spied Susan's clothes nearby and hastily pulled them over her slick skin. He pulled a dirty sheet from the window and wrapped her in it as she moaned deep in her throat. Her eyes fluttered but remained closed.

"Julie," Ted called. "Try to get the chicken wire off that window. It's the only way out."

She nodded and pried at the wire with her bare fingers. Next to the metal table she saw a small bench with an assortment of tools, ones she assumed were going to be used to prepare Susan's body for the feast to come. She grabbed a pair of rusty pliers - shuddering as she realized the rust was actually dried blood - and went to work on the window. One by one, she popped the nails free. She grabbed the loose corner in her hands and began tugging on it.

Ted tossed Susan over his shoulder just as the last of the chicken wire fell to the floor with a clatter.

"I don't see anyone," Julie said. "I think we're clear."

Ted nodded and motioned her to the window. "Go. I'll hand Susan out to you." Julie climbed through the opening into the weedy lot beside the building; fat drops of chilly rain splashed on her skin and ran over her exposed breasts. Ted passed Susan's lifeless body through the window and Julie held her in a standing position, propping her against the side of the drugstore. Ted spotted a dusty towel lying nearby and grabbed it.

"Here," he said, handing it through the window. "Wrap yourself in that."

She smiled and took the towel, wrapping it around herself as best she could while holding Susan against the wall. Ted gripped the windowsill and began pulling himself through as the door flung open with a bang. Jack stood there puffing, his matted hair dripping from the rain, his eyes full of hate. He saw Ted and smiled, growling through clenched teeth like a feral animal.

"I'm going to tear you apart," he said.

Jack stepped forward and tripped over Tess's prone body, falling to one knee in the puddle of blood that had spread from beneath her corpse.

"No," Jack moaned. "NO! What did you do? What did you do to my family?"

Ted leapt through the window without a word. If there was any chance of surviving Jack's rage, it'd evaporated the second he saw his wife and daughter bleeding out on the floor. Ted was fairly positive Jack wasn't used to losing, and he didn't want to stick around to find out.

Outside, Ted grabbed Susan in one motion and tossed her over his back. "Where do we go?"

"Back the way we came," Julie said. "Through the yards, back to the road. If we follow the road out of town, the resort should be a few miles in that direction. We'll be safe there. They won't go anywhere near it."

Ted nodded and slogged through the thick grass and mud.

"THEY WENT OUT THE BACK!" Jack bellowed. "Don't let them escape! They killed my Kathy and Tess!" Jack shrieked as he held Kathy's cooling body in his arms.

"Go, go, go," Ted called to Julie. "We're going to have company."

They followed the path they'd created through the tall grass behind the row of houses, passing the cooking meat. Ted gazed into the empty windows, expecting to see the same pale faces watching them as they passed, but they were empty and dark. It didn't put him at ease, quite the opposite. If anyone gave chase, they'd be sitting ducks. Maybe Julie could escape, but Ted would never be able to run while carrying Susan's extra weight, and there wasn't a chance he'd leave her behind. If it came to that, they'd die together.

Ted heard heavy footfalls on the street out front and felt his hopes diminish. They were already pursuing, and they had the numbers to overcome them in seconds.

"This way," Julie waved.

At the rear of the yard, Ted watched as Julie parted the brush and entered a path leading into the woods. He followed as she placed broken branches in front of the opening, partially blocking them from view.

"How did you know this was here?" Ted asked.

"I saw the men use it once. They bring the remains here, the bones, the stuff they can't use."

Bile rose in Ted's throat, imagining them carting wheelbarrows full of skulls and dumping them in the tangled darkness.

"Lead the way," he said.

As they crept down the path, the church bell suddenly stopped, the final loud *bong* echoing out over the town. Without it, Ted felt even more exposed. The sound had disguised their movement, but now they were at the mercy of the encroaching silence.

Deeper and deeper they went, winding through the woods, trying to remain as quiet as possible. The shouting behind had become more distant. Ted shifted Susan's weight on his shoulder and grunted from the exertion. Julie left the path, pushed through the thick growth, and tromped through wet leaves, scanning the area for something in particular.

"There should be a clearing down here somewhere," she whispered.

"Do we really want to break cover?" Ted asked. "Isn't the point to stay hidden?"

"I'm doing the best I can. Just try to keep up, I think we're close."

"Close? Close to what?"

"You'll see, just follow me."

"At least we have the dark on our side."

"It's always dark here. Their eyes are used to it. Just stop talking and follow me."

After a few minutes where Ted thought they were hopelessly lost, Julie stepped through the bushes and brought them into a wide, circular clearing. Ted stopped and gasped, nearly dropping Susan as his legs threatened to buckle beneath him.

They left one Hell behind and walked right into another.

***

The mound of human bones was at least twelve feet high.

The jumbled pile stood in the middle of the clearing; grinning skulls stared at them as they skirted the edge of the forest.

"Why would you bring me here?" Ted asked.

"It's the quickest route to where we're going," she replied. "Do you think I want to be here? I *knew* a few of these people," she said, pointing at the heap.

"I'm sorry," Ted muttered. "I didn't know."

"No, you didn't, so just forget it. We have a little way to go yet."

"Where?"

"The Triple Seven Motel. Let's get there first and I'll explain everything."

They left the human pile behind and followed what had once been a single road. The asphalt was cracked and broken and surrounded on both sides by thick pine trees. Ted had a million questions, but kept them to himself. Susan began to stir little by little. She tried to speak but only managed scattered gibberish.

"Hold on, Suzie. You're safe. Don't struggle or I'm going to drop you."

"Ted?" she managed.

"Yeah, baby. It's me. Just hold on."

They came to a battered metal gate and stopped. Julie crouched and looked through the trees, talking to herself under her breath. She stood and turned to him with a grin on her face.

"It's there," she pointed. "Thank God it's there."

"What? You didn't *know*?"

"I've heard about it. I just hoped we were on the right track."

"Put me down," Susan uttered. "I can walk."

"Susan, just rest. You took a hell of a blow to the head."

"I know that, I was there," she groaned. "Just put me down."

Ted did as he was told, holding his arms around her waist as she shakily got her footing. She swayed back and forth before steadying herself, holding a hand to her swollen cheek and poking her tongue in the hole left by a missing tooth. It must have come loose after she blacked out. The vision in her right eye was blurred from the swelling. She looked around, saw Julie, and slowly looked up to Ted.

"Who is she? Where are we?"

"In a minute," Ted said. "We're not in the clear just yet."

He looked through the trees and saw what Julie had been talking about. A large sign sat atop a metal pole: The 777 Motel. From their hiding space, the complex appeared utterly deserted. It looked like any other nondescript motel along the backroads of Pennsylvania. It was two floors and laid out in an L-shape at the end of a large parking lot. Shingles had been blown from sections of the roof and lay scattered across the macadam. Several abandoned vehicles sat on rusted rims, surrounded by the sparkle of broken glass. One hung behind a burned-out tow truck, making Ted cock his head and look more closely. From this distance, he couldn't be sure, but it *looked* just like the Barracuda. That was impossible. The other cars appeared to have been sitting here for decades.

The crash had just happened last night.

"Let's go," Julie said.

"Are you sure it's safe?"

"No. I'm not sure of anything anymore, but it's the only idea I have right now."

Ted nodded. It had to be good enough.

Ted grabbed Susan's hand and walked around the gate. She was still unsteady on her feet, but she was giving it her all. He loved her, but he didn't miss her dead weight draped over his shoulder. Maybe this would give them a fighting chance.

As they crossed the parking lot, Ted felt very exposed, but also very alone. If there was anyone tailing them, they were absolutely silent. He listened for the slightest sound but heard only the incessant rain. The thunder had become more distant, but the sky still flickered constantly. Ted had always loved thunderstorms, but being hunted by cannibals during one certainly put a damper on things.

They passed the burned tow truck and Ted stopped dead in his tracks.

"How is that possible?"

It *was* his Cuda, he was sure of it. Same color, same year. The driver's side window was busted out, the nose crumpled in from it where it had struck the tree. He circled the wreck and peered inside. It was unmistakably *their* vehicle. Ted felt lightheaded.

"Come on," Julie whispered. "What are you doing?"

"This is my car," he said.

Julie shrugged and waved him over. It meant nothing to her. How could it?

Ted kicked the rear tire with a grunt. The rubber was dry-rotted, the quarter panels coated in flakes of rust. It was theirs alright, but it looked twenty years older, not twenty hours. He shook his head confoundedly and walked over to meet Susan, who looked at him tiredly. She was just about done in. They needed to rest.

"Inside," Julie said.

Ted wrapped his arm around Susan's waist as she looked up and smiled painfully. He'd never seen her so exhausted.

"I'm so sorry, baby," Ted said, rubbing a hand over her soggy hair. "I never meant for any of this to happen."

"Oh? Here I thought this was your idea of something *special*."

"I promise you," Ted said. "We're never coming to Pine Lakes again."

8

JULIE OPENED THE DOOR TO ROOM 212 AND STEPPED INSIDE. THE interior of the small space was covered in years of dust, but appeared dry. Two single beds sat against the wall; an old television rested atop a dusty dresser, its screen busted and scattered on the worn carpet. A mini-fridge sat against the far wall with its door hanging open; inside was a pile of mouse turds and a dented can of Shasta. The closet was wide open, revealing a row of empty clothes hangers. It appeared no one had been here for years.

Julie closed the door and collapsed on one of the beds; Ted led Susan to the other and gently helped her lie down.

"Should I keep watch?" Ted asked. "They have to know about this place."

"Oh, they know," Julie replied, "but they don't come here. They can't."

"What do you mean they *can't?*"

"It's enchanted."

"What? What are you talking about?"

"There's a spell on this place," Julie said, sitting up.

"You're going to have to do better than that," Ted said.

Julie stood, peeked out the window, and walked to the mini-fridge, grabbing the can of Shasta and slurping it greedily. She held it out to Ted, but he declined. She shrugged and finished the contents in one swallow, dropping the can on the carpet.

"Let me gather my thoughts for a minute," Julie said. "I haven't had a second to myself in ages."

"How long have you been here?"

"Days, years, it's hard to tell. Time is funny here."

Ted sat on the bed next to Susan and rubbed her arm. His wife snored lightly; she'd fallen asleep the second her head hit the dusty pillow.

"You love her," Julie said, sitting on her own bed.

Ted nodded. "Very much. It kills me seeing her go through this."

"You're a good man," Julie said. "I can tell. When a lady runs into a good man, she knows."

"It doesn't take a good man to love his wife."

"It absolutely does. Any man can take a wife, but not every man can keep one."

Ted nodded agreeably. "Can you tell me what you mean about this place being enchanted?"

"Just what I said. The building is protected, has been for ages. An old woman once lived here. The townsfolk called her Grandma Emma, said she had special power. Foresight."

"You mean she could see the future?"

"Something like that. I'm only going off stories I heard at the bar. She was widely respected and wildly feared. She was one of them once, and something went wrong."

"What happened?"

"I don't know. They don't talk about it. She went from being a member of the community to being an outcast. They came after her, called her a devil, chased her from her home. Some real witch hunt shit. They were prepared to string her up and burn her at the stake if necessary, but she was always one step ahead of them."

"So she got away?"

"She held up here. She claimed this place as her own and made it clear that if anyone came here with bad intentions, they'd be dead before they crossed the parking lot. She stayed here for years and put a spell of protection over the entire property."

"Oh my God!" Ted exclaimed. "Grandma Emma! I bet she was the old woman in the woods."

Julie raised an eyebrow.

"On our way here, we were being chased by these dogs or wolves or whatever the hell they were…"

"Emma called them Cwn Annwn. Something to do with Welsh folklore."

"Called them what?"

"Hellhounds. Harbinger's of death. Everything that old woman said was based on some foreign myth or legend."

"Right, well anyway, we stumbled on an old cabin in the woods, and this old lady took us in and gave us tea. She must have drugged it or something, because when we woke up she was gone, like she'd never been there."

"It could be her. I've heard she lives nearby, but no one has seen her for years, which is likely the way she wants it."

Susan muttered in her sleep and Ted ran his fingertips lightly across her forehead. He saw Julie watching him and laughed.

"She used to have awful nightmares, shouting in her sleep, tossing and turning for hours. I found that running my fingers over her head or through her hair would calm her down. She's had a rough ride."

"What do you mean?"

"When she was in college, she was in a horrible car accident. Her roommate died in the crash, and for years she was scared to even ride in a car, let alone drive one. Then later, after we were married, she had a miscarriage…"

"I'm so sorry," she interrupted.

"So was she. She blamed herself for losing the baby. Thought I wasn't going to love her anymore. It wasn't easy."

Julie stared at the floor between her feet and remained silent.

"I didn't want to make you uncomfortable," Ted said.

"No, no, it's nothing. I'm fine. Just tired. I think we should catch a nap and rest. Something tells me that getting out of here is going to require every ounce of strength we have."

"You're sure it's safe?"

"We'll be fine," she assured. She laid back on the bed and shut her eyes. "It feels so good," she moaned. "It's been so long since I've slept in an actual bed."

Ted nodded. "You didn't have a bed?"

"No. Jack's girls sleep in cages so they can't escape. That disgusting place is his bread and butter and he runs it like a prison. It's like he gets off on it, gets off on having *status*."

"That's awful," Ted said. "Did he feed you?"

"Whenever he remembered. Usually table scraps. Nothing

substantial. He kept us weak enough so that we wouldn't try to escape."

Ted grimaced and cleared his throat. "Table scraps, like fucking dogs."

Julie nodded. "If the girls wouldn't eat, Jack and his men would force feed them. More often than not he'd toss a plate of spaghetti in our cages. No sauce. Nothing fancy. The noodles were always greasy and tasted like he made them in old bath water. Maybe he did, who knows?"

"Horrible."

Julie reached out and grabbed Ted's hand, smiling, eyes half open. "I can't thank you enough for getting me out of there. I was sure I'd die. Every day was just as bad as the one before."

She took her hand away and closed her eyes as the storm intensified. Ted listened as the wind pulled at loose shingles on the roof and whistled around the corners of the building. He laid back next to Susan and stared at the ceiling, listening to her breathing.

"I'd kill for a hamburger and fries," Julie uttered.

"You're not kidding," Ted replied.

"French fries were Jacob's favorite."

"Jacob?" he asked.

Julie mumbled something he couldn't understand and began breathing deeply, slipping further into slumber.

Who the hell's Jacob? he thought.

Before he knew it, he too drifted off.

***

Ted was awakened by a sudden commotion.

"What do we do?" Susan asked.

"What's going on?" Ted said. He stood quickly, wiped at his eyes, and joined them at the window.

"There," Susan pointed.

Ted squinted into the gloom and saw them. There were at least forty men and woman lined up at the far edge of the parking lot. Some carried hatchets while others carried homemade clubs or pitchforks. One man appeared to be holding a rusted sword.

"It's a goddamn hangman's posse," Ted said to no one in particular.

A group of men stood huddled together, pointing up at their window.

"They saw us," Susan said in a hushed tone.

"They can look all they want," Julie said. "They know they can't cross the lot."

"I don't understand…"

"Don't worry about it," Ted interrupted. "If what Julie told me is true, we're safe here."

Susan shrugged and shook her head.

"Just trust me," Ted added. "I'm not letting anything happen to you."

Susan grabbed his arm and buried her face in his chest. He wanted to explain everything, but now was not the time.

"They can't hurt us," Julie said, "but they *can* wait us out."

"A standoff," Ted added.

"Exactly."

"There has to be a way out of here."

"I don't know!" Julie shouted. "I didn't know if this place existed at all, let alone a secret escape hatch." She went to her bed and sat with a grunt, holding her face in her hands. "Let me think."

Ted pulled the frayed curtain aside and watched the mob line the edge of the lot. One man put his foot on the curb separating the road and the lot and immediately jumped back as if he'd been burned. It was the first sign that Julie wasn't just telling stories; there was something very powerful at work here.

"What did you do to piss them off?" Susan asked.

"He saved me," Julie said. "He risked his life to get me away from there, and now we're just as trapped as before. Always trapped," she cried.

Susan watched the woman as she sobbed weakly. She frowned, feeling the woman's helplessness leak from her pores like sweat.

"She's in a towel," Susan whispered to Ted.

"That's more than she was wearing when we escaped the bar."

"Where are Kathy and that mutant bitch?"

"They won't be bothering you again," he said. "Won't be bothering *anyone* again."

"Ted? What did you do?"

"What I had to. Let's leave it at that." Susan looked up with sad eyes and swallowed hard. "I had to get you out of there," Ted explained. "Nothing else mattered."

"What are we going to do?"

Ted closed his eyes and shook his head.

When he looked outside, another twenty or so people had joined the ranks of the redneck militia. They tapped the handles of their weapons rhythmically on the asphalt. A warning? A call to action?

That's when he noticed Jack saunter to the front of the line and raise his arm above his head. The mob quieted instantly.

"Julie," Jack shouted. "I know you're in there, girl. I'm not here for you."

Julie jumped up from the bed and joined them at the window, her face a mask of fear.

"I know the other two are with you. Send them out and you can go free."

"Fuck you," Julie whispered.

"They killed Kathy and Tess," he continued, "and I can't abide that kind of behavior in my town. You know we take care of our own. Send them out so they can face their wicked deeds and you can go."

"He's never going to let me go," Julie said. "Not for anything. He intends on killing you, killing us all."

"You want to be free, don't you?" Jack hollered. "You send them to me and you have my word. We'll take them to the church and you can just walk away."

"The church?" Susan asked. "What's he talking about?"

"That's where they pray," Julie said. "To whatever god or devil they worship. They offer sacrifices. *Human* sacrifices."

"Fan-fucking-tastic," Ted blurted.

"Whoever goes in as a prisoner comes out in bags," she said. "They believe by eating the flesh of their enemies, they gain their power and their knowledge, or so I've heard."

"Christ," Susan groaned. "Do they think they're Aztecs? This is 2017!"

"2017?" Julie asked. "The *year* 2017?"

"Of course," Ted said. "Why?"

"I've been here so long," she said. "So long."

"How long?" Susan asked. "You don't look like you're much over twenty."

Julie put a hand to her cheek as her eyes closed in deep though. Just as Ted was going to ask if she was okay, Julie looked up and said, "1991. That's when I got here."

"NO!" Susan scoffed. "Can't be. You have to be mistaken."

"I'm positive," Julie replied. "George Bush was President. *Roseanne* was the biggest show on television."

"It's not possible," Susan repeated.

"Even if you were *born* in 1991, you'd be twenty-six years old now."

"I was born in 1972," Julie said. "My son was born in 1990."

"This is ridiculous," Susan blurted. Ted held his hand up to stop her. "I'm sorry, I don't mean to sound bitchy, but it's 2017. That's all there is to it."

"Not for me," Julie said. "How did this happen?"

"We have bigger problems," Ted said. "Like the ones outside."

"Time. Time is weird here," Julie muttered.

"You'd be in your mid-forties," Susan said. "There's no way…"

"I can't explain it," Julie shouted. "I just know what I know."

"George Bush hasn't been President in over twenty years," Susan explained. "He was followed by Clinton, Bush Junior, and Obama. How can you not remember any of this?"

Julie shook her head.

"Donald Trump is our current President," Susan said.

Julie snorted laughter. "Donald Trump? The hotel guy with the fright wig? Our President? Now I know you're pulling my leg."

"She's telling the truth," Ted said. "He took office earlier this year."

"How? How can that much time have passed?"

"That's what I'm saying," Susan replied.

"I assure you it was 1991. It's a hard thing to forget. I mean come on, do I look like I'm in my forties?"

Susan shook her head but said nothing. She came back to reality with a start as the angry mob outside began shouting and calling Julie's name.

"This is insane," Susan said.

"Suzie, please, just let it go. No one's saying we drove through a fucking wormhole, she's just confused."

Susan looked at the floor, stung by Ted's harsh words. He didn't have time to coddle her, there were more important things transpiring.

"What do you say?" Jack bellowed. "Fair trade, Julie. You're not going to get a better offer."

"I just want him to shut up already," Julie hissed. "If I never hear his voice again, it'll be too soon."

Ted pushed Susan and Julie aside and opened the window. "No deal, Jack," he shouted. "We're getting out of here together."

"Ah, Ted, the murderer. Why don't you let her answer for herself, Ted? This isn't your decision."

Julie appeared at the window beside him, trembling with rage. "Fuck you! Do you hear me? You'll never get me in a cage again. Never! You or your fucking cronies."

Jack laughed. A hearty, deep, belly-laugh. "Girl, you're signing your own death warrant. I'm going to give you to the count of ten, and when

I'm done, I better see that door open. If not, you'll all die side-by-side like one, big happy family."

A few of his henchman laughed like it was the funniest thing they'd ever heard. Jack beamed, drinking in their favor like a fine wine. His arrogance was appalling.

The crowd began counting down from ten excitedly, like teenagers at a high school pep rally.

"Now what?" Susan asked.

"Play their game," Julie said. She went over, opened the door, and walked onto the second floor balcony. The countdown stopped at once.

"That's a smart girl," Jack shouted. "Now just send out the sheep and we'll be on our merry way."

Julie motioned them forward. Ted followed her suspiciously and held his hand up to Susan. "Stay put."

The air outside was damp and cool; rain buffeted the building, blown along on sporadic gusts of wind. Ted turned and saw Susan peeking around the door frame. He winked and turned back to the distant crowd.

"Where's the other one?" Jack called. "No deal if I don't get them both."

"I always wanted to say this, Jack, so listen carefully," Julie yelled. "Fuck you and fuck your twisted inbred family! Fuck your dead wife and your dead mutant bitch of a daughter. Fuck your disgusting bar and fuck your dirty, goddamn greasy noodles." She dropped her towel and stood there naked. She grabbed her breasts and jiggled them in both hands, then turned and bent over, showing her bare ass at a stunned Jack. "Did you see that, Jack? Remember it! It's the last time you'll *ever* see it!"

Behind them, Susan erupted in good-natured laughter. Ted grinned and flipped the crowd his middle finger, then the other.

"That's as good as it gets, Julie," he said. "I'm not showing him my ass."

"You know what else, Jack?" Julie continued. "It wasn't Susan who killed your wife and daughter, it was *me*, and I loved every fucking minute of it! I'd do it again if I had the chance." She laughed, grabbed her towel, and went back inside. Ted waved and followed her, closing the door behind him. Julie wrapped herself in the towel and sat on the bed, grinning like a maniac.

"You didn't kill them," Ted said. "Why did you say that?"

"To see the look on his face. That blank stare as he realized one of his dogs had bitten the hand that feeds."

"Now that we've pissed them off, what happens next?"

They jumped as a raspy, warm voice spoke behind them. The woman from the cabin toddled forward out of the shadows.

"Grandma Emma?" Julie asked cautiously.

"Oh my God," Susan said.

"You got yourselves in quite a mess here," Emma said with a smile. "I guess you'd better listen carefully if you want to get out of here."

***

"You're Grandma Emma," Julie stated.

"You can just call me Emma, I feel old enough without all of this *grandma* nonsense."

"You were at the cabin," Ted said angrily. "You drugged us!"

"I *saved* you," Emma interrupted. "Without my help, the hounds would've been picking your bones by now."

"Why couldn't you have told us? Explained what the hell is going on?"

"We wouldn't have had enough time. I can't take your hand and lead you out of here, so I did what I could. You're still alive, aren't you?"

"For now," Susan mumbled.

"Exactly. *For now.* So are you going to listen to me, or are we going to sit here until you starve to death?"

Emma shuffled to the window and peered out at the angry mob.

"Emma?" Susan asked shyly. "What's going on? How can this be happening?"

"There isn't a simple answer. These monsters have been trapped here off the beaten path for so long, they've learned to make do with what they have. Once Jack arrived and made this his kingdom, everything went downhill. For them, eating and procreating with one another is perfectly acceptable. At first, people tried leaving. Hope hadn't yet become a dirty word, but once Jack got his hands in everything, he poisoned the well. They stopped trying, they gave up and accepted their plight."

"Couldn't you have done something?" Julie asked. "These people respected you."

"I tried. I offered aid and ideas, but Jack didn't appreciate me meddling in his affairs. He slowly turned them against me, convinced them I was the monster. They chased me from my home, burned it to the ground, forced me to take up residence here like a bad dog chained up outside the fence. That worked for a while, but Jack still considered me a threat. They started sneaking around outside, trying to lure me out. Jack wasn't happy knowing I was out of the way, he wanted me dead. I knew I'd be the next one to go to the church if he could get his hands on me."

"I don't understand why they wouldn't want to leave," Ted said. "This place makes my skin crawl."

"Jack convinced them to stay, told them things were better here, that the outside world would never accept them. He opened that filthy titty bar and started making his own liquor, all in an attempt to keep people happy and horny around the clock. He surrounded himself with weak minded people who he'd brainwashed into killing his enemies on sight. Then he created his *religion*, building his following from the ground up through fear and intimidation."

"Why hasn't anyone stopped him?" Susan asked. "I mean, not everyone can want this way of life."

"Anyone who disagrees with Jack's ways is taken to the church and offered up to whatever devil they pray to. Dissension is punishable by death. After seeing your neighbors sacrificed or hung from telephone poles, you tend to fall in line. Never get between a starving dog and raw meat."

"How did you keep them out? How did you do *this*?" Susan asked, spreading her arms to signify the warding spell surrounding the motel.

"They underestimated by capabilities," Emma chuckled. "You can only push an old woman so far. I placed a wall of protection around this motel. Anyone with hate in their heart will never cross the boundary alive. Unfortunately, there were side effects. Consequences."

Ted watched her curiously. "What do you mean?"

"Look around you," she said. "At one time, Pine Lakes was like every other town. Now, there's perpetual darkness. The sun hasn't risen here in decades, and the trees and plants all died ages ago. Messing with the power of the universe often has negative effects. I knew that going in, but I don't regret it. It's more than Jack and his henchmen deserve."

"You could have wiped them out." Julie said. "Put them out of their misery, erased this hellhole from the map."

"There are powers at work here much stronger than mine, ones even I won't tamper with. This place is here for a reason and it's not my intent to meddle with that. All I can offer is help to those who find themselves trapped here. Not those monsters outside, they're beyond anyone's help."

"You can get us out of here?" Susan asked.

"I can point you in the right direction," Emma said, "but I can't go with you. My place is here. The motel, the cabin. Safe havens. I'm just as trapped here as they are, only for different reasons."

Susan frowned, overcome with sadness. She only understood half of what Emma had told them, but it was more than enough. Pine Lakes was a scar on the face of the Earth.

"Does this *spell* explain why time is different here?" Ted pointed at Julie. "She thinks she came here in 1991, but when we crashed in the woods, it was 2017."

"Time no longer adheres to any cosmic rules," Emma said. "Crossing that boundary negates time as you know it. If she says she came here in 1991, then she did, just like you say it's 2017. If that's true, I'm nearly two hundred years in your past."

"What the fuck?" Ted blurted.

"Hard to wrap your head around it? Don't bother, it's not going to change anything. We're here together, for better or worse. We all have a part to play, and a destination. I'm going to help you find yours."

"What about them?" Ted asked. "What do we do about them?"

"I'm going to talk to them," she cackled. "I haven't seen Jack in a long time."

Emma opened the door and stepped outside. No fear, just mild amusement.

"Jack!" she called. "So nice to see you again. I've heard you had some problems."

"The witch returns!" Jack shouted. "To what do I owe this misfortune?"

"What're you doing all the way over there, Jack?" Emma giggled. "Why don't you come a little closer, my hearing ain't so good these days."

"Fuck you, hag!" he returned. "You know, there's still plenty of room in the church when you give up this game of yours."

"I'm fine right where I am."

"I guess you're not going to send your new friends out to me."

"They have places to be, unlike you. You'll die here and live this nightmare over and over again. Do you even remember who you were, Jack? Before you came here and claimed ownership over something you have no right to possess."

"I have every right," Jack said, spitting on the ground between his feet. "It's you that doesn't belong, old woman. I'll do whatever needs to be done to right your wrong."

"You're a broken record," Emma yelled. "You can't find me anymore than you can find that shriveled, old bird between your legs."

Ted, Susan, and Julie crowded around the window as Emma taunted Jack and his minions. The crowd listened to every word, but said nothing. Unlike Jack, they were visibly shaken by the enchantress's appearance. Many had only ever heard tales of her existence; seeing her in the flesh was more than some could take. They backed away from the motel, fearing bolts of lighting would begin shooting from her fingers.

"She-devil," Jack growled. "You'll pay for that."

Suddenly, a small group of men jumped the curb and raced toward the building, weapons held above their heads. Jack screamed at them to return, but their blood lust had taken over. They wanted the bitch's head on a plate, and knew that the one to bring it to Jack would be handsomely rewarded.

One of the men erupted in blue flame as his screams pierced the night. He writhed on the wet macadam as the flesh on his face melted like candle wax. Ten feet to his right, another man fell to his knees, blood pouring from his eyes and nose in a river.

"Get back, goddammit," Jack bellowed.

The two men at the front of the line turned and began running back to the safety of the street, when without warning, they exploded as if they'd been carrying sticks of dynamite. Their remains rained over the parking lot in a hot, red mist as Jacked jumped up and down and stomped his feet. Emma laughed shrilly, clapping her hands, enjoying the show. The final man fell to the ground and burst open as his flesh gave birth to thousands of black, trundling beetles. The mob stared in awe as Emma's laughter died out.

"The magic works," she shouted. "How brilliantly the magic works."

"I'll see your head on a pike," Jack wailed.

"You'll try," she replied, "but you'll fail, as you always do."

Emma turned, reentered the room, and closed the door behind her.

"What are you doing?" Julie shrieked. "You're only aggravating them!"

"I'm proving to them there's a price to pay if they cross me. It'll put the fear in them, give you a chance to sneak away."

"How are we supposed to do that?" Ted asked. "They have the damn place surrounded."

"You go under them," she said.

"Under?" Susan asked.

"The sewer."

Julie groaned loudly.

"I didn't say you were going to like it," Emma said, "but it's better than the alternative." Emma pointed at Susan and frowned. "You're a pretty girl. They'd pass you around the bar like a collection plate."

Julie shuddered. "You don't want that, trust me. I never felt so dirty. The things they made me do…"

"Don't think about that anymore," Emma said. "That part of your life is over."

"So. The sewers then?" Ted asked.

"The sewers," Emma replied. "Follow me."

***

They crawled through a window in the back of the room and exited onto a rickety fire escape. The crowd out front jeered and called for their heads. Somehow, this made Emma giggle intermittently as she led them down the stairs to a small basement door. Inside, it was completely black. Ted listened as Emma opened a squeaky locker door and removed two flashlights, pressing them into Ted and Susan's hands.

"No batteries," Ted said, shaking the flashlight in his hand.

Suddenly the light came to life and cast a bright, white glow into the room. Susan flinched and covered her eyes.

"Don't need batteries now," Emma smirked.

"Are you sure you can't come?" Julie asked. "Your specific *talents* would definitely come in handy."

"No dear, I'm sorry. This is as far as I go." She pulled a musty coat from the locker and handed it to Julie. "Better than nothing."

Julie nodded and slipped it on over her towel.

"Shine your light over here," Emma demanded. "There." She pointed at a circular manhole cover in the concrete floor. "You want to follow the tunnel east. If you get lost down there, there's a chance you aren't coming back. The lights will guide you," she said. "I've made sure of it. If you get turned around, just hold out your light. It knows the way."

"This is insane," Susan whispered. "How do we know they won't be waiting for us at the other end?"

"Listen to me," Emma demanded. "If you don't believe the magic works, it won't. If those lights go off, you could wander in these sewers forever. You won't be the first, and I doubt you'll be the last."

Ted put his arm around Susan and hugged her tightly. She

thrummed beneath his touch with nervous energy.

"Where does it go?" Julie asked.

"Near the edge of town. Still within their reach, but hopefully I've created enough of a diversion to put them off your trail. I have a few more tricks up my sleeve," Emma grinned.

"We can't thank you enough," Ted said, suddenly overcome with emotion.

"You can thank me by getting out of here. You don't belong here. Balance the scales, live your lives. Maybe one day, it'll be enough."

"Enough?" Susan asked. "Enough for what?"

"Nevermind." Emma walked to the cellar door and turned. "You find your own way, and I'll find mine."

She closed the door behind her.

"What the fuck just happened?" Susan asked.

"Emma gave us a chance," Ted said. "It's up to us to take it."

***

Emma walked onto the balcony and waved at Jack and his horde.

"You come to your senses, old woman?"

"Your company is so stimulating, Jack. How can I stay away?"

"Your time here is limited and you know it. Once your half-penny magic wears off, we're coming to get you, and when we do, the streets will flow with your blood. Send out your friends; maybe we can reach some kind of agreement. I'll show you the mercy of a quick death."

"I think they're sleeping, Jack," Emma said. "Even they grew tired of your empty threats."

"Bitch!" Jack roared. I'm going to break you in half and make you eat your own asshole, do you hear me?"

"Don't promise me a good time, my old heart can't take it." Emma spied an old plastic lawn chair and sat down with a grunt. "Why don't you come a little closer, Jack? If you want me, you're going to have to come and get me."

9

THE SEWER REEKED OF ROT AND THE GASSY STENCH OF DECAY and raw sewage; the walls were coated in green-black slime. It was hard not to feel they'd gone from bad to worse, but they trusted Emma and allowed themselves to believe the unbelievable. The tunnel stretched out before them, illuminated by the bright glow of the magical flashlights. Ted held his in front of him and instantly felt it pull him forward. A warm tingle crept into his hand and worked its way up his arm as he splashed through the slow-moving muck at his feet. The sound of their progress echoed off the low ceiling and down the branching tunnels of the subterranean labyrinth. The air was thick and humid.

"Do you really believe this stuff?" Susan asked.

"It's hard not to," Ted replied.

"I keep thinking we're going to run into Morlocks," she said.

"*What?*" Julie asked.

"Nothing. Just thinking out loud."

"Can you think a little quieter? Before the whole town knows where we are."

Susan frowned and choked back a sarcastic reply.

"This way," Ted said, ignoring their banter. Now wasn't the time.

They came to the first branch in the tunnel and stopped. Ted felt the flashlight turn in his hand, lighting up the correct path. He couldn't comprehend how the power worked, but he was glad it did. He just wished Emma could have come with them instead of staying behind to deal with Jack and his minions. Something told him she'd be just fine.

He continued forward as cold water seeped through his shoes and numbed his toes. In the darkness, minutes felt like hours. It was impossible to tell how far they'd come or how long it'd taken. Every tunnel looked the same. Water seeped in through cracks in the walls and dripped from the ceiling. Fat rats with beady, black eyes scampered around their feet, squeaking protests at their passing. Ted heard Susan groan and kick out at one of them with a splash.

"It's okay, Suzie, they're more scared of us than we are of them."

"Speak for yourself. I'm plenty scared."

At the end of the tunnel, they exited into a large round room with a domed ceiling. Torrents of muddy water poured from several pipes in the wall. The floor was littered with wet clumps of leaves and garbage; a large circular drain sat in the middle of the floor. The runoff circled and frothed on its way to a lower level of the sewer. They walked carefully around the edge of the room, keeping away from the rushing water as it hissed and gurgled its warning. Julie covered her nose with her hand to block out the foul stink.

"I hope this leads out of here," she said. "I don't normally walk through waterfalls of shit unless I have a really good reason."

Susan muttered her agreement, shining her light on the center of the room as the whirlpool of detritus circled the drain. She gasped and grabbed hold of Ted's arm.

"There! Look!"

Ted shined his light where Susan pointed and saw a tattered, red sneaker quickly disappear into the watery depths.

"Did you see it?" Susan groaned.

Ted nodded as a shiver ran up his spine. The sneaker contained the remains of a human foot, its splintered ankle bone jutting from the shoe and glistening in the beam of their flashlights. Julie screamed as the other shoe dropped from one of the large pipes and splashed into the foamy water. It was followed by a pale, dismembered arm covered in prison tattoos. A head plopped into the water, trailing filthy blond hair and strings of bloodless flesh from its jagged, stumpy neck. Limbs and torsos circled the drain like a giant, human garbage disposal. Susan gagged and turned away as the beam of her flashlight dimmed.

"Don't look!" Ted screamed. "Focus on your light."

Susan cried out as a severed hand brushed against her shoe. A gleaming wedding ring was still attached to one shriveled finger. Her flashlight flickered.

"Give me the light," Julie shouted over the roar of the water. Susan reluctantly handed it over, watching as the bulb flashed with pure, white light. "You can't let your fear take over. If we lose the light, we're in big trouble."

"You mean worse trouble than body parts raining from the fucking sky?" Susan shrieked.

Ted grabbed her hand and held it tightly. "Come on, don't look. I'll guide you."

"How are you so fucking calm?" she shouted. "Both of you!"

"If we're not, we're never getting out of here," Julie said. "I can't go back to Jack, I'd rather die here and be eaten by rats than ever step foot in that bar again."

"Come on Suzie," Ted said, pulling her forward. "We'll look back and laugh at this…"

"Laugh?" she screamed. "I'm never going to laugh again. Are you fucking serious? This isn't a rained-out camping trip or a flat tire on the side of the road." Another head bobbed past and stared up at them with milky eyes. The room was becoming a boiling cesspool of human soup.

They inched along the wall as the water level slowly started to rise. The drain was clogged with human remains. Suddenly, with a loud sucking roar, the pile of dismembered limbs disappeared into the hole and the water receded, pulling at their feet. Susan felt Julie's hand graze her shoulder as Julie lost her footing and fell back into the swirling water. The flashlight splashed into the waves and immediately went dark.

"Help me!" Julie screamed.

Ted turned and watched as Julie was pulled away by the receding water. Wide-eyed, she splashed frantically, grabbing at pieces of floating garbage to slow her progress. She found her footing and stood shakily, taking a tentative step away from the drain; the flashlight was nowhere to be seen.

"Get out of there," Ted shouted. "Come on!"

She stepped forward and fell on her face, getting a mouthful of gritty water. Sputtering, she tried to stand and realized she couldn't; her leg was *caught*, encircled by something very strong, warm, and pulsing with life. She flipped over on her back and saw a giant, scaly, tentacle snaking from the hole and wrapping around her ankle. It gripped so tightly, she feared it would snap her leg like a twig. The pressure was nearly unbearable.

"Julie!" Ted yelled. "What are you waiting for?" It was then he saw a dozen twirling, black arms poke from the drain and feel along the floor, clutching at anything that touched its sensitive flesh. He put his arm out across Susan's chest and pushed her back, pressing them against the wall in an attempt to keep out of the arms' radius. Julie's mouth opened and closed in a silent scream as the arm wrapped around her midsection and slowly pulled her across the floor. As she neared the hole, her body went limp. Her terrified eyes stared at Ted, stared *through* him, as she was pulled over the rim of the drain and disappeared with a high-pitched wail.

Then silence.

"Oh my God," Susan whined. "What the fucking hell was that?"

"I don't know, but we have to go. Now! Can you keep up?"

"I'll sprout wings and fly if I have to."

The ground trembled beneath their feet as a spout of water burst from the drain and rained down around them. The thick arms snaked back and vanished from where they came as the unseen monster screamed from the abyss. The stench of soggy, rotting flesh filled the room as the creature thrashed audibly in the endless, watery, hell beneath them. Ted's feet slapped the wet ground before his brain could register the motion. He stumbled, caught himself, and continued forward down the tunnel, dragging Susan behind him.

When they stopped running, they were exhausted and felt hopelessly lost in the labyrinth below Pine Lakes.

***

Ted and Susan sat on a waist-high brick ledge as a steady stream of foul smelling water rushed by at their feet. Tunnels branched off in six different directions, and although the light shined brightly, it no longer pulled them in any specific direction. Whatever magic Emma had imbued it with had faded the further away they ran. They prayed the little bulb would stay lit. If not, they'd wander for miles in the blackness, likely never seeing the sky or tasting fresh air again.

"You risked your life for that girl," Susan said. "More than once."

"I couldn't let her suffer at Jack's hand," he replied. "If you could have seen that place, and what he made those girls do." He shook his head and sighed deeply. "All for nothing."

"It wasn't for nothing. You gave her hope. You gave her a chance, which was more than she would've had otherwise."

"Yeah, but maybe she'd be alive."

"Is being trapped in a cage really living? She may be gone, but she died free, Ted. You can't blame yourself."

"I don't blame myself," he shouted. "I blame Jack! I blame this place! This whole damned place."

Susan rested her head on Ted's shoulder and whimpered quietly. "Do you think we'll ever get out of here?"

"I don't know," he said. "I had hope, I really did. How can anyone survive this and ever live a normal life again?"

"I'll take any kind of life I can get at this point."

"Even if it means living in fear for the rest of our lives? Waking from nightmares so real we can still taste this sewer on our lips?"

"It wouldn't be the first time I survived a nightmare."

Ted nodded and snuggled closer. Just when he thought he was the shoulder to cry on, he realized he needed one himself. It was dark, it was cold, and he was absolutely terrified of what waited around the next bend, but he had Susan. He wasn't alone. Where there was love, there was hope.

"We have to keep going," he said. "There has to be a way out somewhere. Nothing goes on forever." A rat trundled by, looked at them curiously, and slunk off into the dark. "Come on."

Susan's legs felt like they were made of concrete, but she focused on putting one foot in front of the other. She kept looking over her shoulder, making sure they weren't being followed. Rats splashed and squeaked in the darkness, agitated by their new guests. The echoes of their passage and of the water lapping at the walls made it impossible to judge location or distance. The reflection from the flashlight bounced off the ceiling and walls in rippling bands of lights.

"Remember that funhouse we went to for Halloween? About eight years ago?"

Ted chuckled tiredly. "Of course. The one in Scranton. I've never laughed so hard in my life."

Susan returned a laugh. "This reminds me of that. All of those damn mirrors. If felt like we walked for miles and kept coming back to the same place."

"Then the guy in the Freddy Krueger costume jumped out and scared you so bad, you peed your pants," Ted laughed.

"Just a little! I knew I shouldn't have had that second Coke."

"I wish I could have seen your face." He abruptly stopped laughing. "That was different. It's fun being scared when there's no real danger. This place, though? H.R. Geiger couldn't have imagined this."

"You're probably right."

Ted was a horror buff, always had been, ever since he was a child and his father would watch the old classic monster movies on VHS. The idea of seeing a vampire or a werewolf or a mummy fascinated him. He'd asked his father once how it was possible for these stupid movie characters to run and fight and still have time to make jokes. How can you look at these abominations and not just want to lie down and die?

Monsters aren't real, Teddy, his father had said. *Movies are works of fiction, they're for entertainment.*

Ted wasn't satisfied by that answer. He wanted more. He needed to know how anyone could put a stake through a vampire's heart and then walk off into the sunset with a beautiful woman on their arm.

Who knows what any of us would do if something like that was possible? I'd like to think we'd behave like some of these characters, he'd said. *I'd like to think we'd be brave and strong and we'd fight for what was ours, that we'd fight for our loved ones and do everything we could to survive. No one knows how they'd act in a time of crisis unless they were looking it in the eye. The human spirit is strong, Teddy. Our survival extinct would kick in and we'd fight.*

Ted was young and only understood half of what his father had told him, but now he finally got the point. After everything he and Susan had seen, after everything they'd done, they were still alive. They were still fighting. The will to survive was stronger than he'd ever imagined, and they were living proof.

They inched along cautiously as their conversation faded. The further they walked, the quieter the underground became. The steadily flowing trough of water had slowed to a trickle. Their footfalls had become muffled.

"Do you think anyone is looking for us?" Ted asked.

"Probably the whole damn town by now."

"No, not them. Our parents. Our friends. Do you think they're wondering where we are?"

"I don't know," she huffed. "I don't even know how long we've been gone. On one hand it feels like hours, and on the other, if feels like forever. Maybe it *has* been forever. You heard what Emma said, time isn't the same here, whatever that means. It's so confusing."

Ted stopped short and Susan ran into him with a quick squeal. The tunnel ended abruptly, falling off into nothingness. He shined the light into the shaft, unable to see the bottom.

"What now?" Susan asked.

"It just disappears," he muttered.

"There's a ladder," she said. "There."

Metal handholds arched above the brick; a steel ladder ran along the side of the drop and vanished at the edge of the flashlight's beam.

"Do you think this is the way out?" Susan asked.

"I don't know, but we either find out or we go back."

"I can't go back, Ted, I just can't."

He nodded and wrapped his arms around her. "Then we go down."

He tucked the flashlight into his pants and wiggled it to make sure it was secure. He turned, grabbed the metal rungs, and hung his foot over the precipice.

"I'll go first."

***

They descended further and further into the abyss. Ted's arms and legs trembled from exertion. After fifty feet, Ted stopped counting.

"It's like climbing down the side of the Empire State Building," Ted puffed.

"We've got to be close," Susan replied. "I don't know how much longer my arms and legs are going to hold out."

The ladder was covered in rust, but seemed solid. Parts were slathered in gelatinous slime that made the descent even more precarious. Ted thought if this led them to a dead end, they'd never have the energy to climb back up.

"What do you think happened to Julie?" Susan asked.

"I don't even want to think about it. That *thing*. What the hell was that? I've heard legends of massive alligators living in the sewers, but that was no damn alligator."

"Maybe she got away. Escaped."

"I wouldn't count on that. For her sake, I hope I'm wrong."

"What was that place like, Ted? Jack's place?"

"You don't want to know, babe, trust me. It takes human bondage to a whole new level. Jack really set the high water mark when it comes to depravity. I'll die before I'm caught, Susan. If it comes to that, I'd rather die than be a prisoner there. It's gotta make Guantanamo look like a fucking ski vacation."

"I don't understand how a place like that can exist in a sane world.

So far off the map. So backward."

"I'm trying not to think about it. Therapy expenses are already going to be off the charts."

Susan chuckled. "Well, now is a great time to finish that book of yours. You certainly won't be struggling for ideas."

"Isn't that the truth?"

They descended another twenty feet in silence before finally reaching solid ground. Ted leaned against the wall, breathing heavily. His legs felt like rubber and his hands were covered in rusty grit and muck. He wiped them on his pants, removed the flashlight from his waistband, and shined it around the room. They were in a massive chamber, too large for their flashlight to reach the sides. The ceiling arched over thirty feet above their heads. The feeling of claustrophobia from the tight tunnels above didn't dissipate. The darkness wrapped around them just as tightly as the brick and mortar of the labyrinth.

Ted watched Susan jump from the ladder and test her footing. She exhaled deeply as she rubbed life back into her sore arms and legs.

"Now what?" she asked, startled by the booming echo of her voice reverberating off the high ceiling.

"We go forward, hug the wall. If there was a way in, there has to be a way out."

"Does logic even apply?"

"Good question. I guess we're going to find out."

Thirty feet to their left, they found the chamber wall. They side-stepped, keeping their backs to the brick, shining the light into the darkness. The wall curved ever-so-slightly, bending to the right so Ted couldn't see more than twenty feet ahead. Their pace slowed.

On their right, something scurried in the darkness, its feet slapping on the wet ground. Human feet.

"Jesus Christ," Susan whispered. "What is that?"

"Just keep moving."

A figure appeared at the furthest reach of the flashlight beam, nothing more than a hunched silhouette. It watched them pass but made no effort to approach. It matched their pace, keeping to the shadows.

"Look," Susan pointed.

Ahead, orange light flickered and cast human-like shadows on the far wall. They weren't alone.

"We know you're there," a voice called. A thick, wet, guttural croak devoid of emotion or intent.

Their pace quickened as they tried putting distance between them and whatever lurked in the murky light.

"We're not going to harm you," it said.

Susan whined and clutched at Ted's shirt. The bend in the tunnel stopped and Ted caught a glimpse into the chamber ahead. He stopped, moaning at the sight. Four separate burn barrels raged with crackling flames, illuminating dozens of moving figures. Some were huddled around the barrels while others wandered aimlessly on the fringe of the firelight. Groups sat on the ground in piles of soggy sheets and sleeping bags; a few scattered, grime-covered mattresses dotted the floor nearest the center barrel. It again reminded Susan of the documentary she'd seen about New York City's homeless population; hundreds of men, women, and children huddled around the fire, living beneath a bridge to keep out of the elements. This was similar, except these *people* were completely nude, exposing their pale flesh, riddled with sores that seeped a thick, viscous, liquid.

"We have to go back," Susan trembled. "We have to get out of here."

"We'll never make the climb, Susan. We have to take our chances."

"You have nothing to fear from us," the voice called. "You're running, anyone can see that. Was it Jack?"

"What do you want?" Ted asked. "We don't want any trouble, please. Just let us go on our way."

"You're free to do whatever you like, we're not going to stop you."

Susan didn't believe a word. If she'd learned anything since the Cuda left the road, it was to trust no one.

"I know what you're thinking," it said. "We're not like Jack and his people. We're here *because* of them, chased underground by his savagery."

"Why haven't you left, then?" Susan asked. "Why are you still here?"

"We don't have a choice. It's safe here."

The figure approached slowly, walking into the light, covering its face with an arm the color of eggshells. Susan gasped and covered her mouth. It was a man, only discernible by his flaccid penis peeking through a tangled patch of silver-white pubic hair. He walked hunched, his other arm dangling between his legs and nearly touching the floor. The nails on his hands and feet had become broken, brown claws, coated in sludge and muck.

"Can you lower your light, please?" the man asked. "It hurts my eyes."

Ted did as he was asked as the man lowered his arm from his face. Susan choked back a cry and gripped Ted's arm painfully.

The man was pale as a corpse. His thin lips were pulled back over cracked and broken teeth; his tongue a bloated, pink snail flicking around in his small mouth, his ears stunted and shrunken, poking from the side of his bald head like cauliflower.

His eyes…

"Oh my God," Susan muttered.

"I know what you must think," the man said, "but I look scarier than I am."

The man's eyes rolled around in his skull like wet marbles. All the color had been drained from his irises, leaving them the color of old milk. He was completely blind. His nose twitched like that of a rabbit, picking up their scent to compensate for his lack of sight. He reached out toward them and Susan screeched and jumped back, pressing herself tightly against the wall. The man pulled his hand away and backed up a step.

"Don't touch me!" Susan yelped.

"No, I won't, please. I'm not going to hurt you."

"Who are you?" Ted asked. "What is this place?"

"This is home," the man said. "Who am I? I don't know. I might have known once, but not anymore. My previous life is a blur."

"Your previous life?"

"Sure. Do you think I was born here? I mean, some of us were, but many of us started just like you. We had lives, families, jobs. Now this is all we know. Jack took everything away."

"Jack put you here?" Ted asked.

"We were forced underground. Disagreeing with Jack and his ways is a surefire way to wind up here. They hunt, and they don't give up until you're on the end of a spear."

"So leave," Susan cried. "You can't live here forever."

"We can and we will. There's nothing for us up top. We've been here so long; this is our home now. I can't even remember what the sun felt like." The man hung his head.

"We can help you," Ted blurted. "Find a way out."

"We know of ways out," the man said, "we just can't use them. This is where we live, and if you don't want to be trapped here with us, I suggest you leave as soon as you can. *If* you can."

"I don't understand," Susan said. "If you know a way out, why would you want to live here in this filth?"

"Susan…"

"No, she's right," the man said. "Do you think we haven't tried? We have. Hundreds of times. Every time we think we've found something, the tunnel stops at a dead end, a cave in, a drop to the levels below this one."

"*Below*," Susan said. "You mean there's more below this?"

"It's endless," he replied. "You don't want to go down. There are worse things than death, and all of them live beneath your feet."

"Then how do we leave?" Ted asked. "You said there are ways out."

"I can show you, but I can't follow." The man shuffled toward the center of the chamber where others turned at his approach, sniffing the air, identifying him by smell alone.

"We have company," a woman croaked.

"They're passing through," the man replied. "I'm going to show them the way out. Then they're on their own."

"The way out," she cackled. "That's a good one. I have a better chance of Clark Gable crawling out of my twat." She grabbed her naked crotch with one filthy hand and laughed harshly. Susan turned away, disgusted.

"Don't mind her, she means no harm."

"They smell so new," she said. "The fresh air clings to them like fleas." The group had turned in their direction, an assortment of grotesque albinos covered in the sloppy film of decay. They too were blind. A small child sat on top of a pile of trash, hungrily gnashing on the remains of a giant rat. His face and chest were smeared in fresh blood; a pile of entrails lie at his feet. He stopped chewing and held the corpse out in his hand. Ted looked away. The boy shrugged and went back to his meal.

The group milled about curiously, but showed no signs of aggression.

"You have company often?" Ted asked, not expecting a reply.

"Often enough. Not many stay. They wander off, go deeper, get lost. Now and then you hear them screaming in the darkness, but none make it back. This is the last stop for newcomers."

The smell of their unwashed bodies grew stronger as Ted and Susan closed in on the circle of light; a cloying mixture of sweat, excrement, and the swampy, fishy stink of stagnant water. Nearby, Ted watched a man roll over on a waterlogged mattress and piss on the ground next to his bed. He wore a small, dirty towel around his shoulders.

"That towel," Ted shouted, rushing forward. "Where did you get that towel?"

The man shrank away and pulled it tighter around his skinny frame. "It's mine," he whined, "and you can't have it!"

"No, I don't want it. I need to know where you found it."

"Ted, calm down," Susan said, putting a soothing hand on his arm.

"He has Julie's towel!"

"It's a white towel. There are millions of them. It doesn't mean it's hers."

"Where'd you get that towel?" he repeated.

"I found it, fair and square. I'm not giving it up."

"I don't want the fucking towel, I just need to know where you found it."

"It just washed down," he said. "Stuff always washes down when it rains."

"Did you see a girl? Did she come through here?"

"See? Are you making a joke?"

"No! Goddammit, you know what I mean. Did a girl come through here. She was wearing that towel when we saw her last."

"No girl. I would've noticed. Just a towel, and you can't have it."

Exasperated, Ted hissed and turned to Susan. "It's like talking to a wall."

"They can hear you," Susan whispered.

"It's okay," their guide mumbled. "No one came through. No one but you. I'd tell you."

"She was a friend. I saved her from Jack only to watch her get sucked down into the sewer by some goddamn monster."

"Fang," the man said. "We call it Fang. It guards the sewer. Lucky for you, there's more than one exit. There's no getting around that thing. Its appetite is insatiable."

"It took Julie," Ted said.

"Then your Julie is no longer among the living. No one comes back from its nest."

"What the hell are we talking about?" Susan screamed. "Like the Loch Ness fucking Monster?"

"You've seen it," the man said. "How can you doubt its existence?"

Susan deflated and shook her head.

"Your friend is dead. Forget about her and focus on yourselves."

Susan screamed as strong fingers wrapped around her ankle. She looked down as a naked woman pulled herself into a kneeling position and sniffed Susan's legs.

"You smell like fresh bread," the woman said. "All buttered up and ready for the oven."

"Get away from me," Susan said, kicking the woman away.

"Leave them alone," their guide shouted. "No one's going to harm them."

"But they smell so tasty," a man grunted. "Why are we eating rats and rotten meat when we can have it fresh and warm?"

Others began inching forward, crowding around them, noses wiggling in a frenzy.

Another woman, wearing the remains of a football jersey over two misshapen breasts, reached out her bleached fingers and squeezed Ted's balls harshly. He squawked and jumped away from her clutching hand. "You said nothing would happen to us," Ted shouted.

"It's been so long since I felt the touch of a man," the woman lamented. "Just stay a little while, huh? Stay and keep me warm."

Their guide slapped the woman across the face and she fell back into a scummy puddle with a cry.

"These people are going on their way," he shouted. "If they don't belong here, we ain't keeping them."

"Don't you want a taste?" the woman asked, slobbering. "Aren't you tired of eating shit?"

"We're not like Jack!" he screamed. "We're not going to become what we fought so hard to escape."

"Then let them go," a man shouted. "We don't have to hurt them, but we can *use* them," he laughed.

A small child bounded toward them on all fours like a naked chimp. Ted kicked out and sent the child sprawling.

"You don't hurt my boy!" a woman shrieked.

"GO!" the guide shouted, grabbing Ted by the collar. "Get out of here now while you still have a chance. There's a tunnel at the end of the room. Don't look back. I can't stop them when they get this way."

"You said they wouldn't hurt us," Susan said. "You promised we were safe."

"I'm sorry," the man babbled. "It's out of my control."

A naked man hit Ted in the chest with a sinewy arm, knocking him back. Ted swung the flashlight and connected with the man's skull, dropping him to the ground as his scalp bled onto the floor. Others rushed forward, but kept their distance. They may not have sight, but their hearing had been finely honed over generations of living in the dark. They huddled against each other, tripping over flailing limbs, scratching at the ground aggressively with jagged talons.

Ted grabbed Susan by the arm and looked into her horrified eyes. "Run," he whispered. "Run and don't stop for anything. Do you hear me? If we get separated, you just keep running. One of us has to get out of here."

A hand reached around Susan's arm and tried pulling her into the crowd. Ted swung the heavy flashlight on the man's forearm, snapping it like dry kindling, exposing the splintered bone. He pulled his fractured arm to his chest and ran back into the crowd, wailing.

"Just leave us alone," Susan screamed.

She felt Ted's larger hand grab her own and hold it tightly. With a jerk, he pulled her along behind him. She fell to her knees, skinning them on the harsh edges of exposed brick. Ted pulled her up and began running as the angry crowd gave chase. The beam of light bobbed ahead of them as they rushed toward the far end of the massive chamber. Their pursuers grunted and chattered and squealed as their bare feet pounded the floor. All signs of their humanity had vanished; they regressed into a pack of feral dogs, slavering over the warm scent of their prey.

Ted saw the arched tunnel opening at the end of the room and pulled Susan in that direction, praying she had the stamina to stay on her feet. The horde was only inches behind. If the man was right, this could be their only way out.

It was the only choice they had left.

***

The only advantage was that the tunnel was a straight shot forward. There were no branching tunnels, no drop-offs, and so far, no dead ends. The clan of albinos were still in pursuit, but had dropped back to a safe distance, allowing Ted and Susan to catch their breath. The tunnel had been on a steady incline for several minutes, giving them hope that they'd eventually reach higher ground. How far down were they? One mile? Three? It seemed they'd been steadily going deeper and deeper into the subterranean tunnel system ever since leaving the surface.

Briefly, Ted thought he heard the distant rumble of thunder, but sound was strange down here. It was impossible to tell where the noises were coming from. Ted slowed and shined the light behind them, confused by what he saw. He slowed to a jog and finally stopped. Susan pushed him, shouted at him, beat at his shoulders with an open hand. She was sure he'd given up until she saw the puzzled look on his face.

"What? We have to go. Now is not the time for sightseeing."

"Suzie, look," he said. He raised the flashlight and illuminated the pale bodies as they fell forward and disappeared. A new tunnel had opened in the floor beneath their feet, spilling them into the depths of the sewer. Their shrill cries echoed piercingly as they tumbled into the abyss. Those fortunate enough to stop in time stood motionless, their heads cocked to the side, listening to the terrified chorus of voices emanating from below. The tunnel trembled as something came to life beneath them. Those remaining turned on their heels and sped back to the chamber as dark tentacles burst from the opening in the floor. At once, six of the once-human monsters were scooped up and pulled into the bowels of the sewer where they were loudly torn to ribbons.

"That doesn't make sense," Susan muttered, wiping her eyes with her balled fists. "There wasn't a tunnel there a second ago."

"Nothing makes sense here. Nothing."

The tremors beneath their feet subsided as Fang finished its meal and splashed away, momentarily sated.

"Remember what the man said," Ted whispered. "They've tried to escape but keep running into dead ends and drop-offs. I think we've just witnessed what he was talking about."

Without warning, one of the albino monsters leapt over the gap, arms flailing, mouth open wide to display its broken teeth. A pair of massive breasts swung like pendulums as it leapt toward them with a shriek. Ted swung the flashlight blindly and hit the beast in the side of the head with a loud crack. It stumbled and fell sideways into the slime-covered tunnel wall. Ted raised the light again to finish the job, suddenly stopping and staring as the creature melted into the brick with an explosive bellow. Its eyes rolled in its bloody skull as it tried to free itself, but its struggles were in vain. It melted into the wall, its skin smoldering and dripping down the cracked brick, as it vanished in a final puff of putrid smelling steam.

Whatever magic was in play in this cursed place was keeping *them* from leaving. A fine balance existed here between the real and the obscene; a balance that thankfully kept those blind demons from spilling out into the world.

Susan exhaled a shaky breath and looked at her husband for answers, but none were forthcoming. Instead, he shined the flashlight up the ascending tunnel floor and slowly crept forward. Getting out of this stinking labyrinth was the only priority. Albino man-things be damned.

"Please God, let this lead outside," Susan said.

"You might just get your wish," Ted replied. "Do you feel that?"

Susan shrugged.

"Air!" he said. "I can feel it on my face. We're close."

Susan sniffed and realized he was right. There was a different smell, a fresher smell. It would never be confused with a summer garden, but anything was better than the musty stench of rot that assailed them under ground.

"Come on," Ted called, grabbing Susan's hand and pulling her behind.

They jogged for several minutes, always up toward the hope of freedom. Ahead, dim, gray light spilled around the arched exit. It was the most beautiful thing Susan had ever seen. She started giggling like a schoolgirl, unable to get herself under control, tripping and stumbling and rushing forward blindly to the circle of muddy light.

One hundred yards to go and the flashlight went dark, plunging them into dim shadow. Ted's air rushed from his lungs like he'd been gut-punched, but Susan squeezed his hand reassuringly.

"We don't need it," she said. "We're out, Ted. We're actually *out*."

"We don't know what's out there. It would've come in handy." He tossed the heavy flashlight on the floor where it rolled away into the darkness.

"Sure, so would a map and compass, but we have to work with what we have."

Ted nodded and kissed her on the forehead. "Then let's do it. I've had enough of this place for ten lifetimes."

"Amen to that."

The tunnel widened as they approached the exit; the light had taken on an ugly reddish-gray hue, and the pattering of rain intensified as they reached the tunnel's mouth. Susan was disheartened. She'd do just about anything to feel the warmth of the sun on her skin and have a dry place to rest her head. The rolling thunder brought her back to reality.

"Are you ready?" Ted asked.

"I haven't been ready for anything since we left the house, but I don't really have a choice, do I?"

Ted shook his head. "No, but it's a vacation you're never going to forget."

Susan snorted laughter. "That's one way of looking at it. Too bad we didn't bring the camera. Could you imagine dinner parties?"

"Sure," Ted chuckled. "In this picture you can clearly see Fang, the Pine Lakes sea monster, and here's the motel where we stayed. Notice the crowd of curious townsfolk stopping to pay a visit."

"Here's the local *bruja*, giving us directions to some of the town's hot spots."

"And our tour guide, *Whitey*, local clan chief of a previously unknown camp of albino sewer dwellers."

"Too bad they didn't have a gift shop!"

"What the fuck is wrong with us?" Ted asked.

"It's not us I'm worried about," Susan replied.

They walked hand-in-hand, cautiously scanning their surroundings, testing their footing on the rocky shore of a massive lake.

A lake full of bobbing, white flesh.

10

"OH GOD, NO," SUSAN moaned.

The Pine Lakes region was dotted with bodies of water, scenic beaches, and nature trails. The resort was full of wildlife; deer and squirrels would come right up to the cabin and eat out of your hand. It was one of the region's most appealing qualities. Before the resort closed for the winter, one was given the chance to behold nature's beauty in action as the trees turned gold and the frosty air painted the flora in a shiny coating of silver.

There was no evidence of nature's beauty here. The surrounding forest was dead and black; desiccated leaves clung to twisted branches, rasping harshly in the sour breeze. The sky had turned crimson; fat storm clouds floated overhead like giant bags full of blood. The bank of the lake was littered with detritus, floating in black water that lapped the sand in thick, foamy curds.

As far as the eye could see, corpses floated closely together, a human blanket undulating on the water's surface like a melting ice floe. The air was thick with the foul, gassy stink of decay and clouds of fat flies buzzed lazily over putrefying flesh.

"What *is* this?" Susan asked.

"A dumping ground," Ted replied. "The *smell*!" He covered his mouth and nose with his arm, breathing shallowly. The sea of bodies glistened with rainwater; arms and legs flopped around lifelessly; mouths hung open in silent screams; milky eyes stared unseeing into the sky, filling with metallic-smelling water.

Susan was suddenly relieved that the flashlight had given up the ghost. This was one atrocity that didn't need further illumination.

"There's a path," Susan pointed. "Maybe it leads back to the road."

"What if Jack and his crazies are up there waiting?"

"Do we have a choice?"

"No. I guess we don't."

"Besides, anything is better than this…"

Her words were interrupted by a harsh gasp at her feet. A face broke the surface of the water and gulped in the noxious air. The woman got to her knees, choking out gouts of filmy water and splashing frantically in the thick, sludgy muck at the water's edge.

"Help me," the woman spluttered.

"Julie?" Ted shouted.

"How many other naked blonds have you seen today?" she spit.

Ted waded into the lake and grabbed Julie by the arm, pulling her onto the rocky shore where she collapsed and coughed the remains of the slimy water from her lungs.

"You're alive!" Susan said.

"Am I? It's getting harder and harder to tell."

Ted knelt beside her and put a hand on the clammy flesh of her abdomen. "How did you get out of there? We thought you were gone. We saw that thing grab you."

"I'm not sure," she coughed. "One minute it had me and the next I was being flushed through the sewer like all the other shit. The *things* I saw down there," she sobbed. "You don't even want to know."

"Can you stand?" Susan asked. "We can't hang around here."

"You're fucking brilliant," she said. "I was just getting comfortable. Who brought the picnic basket?"

"I'm sorry…" Susan began.

"No," Julie interrupted, "I'm sorry. You didn't deserve that."

Julie sat up with a groan as Ted and Susan grabbed her arms and helped her to her feet.

"Jesus Christ," Julie hissed, looking out over the sea of bodies. "Out of the frying pan and into the lake."

"Come on," Ted said. "There's a path."

"A path to *what?* How do we know it won't lead us to another nightmare?"

"We don't," Susan said, "but we're running out of options."

"I need to rest," Julie said. "I can't go any further, not yet."

"We can sit for a few minutes," Ted said, "but that's it. We're *not* staying here."

Julie nodded and allowed them to lead her into the forest. Julie spied a fallen tree and sat with a grunt, wiping thick film from her arms and legs. It plopped to the forest floor like jelly.

"Do you think we're ever going to reach the resort?" Julie asked. "I mean, do you *really* believe there's a way out?"

"I do," Ted assured. "I have to."

Julie nodded sadly. "What if I'm not allowed in?"

"Allowed in? What? Because you're naked and…"

"No, not because I'm naked, Ted." She sighed deeply and collapsed into herself. "What if I don't deserve to be saved?"

"What? You're talking nonsense," Susan said. "Of course you deserve to be saved. We all do."

"I'm not so sure. I've done some terrible things."

"We've all done terrible things," Ted said. "That doesn't mean we need to punish ourselves for them." Ted looked at Susan questioningly.

"Not like the things I've done. I'm an awful person. Being locked in a cage is more than I deserve."

"Now come on," Susan said. "No one deserves *this*. How can you even think that?"

Julie sucked in a deep breath and held it as tears leaked down her face. She brushed wet hair from her forehead and looked up at them with the saddest, most tortured stare they'd ever seen. Her pain was all-consuming; it washed over them like high tide.

For five minutes, Julie wept loudly, completely inconsolable, trapped in some private torment. When her cries died, her eyes cleared, and she sat up straight. She wiped snot from her upper lip and took a deep breath.

"I've only ever told this story to Jack and Kathy," she said, "and I'll understand if you leave me behind."

"We're not going to leave you." Ted said.

"Don't say that. Not yet. Let me get this out first, then you can make that decision."

"Julie," Susan soothed, "nothing can be so bad that we'd leave you behind."

"Well I guess we're going to find out."

***

"When I was fifteen I had my life pretty much together. Up until then, I was a smart kid, full of life, a good student. My bedroom was papered with scholastic awards, attendance honors, trophies from softball and swimming. Damn, I was a great swimmer. Like an eel. I just slid through the water. I was at every meet. I cleaned house on the 500 Meter Freestyle, and my backstroke was a thing of beauty. My swim coach was sure I'd be a contender for the Olympics some day, and I believed it, every word. It was my ticket out of Lebanon County. I didn't hate where I lived, don't get me wrong, but I didn't want to be there my entire life. I think your brain starts to atrophy the longer you stay in one place. I had my goals set higher than that.

"In the summer of '88, my father was diagnosed with stage four prostate cancer. I didn't know it at the time; he didn't want me to, but there was no disguising the fact that something was terribly wrong. He lost so much weight and his skin turned yellow and brittle like old newspaper. My mother finally told me what was going on four months after his diagnosis, and two weeks before he died in their bed. There was nothing I could do, nothing anyone could do by then. I didn't blame my mother for not telling me; I knew she was trying to protect me, but sometimes the choices parents make to protect their children actually hurt them in the long run.

"When I returned to school, I didn't fit in anymore. I could see the way the other girls looked at me, like I was damaged goods, the girl with the dead dad. There's no long involved story about how I slowly faded into the background and let my grades slip, it happened overnight. I was kicked off the swim team, and I was *fine* with it. I was dying out there, like an injured seal floundering around with a busted flipper. In no time at all, it was like I'd completely forgotten how to swim. My coach watched helplessly, and I'd hear him talking to other teachers about me. *She was gifted. A real champion swimmer. It must be drugs.* The usual shit. I wasn't on drugs. It never crossed my mind until I heard him talking about it. All of a sudden, I wanted to see what all the fuss about.

"Not all of my friends were straight-edge. I knew that, but I let them do their thing and they let me do mine. The first time I asked my friend Charlene for a hit off her joint, I think I nearly killed her. She choked on it for a minute or two before passing it to me, her face purple from hacking. I was a terrible pot smoker. I coughed out more than I inhaled, but just like everything else, practice makes perfect. By Christmas break I was a full-blown pothead. I couldn't survive without it. I'd smoke a half ounce over the weekend, every weekend, sometimes more depending on who was holding. I became the party girl. I lost some friends, but gained others. It was those *others* that opened my eyes to pills and powders. How did I live my life not knowing this stuff was out there? I thought I'd rediscovered some lost art.

"My junior year in High School was a blur. I'm not sure how I got there most of the time. I was still high from the night before. I'd take something to perk me up in time for class, ride the high as long as it would last, and hit the bathroom a few times a day to get that extra bump I needed to see me through the day. Eventually, it wore off. I was doing more and more and getting less. My grades slipped even further, and by the time I started my senior year, I was onto the harder stuff.

I starting dabbling in needles. My problem there was that I hated wearing long sleeves, so by the time my arms started showing signs of my vice, I decided to stop going to school altogether. Junkies don't feel self conscious in front of other junkies. We'd often show off our tracks like they were war medals. I didn't realize how fucked up that was at the time. By then, all my old friends were gone, so I started making friends with all the wrong people to replace them.

"The problem with heroin, other than the obvious, is you can never get enough. You'd jump off a bridge to chase that dragon. I stole money from my mother, who at that point was in her own addiction of self pity and willful ignorance. She knew what was going on. She blamed herself for it, for how she treated the situation with my father, but I wasn't in the game of feeling bad for others' mistakes. I felt bad enough for my own.

"Once the money ran out, I found other ways to get my fix. Sex and blowjobs would earn me enough to get by some days. Threesomes. Gang bangs. I did whatever I needed to do, and I was so far into my addiction that I didn't realize there was anything wrong with my behavior. The year I was meant to graduate, 1990, started with the death of my mother. She'd burned herself out, fed into her depression, slowly withered away until there was nothing left to hold onto. Was it my fault? I don't know. I'm sure I didn't help. My father's death put her in the ground, but my addictions likely shoveled the dirt over the coffin. On Valentine's Day, she hung herself from the rafters with an extension cord. I found her a week later. I called the police, left the house, and never went back. I didn't go to her funeral. Don't even know where she's buried. I assume my aunt took care of that.

"Once my mom was gone, I really hit it hard. The drug was the only thing I was living for, and it was getting harder and harder to find guys willing to pay me for my *services*. I became the problem. The untouchable. I moved in with a guy, Jay Bigham, not because I loved him, but because he fed me what I needed. We walked the road of mutual destruction, content in knowing we didn't have to do it alone.

"I found out in July that I was pregnant. Jay had knocked me up, just like he'd knocked up countless others. To celebrate, we tied each other off and got higher than we've even been. I came to, but Jay didn't. Jay never did anything again. He died on a stained recliner with foam bubbling from his lips. I knew I'd reached the bottom of the barrel

"I walked away from Jay. No one cares about another dead junkie. I disappeared into the night like a ghost and never looked back. I got clean, but only after leaving two dead bodies in my wake. I got clean by myself. I got a job, rented a small apartment, watched my tummy get bigger and bigger as the spark of life inside me ignited into a raging fire. I prayed the kid wouldn't be another victim of my bad choices.

"I gave birth to an absolutely beautiful, seven pound baby boy. Every finger and toe was another blessing. I swear when they handed him to me, he looked up with those gorgeous blue eyes and he smiled. Everything was going to be okay. Nothing bad could exist in a world with such perfection. I named him Jacob after my father. I showered him with gifts, at least as much as I could on a waitress's wage. The owner of the diner, Rita, watched Jacob when I worked. She was a wonderful woman, a real angel. Didn't charge me a dime. She saw the fading scars. She knew I was walking a tightrope, but she gave me the chance I needed to get my shit together. She didn't ask questions.

"I repaid her by skipping out early one night to hang out with a guy I'd met at the diner. He was cute. I was always a sucker for a cute face. The appeal was in the anonymity. He didn't know about my past, and he didn't ask questions. I knocked on Rita's door at three in the morning and knew I'd crossed a line. She asked me if I'd gotten high. I couldn't blame her. It's the first thing I'd think if I was in her shoes. In no uncertain terms, she warned me if it ever happened again, I'd not only be out of a job, but she'd make sure I'd never see Jacob again.

"After some time, I explained my past to her. She nodded in all the right places. It was a story she'd heard before, one she was familiar with. I tried telling her I'd met someone, someone I enjoyed spending time with, and she gave me the rope to hang myself.

"The man's name was Cameron. We just clicked. Rita allowed me twice a month where she'd watch Jacob so I could meet Cam. A few times, I took Jacob along. If this was going to be anything, Cam had to know my baby boy. I was very adamant about it. One Saturday evening, Cam told me to let Rita watch Jacob, said he had a surprise for me. I was skeptical, but curious. I left Jacob with Rita and drove over to Cam's apartment, and wouldn't you know it, my came in the shape of a syringe filled with clear liquid. I'd been clean for a year at that point, and it took me ten minutes of half-hearted arguing to tie off my arm and run into my demon's embrace. That particular demon doesn't take no for an answer, not like I really tried to fight. We welcomed each other with open arms.

"I went to pick up Jacob two days later. I fed Rita lies she didn't believe. She saw it in my eyes, heard the tremor in my voice. I came at her like a honey badger! I screamed, ranted, threatened to call the police. When that didn't work, I hit her. Punched her right in the face. She was in her mid-sixties, it didn't take much. She went down and didn't get back up. I grabbed my son, buckled him into his car seat, and tore out of her driveway like the princes of Hell were on my tail. I had no idea if I'd killed her. All I could think of was getting as far away as possible. I thought of going to Cameron's place and decided against it. Someone would find me there, and at that moment I didn't want to be found. Not ever again.

"I drove and drove and drove. I had no idea where I was going, but as long as there was road to follow, I pointed the car forward and kept my foot on the gas. Instead of feeling better, I started feeling worse. The drug was wearing off. My hands were starting to shake, and Jacob was in the back seat screaming his little head off, likely hungry, likely wet. He wouldn't stop screaming. It went right through me. It was like a toothache, like raw nerves pounding signals deep into my skull. It went on for miles. Eventually it just became part of the drone that swirled in my head. I blocked it out. I kept my hands on the wheel and tore up the miles, praying for another fix. Anything to make it all go away.

"I turned onto a side road; my eyes were getting foggy and I didn't want to risk getting into an accident. I just needed to stop for a bit, rest, clear my head. The road wound down into the woods, narrowed, and grew darker as I left the lights of town behind. By then I was on autopilot. I saw the world passing by out my window, but I was oblivious to it. The road opened into a wide, empty parking lot, and at the far end was a boat launch. I didn't know I was going to do it until the car splashed down twenty feet from shore.

"The car filled quickly. I put my head back and listened to Jacob wailing in the back seat, and I wondered how my life had come to that moment. That little boy was the only thing I had in the world, and there I was, water gurgling up through the floor as the car slipped beneath the surface. I remember thinking of some stupid movie I'd seen once, where a submarine gets depth charged and sinks, only to leave the crew struggling inside, trapped by rising water. Isn't it funny, the stupid shit your mind latches onto in moments of crisis?

"Jacob was still screaming. I can't imagine how terrified that poor boy must have been, but my mind was a million miles away. I reached into the back seat and grabbed his pudgy, little fingers, and this amazing calm came over him. He sniffled, looked at me, and giggled. The sweetest sound you could imagine. He clutched my hand tighter and shook it, kicking his tiny legs and jumping around in his seat. In that final minute before the car filled with water, he was happy. Maybe he knew? Maybe he was ready for it to be over just as much as I was. What was I ever going to be able to do for him? A junkie.

"I held my breath and let the water take me. Jacob thrashed and kicked and reached out for me in the dark, wanted me to take his pain away. I was all he ever had, and that's a shame when you think about it. If children could choose their parents, I'd be the last in line.

"Jacob stopped moving, and in that moment, my world exploded. What the fuck was I doing? How could I punish that sweet little boy for my lifetime of mistakes? My lungs burned from lack of oxygen and something in my head snapped, like a light going on in a dark closet. I saw everything clearly for the first time in years. How I could clean up my act, how I could be a good mother to Jacob and give him the attention and love he deserved.

"I rolled the window down and shot from the car like a torpedo. Somewhere inside of me was the teenage swimming prodigy that had once been. I reached the surface in seconds, treading water, filling my lungs with precious air. I was going back down to save my son. There was no way I'd be able to live with myself knowing what I'd done. I'd become something I hated, and although it took years to lose myself in the trappings of teenage burnout, it took only seconds to see there was another way.

"The water wasn't very deep where the car was; fifteen feet, twenty at most. I dove and felt around in the dark; I couldn't see anything. If I could just find the car, my mind would figure out the rest, but all I came up with were handfuls of the lake bottom. I scoured the ground in every direction until my lungs were ready to burst before coming back up and doing it again. I'd gotten so disoriented, I wasn't sure if I was even looking in the right place.

"I searched and searched until I was utterly exhausted. I couldn't keep my head above the surface anymore. What had I done? I let my little boy drown. Not just let him drown, but led him right to the door and walked him inside. I collapsed on the beach, shivering, empty, broken. I deserved to be the one floating down there in the dark, not him, not that precious little boy with so much life left to live. I never thought I'd stop crying.

"The next morning dawned cold and gray. My prayers for death went unanswered; I didn't get an easy way out. Jacob didn't have a choice, so why should I? I thought of killing myself. Walking into the lake and letting the water take me away, join my baby boy in his watery grave. When I started walking, it wasn't toward the lake, but away from it. My feet carried me away from the scene of my heinous crime, but no matter how far I walked, I knew there was no way to outrun what I'd done.

"I didn't see a single, living soul. Not a car passed. The sky got darker, and I assumed I'd been walking all day, but it didn't *feel* like that much time had passed. I saw the sign for Pine Lakes and had every intention of turning myself in and paying for my crime. Put me in the electric chair! Hang me from the highest tree! I welcomed it.

"When I wandered into town, Jack and Kathy were there, sitting on the sidewalk in front of the drugstore like they were waiting for a fucking parade to roll through. I broke down and told them everything. They were so... *understanding*. I couldn't figure them out. Why didn't I see through them right away and realize something was terribly wrong? They fed me, they gave me dry clothes and a place to sleep. I lost track of time in that never ending darkness. I pleaded with them to show me to the police station and let me begin atoning for my grievous sins, but they convinced me I didn't deserve that kind of life. They said I'd make up for my crimes in other ways, and that only God could judge me for what I'd done.

"Jack's plan for atonement meant working for him at the bar, performing stunts for his clientele, sexual favors, locked in a cage like an animal. I got used to the treatment, and at first, I welcomed the abuse. It was about a week later when Jack unlocked my cage and said he had a *present* for me. A fucking present for good behavior. He let me wear clothes for the first time in days. They felt heavy and smelled of mildew. He walked me through town, showing me off, telling his cronies about my sins and how I'd be held accountable. Jack reveled in his position as judge and jury when all I prayed for was the executioner.

"I wondered if my walk across town was building up to something. Would they put a bullet between my eyes? Justice for Jacob? Jack held my arm tightly, painfully, laughing the whole time. 'You're going to love this,' he said. Love what? The streets were lined with people, more people than I'd seen in Pine Lakes since I'd arrived. There were carts set up on some of the sidewalks, like food vendors at a carnival. Whatever Jack had in store, these crazy fucks were celebrating it like the Fourth of July.

"When we turned the corner, I got my first glimpse of their church. It was like everything else in town: peeling paint, windows shuttered, front steps covered in trash. It took a minute to realize that was where he was leading me. A throng of people stood on either side, parting for Jack as he walked me to the front door. They were a ragged lot. Broken smiles for broken people. They smelled like a locker room.

"Walking inside, I was suddenly hit by a wall of heat. The crowd hushed as Jack walked me down the aisle, like it was my wedding day or something. I looked up and noticed the bodies, dozens of them, hanging from the rafters. Offerings? Punishments? Was I the next one to get strung up and dangled from the ceiling? Fine. I accepted that. I thought I was beginning to understand Jack's form of vigilante justice. Turned out I knew nothing of how deep his insanity ran.

"At the end of the aisle stood a large marble altar. I'm sure it had been beautiful once, but now it was covered in dried blood, large crimson patches that had stained the surface. Dead, dried flowers were spread across it, and wrapped in a dirty blanket was a small body.

"Jacob's body.

"I stared at Jack in absolute horror. They fished Jacob's corpse from the lake and brought him here, and for what purpose? To torture me? I tried to run to escape coming face to face with my crime, but he wouldn't let me. He grabbed me by the back of the neck and pushed my face down until it was only inches from Jacob's cold body. I could smell the stink of the lake in his thin, brown hair. His body was bloated, his eyes drilling into mine accusingly.

"Jack laughed and pushed my head down further until my cheek rested on Jacob's frozen stomach. 'Do you feel that? Cold. Look at him and realize what you've done.' How could I not know what I've done? The crowd of spectators giggled at me behind their hands. He grabbed my hand and placed it on Jacob's stomach. He was so cold. So lifeless. A child's doll. I tried to pull away, but Jack wouldn't allow it. Instead, he pressed harder and harder until my hand sank into Jacob's tiny, distended belly. Brown water gurgled between his lips, bubbling up and over his chin, over his chest, over my trembling fingers. Filthy lake water that smelled of seaweed and mud.

"I screamed and screamed until my vision went black. I wanted to stay there in that darkness forever. All I could smell was the lake. Taunting me. Reminding me of what I'd done. When I awoke, I was back in the cage, naked, shivering. A plate of cold spaghetti noodles sat on the floor, covered in flies and pulsing with maggots. He forced me to eat it. When I vomited, he forced me eat that as well. 'You wanted to atone for your sins,' he said. 'Start fucking atoning.'

"I've been there ever since. I don't know how long it's been. Time meant nothing to me after that day. I've been beaten more times than

I can count. Raped. Pissed on. Mocked. Constantly reminded of why I was here and why I deserved the treatment I was getting. Eventually I stopped fighting, because as fucked up as it was, and as fucked up as Jack is, I knew he was right. I did deserve it, and more. I could spend a million years in that cage and never come close to making up for what I did.

"I shouldn't have allowed you to take me from that place. It's where I belong."

***

When Julie finished talking, the overwhelming silence crept in. Ted stepped from one foot to the other, unable to gather his thoughts into any coherent form of speech. Susan remained sitting on a large boulder, rubbing her arms with her hands, staring dazed into the dim red light. Ted recognized the look and knew immediately how the next few seconds would play out. Trying to intervene would only make him part of the collateral damage.

"You fucking monster," Susan hissed. "You fucking degenerate, junkie, whore."

Julie looked up, stunned by Susan's vehemence, but she didn't respond. She'd just told them how she killed her own child. She didn't expect sympathy and a warm shoulder to cry on. Her muscles tensed, expecting Susan to lunge at her.

"Every day of my life I've punished myself for losing my baby. I've sunk so fucking low, beaten myself up, risked losing my marriage, and here you sit, telling us how you murdered your own flesh and blood like you're regaling us with a campfire story!"

"Okay, Suzie," Ted said, stepping closer. "Calm down."

"Calm down? Were you listening to the same thing I was? Do I have to spell it out for you?"

"It's okay Ted, I deserve this."

"Don't you fucking talk to him!" Susan shrieked, jumping from her rock and taking a defensive stance. "You will never earn the right to talk to him ever again. Do you understand me? Never!"

Julie nodded and looked back at the ground.

"Oh my God," Susan cried. "How? How could you do it? That baby didn't do a fucking thing to deserve a mother like you. You disgusting waste of a human being."

"Okay, babe, please. Don't you think she's suffered enough?"

"I absolutely do *not* think she's suffered enough, not *nearly* enough for what she's done. Anything she's endured in Pine Lakes is too good for her. Put *her* at the bottom of the lake, let her feel what her son felt. Let her be completely helpless, crying out for help that will never come. I can't even LOOK AT HER!"

"Susan, I wasn't in my right mind," Julie pleaded. "Do you think I wanted things to play out like this?"

"I don't care how you wanted things to play out. You're going to hide behind excuses? Blame your dead father or your checked-out waste of a mother? People try for *years* to have children, and some of us aren't so lucky. You spread your legs and BAM! Pregnant. All the shit you pumped into your body and you gave birth to a healthy baby boy, and what do you do? You fucking drive him into a lake and let him drown!"

"What do you want me to say?" Julie yelled, standing from her log and stepping forward. "That I'm sorry? Because you'll never understand how sorry I am."

"Shove your sorry up your ass you fucking pig!" Susan lunged and punched Julie in the eye with a loud crack. Julie stumbled back and fell into the wet leaves, covering her face with her hands to ward off another blow. "I'm not going to hit you again. It's too good for you. I just want you out of my sight before I do something I'm really going to regret."

"Suzie, please," Ted soothed. "Get a hold of yourself. We can't do this right now. We'll figure something out."

"I've already figured it out, Ted. We're going to leave her here to rot."

"They'll find her and they'll kill her," Ted said.

"Exactly! Let her fend for herself; leave her alone and scared like that little baby boy. Let them take her and string her up and use her like a pinata. I don't care."

"Susan, we can't…"

"Don't you dare tell me what we *can't* do. That's precisely what we're going to do, and it still won't make up for what she's done." Susan fell back on the boulder hard and started crying tears of pure rage. "She killed her baby boy. She fucking *killed* him. All I ever wanted was a child, Ted. It was taken from us! We were robbed! Why would she be allowed to have a perfect child and cast it away like a bag of trash?"

"It's not up to us to judge her, Suzie. As much as I want to, as much as I want to let you hit her over and over again, it's not our place to dole out her punishment. Let her punish herself."

"She's not coming with us. I can't stand the sight of her. Prison is too good; let Jack have her."

Julie curled up in a ball on the sodden ground and cried quietly. Ted didn't know if she was even hearing any of their conversation or if she'd checked out. It no longer mattered. Susan made up her mind, and by doing so, had made up Ted's mind as well. Right or wrong, Ted would never turn his back on his wife. That was one bond that couldn't be broken; the one thing Ted held onto with every fiber of his being. Their souls were intertwined, and wherever she wanted to go, Ted would follow.

Susan grabbed Ted's arm and stood, testing her legs. Julie crawled back a few feet and put her back to the fallen tree. Ted grabbed his wife's hand and started pulling her away when Susan stopped, looked down, and spit on Julie's naked skin. "Whatever happens to you, it'll never be enough. If you follow us, I'll kill you myself."

Julie nodded slowly and uncovered her head. "I'm sorry…"

"Don't you dare!" Susan shouted. "You don't get to be sorry."

"Come on," Ted said. "It isn't worth it. Let's go."

Suddenly, the silence was broken by an excited voice shouting from somewhere above. "I see them," it hollered. "They're in the woods down by the lake."

"Jesus Christ," Ted whispered, "they know we're here."

He and Susan ran before they had a chance to figure out where they were running to. They listened as voices called out angrily behind them, heard the sound of heavy feet pounding through the brush. They were close. Ted looked over his shoulder, worried they'd made ground. He still couldn't see them, but the sound of their approach was impossible to ignore.

Ten feet behind them, a shape bobbed in the shadows, puffing loudly, legs pumping.

Julie had followed.

11

Ted had no clue if they were running in the right direction. It was so easy to get turned around in the tangled growth; the strange red sky painted their surroundings in muddy shadow, making everything blend together confusingly. Branches ripped at their flesh and pulled at their hair as they focused on putting one foot in front of the other.

"That bitch is following us," Susan panted.

"Not now," Ted warned.

An arrow whistled past Ted's head and lodged in a nearby tree with a heavy *thunk*. He stumbled and felt Susan's strong hands grab his shirt and steady him as another arrow zipped over his head.

"I don't know how much longer I can run," Susan groaned.

"As long as it takes," Ted said. "I don't want to wind up being someone's dinner tonight."

To their left, up a steady incline, Ted saw a fire burning. He turned in that direction, aware of the danger, but helpless to stop his body from responding. Moths to a flame.

"The road is up there," Julie shouted. "That's the way out of town."

"We don't need your help," Susan called over her shoulder. "Leave us alone, we're done with you."

"Please! Just help me out of here and we'll go our separate ways."

"I'm not helping you do *anything*! You lost that right. You're on your own."

Ted saw a warped, battered guardrail at the top of the hill. Julie was right, this was the way to the road. He fought with himself over Julie's fate. On one hand, he knew he'd never be able to look at her again, not after what she'd told them; on the other, the woman knew more about the area, and would likely be helpful in getting them out of this mess. Susan would never agree to allowing Julie to rejoin them, so he kept his thoughts to himself. When Susan said she'd kill Julie, Ted was certain she wasn't just posturing.

Several more arrows whipped over their heads as they steadily climbed to the road; the brush here was so thick not even an expert marksman could sink an arrow with any accuracy. Just as the thought crossed Ted's mind, Julie cried out and fell into the bed of wet leaves. He stopped and turned, watching Julie writhe on the ground with an arrow jutting from beneath her right shoulder blade. The crimson sky made Julie's blood appear black as it ran over her side and into the moss and dirt.

"Come on," Susan said. "If they want her, they can have her."

Ted frowned, nodded, and turned away. Leaving her didn't feel right; it went against everything in his nature to let her bleed out on the forest floor when he was only steps away. Julie had sealed her fate. If she'd left the door ajar, Susan had effectively slammed it and nailed it shut.

"Please," Julie pleaded. "Please help me. I don't want to die like this."

Ted and Susan kept moving. "Please! I know I don't deserve your help, but you know what they're going to do to me."

"We can only hope," Susan muttered, and kept walking.

They put distance between them and Julie, stopping at the guardrail and peering both ways along the broken street. Pine Lakes was no longer in view, but still Ted heard the commotion back at the Triple Seven. At least the entire angry mob wasn't hunting them. Ted crawled over the rail and grabbed Susan's hand to help her onto the road. In the dim light, he watched Julie crawl to her feet and stagger after them, the arrow waving from her back. Her labored breathing sounded wet. Bubbly.

Their pursuers closed the distance behind them. The forest was alive with the sounds of short whistles and shouts, some form of communication. Down the road, a large group broke away from the pack and began running toward them, carrying their handmade weapons above their heads. Emma had either gone back to her hiding place in the forest, or they'd gotten to her. Ted and Susan fled in the opposite direction as Julie pulled herself over the steel guardrail and fell to the road with a grunt. Ted watched her struggle to her feet and noticed the tip of the arrow had pierced through the flesh right above Julie's right breast. Blood ran over her stomach in a thin trickle. The arrow had gone right through her.

The further they ran, the darker it became. The deeply pitted road made it nearly impossible to run; they kept tripping, stumbling, twisting their ankles in potholes and crevices in the street's surface. The approaching mob didn't have that problem; they knew this road inside and out. The crowd laughed as time and again Ted and Susan tripped over the uneven asphalt, losing ground each time.

After what felt like hours, Ted came up short and nearly fell to the road. A massive mound of dirt - at least fifteen feet high - stood in front of them, blocking the road. At its base was a layer of bones, bleached white and brittle from age. Ted stepped through them, pushing aside skulls and vertebrae with his foot. Smaller bones crunched and crackled beneath his feet; some animal, mostly human. He winced, wondering who they'd belonged to, what they'd gone through to get here. Hollow eyes and grinning mouths mocked his passing.

"Watch your step," he said as Susan waded through the pile.

"Who are all these people?" she moaned.

"I don't know, but I don't want to join them. Come on."

They climbed the mountain of loose dirt, careful not to slide backward. Arrows clattered to the street below them as the crowd got within range. Their shouts and jeers had become louder and more frantic. Ted reached the top of the heap, collapsed, and pulled Susan up behind him. They lie on their backs, panting, staring into a sky the color of rust. At the base of the mound, Ted heard bones being pulverized by passing feet. He looked down and watched Julie scrabble over the pile. It hurt him to watch her struggle; hurt him to see blood dribbling from her wound and spattering the remnants of the dead, but Susan was right. She no longer deserved their help. Julie pawed at the soft dirt and began ascending the mound.

"Where do you think you're going, girl?" a voice shouted. Jack's voice.

The group had caught up and formed a line at the boundary of bones. Jack stood in front, leading the cavalry, a giant ax held in his fist.

"You three are some trouble," Jack said. "Ask yourselves what lies on the other side of this pile."

"Anything is better than this," Susan yelled.

"Is it? I wouldn't be so sure of that," he chuckled.

Jack raised the ax above his head and threw it with all his strength. Ted watched it approach in slow motion, reaching out to Susan, trying to pull her out of the way, but he realized a second too late that Jack's aim was true. He opened his mouth to scream but nothing came out. The sharpened blade gleamed in the red light as it spun end over end toward them. He closed his eyes, ready for the meaty thump as it dug deep into Susan's flesh. All of this had been for nothing.

Suddenly, the air in front of them blazed with brilliant blue light and the ax disintegrated, covering them in black ash. Ted reached out with a trembling hand and wiped the black dust from Susan's shoulders; his hand was covered in oily smears.

"Well, would you look at that," Jack grumbled.

"What just happened?" Susan asked.

"Just because you've breached the barrier doesn't mean a thing," Jack cried angrily. "Do you think you're the first to cross the border?"

"It's a pile of dirt, Jack, not Mount Olympus," Ted shouted.

"The extent of your knowledge could slide through the eye of a needle. Do you think you turned up here accidentally? Everything happens for a reason, boys and girls, and you're going to be in for a rude awakening when it finally hits home."

"You and your posse are so smart and all knowing and yet you're still here in the town that time forgot. Living in the dark, eating each other for survival. There's *your* rude awakening, Jack."

An arrow raced toward them from the tree line, and just as before, it burst into blue light and vanished. Ted chuckled. Whatever magic the old woman had used to protect the motel must also protect the exit. It wasn't that Jack didn't want to leave this place, he *couldn't*. Emma had sealed the borders, quarantined the plague that was Jack and his men. The look on Jack's face said it all. He knew he'd lost.

"You two will suffer for this," he shouted. "Do you think you're just going to walk away?"

"That's exactly what we think," Susan said. "Maybe your luck has taken a turn for the worse. You better empty out, Jack. This time tomorrow, this place is going to be overrun with police. They'll burn it to the ground, burn you *all* to the ground."

Jack laughed unexpectedly. "Honey, ain't no one coming here. You can bet the house on that. This is."

"You're welcome to it," Ted said. He stood and looked at the assembled mob, suddenly feeling like king of the hill. Susan stood next to him; Ted felt the heat baking off her skin, felt her perspiration soaking through her clothing. The mob lowered their weapons and stared at them with angry, bloodshot eyes.

Jack stood still, arms crossed over his large chest. "We're going to take that one back with us," he pointed.

Ted looked and saw Julie a few feet below. Her movement had slowed; she breathed harshly, gasping for air, reaching a pale hand toward them.

"Please," she begged.

Susan stepped back and shook her head slowly. "Never. Not after what you've done."

"So she told you her little tale," Jack said. "Pleasant story, isn't it?"

Jack stepped forward and crushed a skull beneath a massive boot. "Come down, Julie. You know you aren't going anywhere. It won't be *allowed*."

"No," she cried. "I won't go back. I won't."

An arrow hissed from the crowd and buried itself in Julie's thigh.

A second arrow pierced the flesh of her other calf as she shrieked into the night.

She peered up at Ted and Susan, eyes full of pain, both physical and emotional. The game was at an end.

"Go," she said. "You don't belong here. No one belongs here, but we all pay for our sins in different ways. Find the resort."

"Come on, girl," Jack called. "We have plans for you."

Julie crawled another foot up the side of the pile, her body shaking from pain and exhaustion. Still she soldiered on.

"Come down here, now! If you're lucky, we'll let you live."

"Live? I haven't lived since I got here, and that's my fault, but I'm not going to let you punish me anymore. It's not your right to punish me. I'll pay for what I've done, but not at your hands."

A machete spun through the air and buried itself in the dirt next to her head. She crawled another foot.

"You will be judged!" Jack growled.

"Yes," Julie said as blood frothed from her mouth, "but not by you."

Julie dug her feet into the soft earth and pushed herself to the top of the mound, reaching a hand over the edge, brushing Ted's shoe with probing fingers. Ted stepped back, pulling Susan with him. Whatever was happening here, it was out of their hands now.

She pulled herself up and over the edge of the bank and sat at their feet, staring out over the crowd, arrows jutting from her flesh. Slowly, she stood, spreading her arms and pointing her face to the sky. The blood dribbling down her back stopped and began smoking, sizzling on her flesh. Susan gagged and turned away at the stink, but Ted couldn't peel his eyes away as Julie's flesh rippled with unknown heat.

"Maybe I'll see you in Hell, Jack," she screamed. "I'll be waiting to tear you apart."

Giant welts appeared on Julie's back before the flesh tore open, bleeding bright orange light from within. The skin on her shoulders crackled and bubbled and turned black as the flames raced up her spine. Holes opened in her flesh, pouring thin shafts of light into the sky. White smoke poured from her hair before bursting into flame, turning her head into a blazing torch. Julie screamed as her body was consumed, screamed until the fire shriveled her lungs. Teeth exploded in her mouth like fireworks. Her blazing body slumped and she fell to her knees, pawing at her face with hands that had become blackened mitts. The light hurt Ted's eyes.

In a gust of hot wind, Julie collapsed and tumbled to the bottom of the hill. By the time she reached the carpet of bones, she'd become just like them. Her blackened skeleton burst apart and came to rest amidst the others, her skull rolling out into the road with gray smoke drifting from its empty eyes.

Julie had chosen her own fate.

Jack rumbled deep in his chest and belted out the loudest, most primal cry Ted had ever heard. Jack ran to Julie's smoking remains and kicked her skull like a football, sending it sailing over the guardrail and into the forest. Susan turned, wrinkling her nose at the hot stink of singed flesh and hair. She watched Jack jump up and down like a child, crushing the bones beneath his feet to powder. He was so used to having his way that losing control so completely was a simple joy to behold.

Ted laughed.

"You think this is the end? You think she *won*?"

"Win or lose, she's no longer yours to control," Ted said, "and neither are we."

"She'll beg to come back to me," Jack hollered. "She'll scratch at the walls of her prison until her fingers turn to mush, and scream until her throat bleeds my name!"

Jack screamed and punched the man standing next to him, dropping him to the road. He grabbed the man's machete and cleaved his skull in half in a spray of blood and meat. The crowd backed away, dropping their weapons with a clatter. Jack cut through them like thick vines, leaving scattered limbs in his wake.

"This isn't over," Jack panted. "There will be more. There's always more." He dropped the machete, breathing heavily. Sweat popped from his pores and ran down his quivering face. "She'll rot in Hell and you'll join her. Mark my words."

"You're already there," Ted said, "and you're too fucking stupid to realize it."

"Better to reign in Hell than serve in Heaven." Jack turned and scuffed his feet in the thick pool of blood beneath his boots. As he walked away, he left tracks to mark his passing. The crowd dispersed and disappeared into the darkness, back to Pine Lakes where the shadows crawled over the dead.

Ted and Susan stepped carefully across the top of the pile and descended to the road on the other side. The town, Jack, and Julie's memory left in the dust of the past. Susan stopped Ted and wrapped her arms around him in a great bear hug. The smooth flesh of her cheek nuzzled into his neck as she cried harshly. Ted smelled the scent of ashes in her hair.

"We're dead," Susan moaned, the sound of her voice muffled and thick.

"No baby, we're free! I've never felt so alive!" he shouted.

"It's not over, Ted," she cried. "You don't understand."

"What are you talking about? Baby, we won."

"We're dead. We're *actually* dead."

"You're talking crazy," Ted said, pushing Susan away and holding her at arm's length. "We've been through a lot. You're not thinking straight."

"No, Ted, I'm thinking straighter than I have since we got here. It's the only thing that makes sense."

"*What* makes sense?"

"We never survived the crash," she said, pausing and staring directly into his eyes. "We died, Ted, and this is Hell."

***

Ted didn't say a word to Susan as they left the town behind them. What was there to say? He feared Susan had left a fragile part of her sanity behind at the pile of bones. Had they escaped this insanity only to dive headfirst into another? The red sky had given way to low, gray clouds; the forest on either side had become lusher, more fragrant, more natural. Susan walked with her head down, staring at her feet, muttering to herself.

"Baby? What's the first thing you want to eat when we get home?" Ted asked, trying to lighten the mood.

"The first thing? What?"

"I could go for some Kentucky Fried Chicken. Big bucket of grease with a side of mashed potatoes and coleslaw. And biscuits! I could eat the ass out of a horse right now."

"Wonderful."

"What about you? What do you want?"

Susan seemed to think it over before stopping in the middle of the road. "I want you to look at me like I'm not crazy!"

"I don't think you're crazy," he said, choosing his words carefully. "After all we've been through, it's hard *not* to think something is off."

"We're the ones who are off," she mumbled. "They said we don't belong here, and they're right, Ted, they're absolutely right."

"I know this is crazy, but that's all it is. A town full of rednecks with nothing better to do than…"

"Ted!" Susan interrupted. She stopped and wiped her face with her hands. "It's more than that and you know it! You have to!"

"I don't know what you want me to say," he said, throwing his hands in the air.

"I want you to acknowledge the fact that something has gone very wrong here."

"Of course I do! It's been a fucked up day."

Susan sighed harshly. "Is that what you really believe? That we've had a string of bad luck?"

"Yes, that's what I'm saying."

"Then you're the one who's crazy," she shouted. "Can you explain any of this rationally? The hounds? The cave? Emma and the motel? Witches and spells? Albino monsters living in the sewer with a sea creature guarding the exits? Does any part of that sound like something you've ever heard of outside of a movie? A woman burst into flame in front of our eyes! For Christ's sake Ted, you have to see it!"

"I don't accept that," he muttered. "It isn't possible."

"And this is? A forgotten town on the edge of the Twilight Zone with cannibal inbreds? Hollywood couldn't write this shit if they locked everyone in a room for a hundred years and forced them to pen a script at gunpoint!"

"Fine!" Ted yelled. "You tell me what you think is going on."

"I already have," she sighed. "I know you don't want to hear it, but nothing else makes sense."

"That we're dead? That we died in the crash and this has all been some crazy dream?"

"Not a dream. It's happening. Whatever this place is, it's real."

"I can see and hear," Ted shouted. "I can *feel*. Could I do that if I was dead?"

"You're not understanding what I'm saying."

"I hear you, every word…"

"But you're not fucking listening!"

Ted lowered his head and shook it furiously, planting his hands on his hips. "Then start making sense!"

"Emma said those woods are on a very thin line. Do you remember that?"

Ted nodded.

"What if that thin line is the one between the living and the dead? Heaven and Hell? She said she's trapped here, that she can't leave. She just people on their way. What if her punishment is to help others through this place? Help them find their direction."

"To Heaven or Hell? Do you know how that sounds?"

"Of course I do," she agreed, "but nothing makes sense here. Nothing we've seen or heard can be explained away."

"You really believe it, don't you?"

Susan nodded. "One of those hounds dragged you away into the forest, to a burning cave, a fiery hole in the earth."

"And I got away."

"Then maybe that wasn't your door, your way out. I think Pine Lakes lies between two paths, a stopping point between one or the other, and that decisions here decide which direction you end up taking."

"Stop, Sue, please," Ted said. "I can't listen to this. It's been hard enough without losing you."

"You're not losing me. I'm right here!"

"No you're not. You're living in some fantasy because that's the only way you can deal with this. I'm just not willing to come along for the ride this time. I'm sorry."

"You're sorry? Were you there when dead children crawled out of the ground? Oh, that's right, you were the one stabbing them with a sharp fucking stick!"

"What are you talking about?"

Susan looked at him, shocked. "Are you being willfully dense right now?"

"That's really nice, Sue, really nice. Why don't you just blame this entire thing on me, huh? I crashed the car on purpose, right?"

"Ted, calm down. You really don't remember?"

"There's nothing to remember. We crashed the car, and I'm sorry you've had to live through that again, but…"

"You don't remember," she whispered. "What about the cabin? Emma's cabin?"

"What about it?"

"What are you doing right now? Are you trying to prove a point?"

"Prove a point? No. Why? You're being silly, babe. Let's get going, okay? We can call from the resort and put this behind us. I hope the wrecker can get the Cuda out of the woods. Maybe I can put her back together."

"The Cuda's not there anymore, you know that."

"Of course it is! Where else would it be?"

Susan was getting frightened. Ted's sense of humor was, at times, completely misplaced, but even he wouldn't go this far to play a prank.

"We saw it back at the motel, in the parking lot. Remember?"

"So they *did* get it out!" he exclaimed. "Thank God! I bet that's going to cost us an arm and a leg."

"Ted?"

"Wait! Did you call for help at the motel?"

"No, we couldn't…"

"No big deal. The resort has a phone."

Ted started walking, whistling a tune under his breath like he was taking a stroll to the convenient store.

How is this happening? Susan thought.

"Ted? Is there a town called Pine Lakes?"

"A town?" Ted thought for a moment and wrinkled his brow. "I don't think so. Why?"

"Nothing," she muttered, "just curious."

"There a Pine *Grove*," he continued. "Pine *Creek*. Pine *Crest*. Twin Oaks. Elmview. Whole bunch of places named after trees," he chuckled.

My God, I'm losing him.

They walked for a mile without saying anything. Susan was afraid to engage in conversation, scared of what Ted would say next. Was he losing his mind or was she losing hers? She was no longer certain.

A chilly wind blew down the road, whipping the trees and blowing ash from Susan's hair. She shivered and looked into the sky, surprised to see the clouds slowly breaking apart and revealing a sprinkling of stars. It was beautiful. She scanned the sky for familiar constellations but found none; these stars looked *different*. Odd pairings and groupings of light she didn't recognize.

When she started dating Ted, they'd often go to the lookout above their hometown and gaze at the sky. It was Ted's way of being romantic. He'd point out constellations, the hazy belt of the Milky Way, the quickly winking specks of light he said were orbiting satellites. He was fascinated by astronomy. He studied it frequently before the Barracuda became his main obsession. Susan frowned at the irony. Maybe if they'd just kept looking at the sky, none of this would have happened. It was amazing how one simple decision can change the entire course of your life.

"It's clearing up," Susan called ahead. "You can see the stars."

Ted looked up and pointed. "Right there is Ursa Minor, Cassiopeia,

Sagittarius. Wait. That's weird, they should be there. I don't recognize that one there." He pointed at a large cluster of stars that resembled a smiling face, two red giants spread apart to look like eyes gazing down at them. "The air is clear out here. We can't see all of this in town," he said. "That's the only explanation. The stars don't change."

Susan sighed and went back to moping. She'd hoped Ted would see the alien sky and realize that something was different, something had changed, but he simply went on walking. When a strange green moon peeked between the clouds, she didn't have the energy to point it out to him. It wasn't their moon. It was pocked with millions of years of meteor strikes and surrounded by a glistening cloud of rock and ice. Susan watched as it was swallowed by clouds once again. The brief glimpse of the cosmos was a fleeting one, but Susan had seen enough.

More than enough for one lifetime.

**

"I have to get my ass in shape," Ted said. "All this walking is killing me."

Ted stopped and sat on the guardrail, allowing Susan a chance to catch up. She sat next to him and put her head on his shoulder. It was the one thing left that felt familiar. He saw the gray ash on her shoulder and brushed it away absently, his face crunching up with curiosity.

"We're in pretty good shape for our age," Susan said.

"Do you remember when I had my *mid-life crisis?*" Ted laughed. "When I started going to the gym at the ripe old age of twenty-six?"

Susan laughed. Real laughter. "Yeah, it lasted a week until you realized a mid-life crisis was too much work."

"Do you think maybe that's what marriage is all about? Finding someone who can tolerate your various levels of absurdity over the years?"

"Quite possible. I was knitting at thirty. Remember that sweater I made for you that Christmas? With the reindeer on it?"

Ted laughed so *hard* he nearly tumbled off the guardrail. "I tried so hard to love that sweater. The deer looked like otters! I didn't have the heart to bury it in the yard."

Susan laughed with him, feeling almost normal for a second. It felt like any other chilly night at home, sitting with drinks on the deck, huddled up in sweatshirts, just enjoying the conversation. Susan realized Ted remembered everything up to the crash, but just like flipping a switch, had forgotten everything that had happened since. It filled her with overwhelming sadness. She'd never felt so alone.

"What do you think comes next?" Ted asked.

"What do you mean?"

"When we're fifty, sixty, seventy. Didn't you ever wonder what we'd be like when we're old?"

"Sure," she said, holding back tears. "I think everyone wonders what their life will be like when they get older. Where will they work? Where will they live? Who will their friends be? Aging is one of life's mysteries. No one ever knows what's waiting for them around the bend."

"We'll still have each other." Ted kissed her cheek, so sweetly and innocently that she wanted to break down into tears. He looked at her, confused.

"What's wrong, Ted?"

"How did we get here?"

"We walked," she said. "You must have hit your head, babe. It'll come back to you."

He nodded quickly, accepting Susan's words for fact. He stood, stretched, and held out a hand to help her up. "You ready? This is nice and all, but I'd kill for a soft pillow right now."

"I couldn't agree more." She held his hand tightly as they walked to the center line and followed the road into the night.

Susan couldn't help but think they were approaching a point of no return.

What if I'm wrong? she thought. As much as she feared Ted losing his mind, it was an even more terrifying idea that *she* was the one losing hers. What if she was the one imagining all of this? Where did that leave her?

There was no way to tell, not until they reached the resort.

12

"I think I see it," Ted said, breaking their silence. The harsh cry of a night bird echoed over the tops of the trees.

"We're really going up there?" Susan asked.

"Of course! Why the hell did we come all this way if we're just going to turn around?" He grabbed her hand and kissed it playfully. "Come on."

"Let's just wait here for a second," she said. "Let me catch my breath."

"Are you okay?" Ted asked, concerned. "You look pale."

"I'm okay," she lied. "Just tired."

"I know, it's been a long night."

A long night? It's been an eternity of long nights.

Ted looked at the winding road leading up to the resort and sighed. It was sometimes tricky navigating that road in the car, but walking was going to be a nightmare. Nearly a mile of hairpin turns on a steady incline to the parking lot. It looked strange in the near perfect darkness; the overhead lamps had gone out, and the usual smell of wood fires was oddly absent.

"Something's wrong," Susan muttered.

"The storm must have knocked the power out," Ted replied.

"No, that's not it."

"Suzie, are you sure you're okay? Your hand is shaking."

"Yes. No. I don't know. I don't like it here, it feels *wrong*."

"It's just the resort, babe. What's gotten you so skittish?"

Susan struggled with the idea of trying to get through to him, make him remember what had happened, but she didn't see a point. It would just make her seem even crazier. She still smelled the ash from Julie's body clinging to her skin, but Ted was oblivious. Lost.

"I don't know. I'm sure it's nothing."

"If you want to wait here, I can go on alone. Make a few calls. I'm sure the resort security won't mind coming down to pick you up."

"And wait here in the dark alone? Are you crazy? This dark is different. It's a *darker* dark."

Ted was concerned by his wife's behavior. Too many hours on the road had apparently worn her nerves down to a nub. He'd seen her this way before and it never ended well. They couldn't stand in the road all night and wait for someone to save them, they needed to act.

Suddenly, the sky lit with a brilliant white light, followed by the shrill, warbling siren they'd heard in the forest. A ball of white flame rose into the air and hovered above the resort. Ted watched it like a young boy at a fireworks display as Susan clutched at his arm. It was obvious by Ted's demeanor that he had no previous remembrance of the lights from the forest. Susan remembered all too well and still had no explanation for their seemingly random appearance.

In the distance, a chorus of dogs howled into the night.

"See baby, someone's up there," he smiled.

Susan tried wearing a brief smile, but it died on her lips.

The ball of light flickered and vanished. The phenomenon was not repeated.

"That was weird," Ted mumbled. "What do you think that was?"

Susan shrugged, refusing to answer.

"Let's go find out, huh?"

"If that's what you want."

They approached the driveway, glancing at the large green sign at the base of the road. 'Pine Lakes Resort & Campground. Established 1968. Enjoy Your Stay.' It was the first familiar thing Susan had seen in ages, but the jury was still out on how it made her feel.

They began the journey, steadily climbing the mountain as the road wound through tall pine trees. There wasn't a sound; not a breath of wind stirred in the canopy as thick clouds swirled overhead. They hadn't outrun the storm after all. Susan just hoped they'd reach shelter before they were trapped outside; she felt like she'd never be warm again.

"I love this place," Ted said. "Seriously. If I could stay here forever, I would."

Susan cringed at his words.

"I'm fine with just visiting."

"It always smells so fresh, so clean, not the smell of exhaust and people living on top of each other. It's just the atmosphere, you know? The fun of," he laughed. "Hot dogs on the fire, cold beers on the porch, the sound of the lake rippling and lulling you to sleep. It's kind of poetic, don't you think? I hope they held our reservations. I know we're late, but I'm sure they'd understand the circumstances."

"I don't know, babe."

"I certainly hope so. There's no point ruining the entire weekend. At least we can get a good night's sleep and worry about this other shit in the morning when we're well-rested."

Ted was seemingly happy enough talking for the both of them. Susan's replies were short, often nothing more than grunts of agreement. Her skin tingled, her eyes burned from weariness yet she never felt more awake in her life. Ted just went on prattling about the forest, the lake, and the food at the lodge as if it was any other day, not a nightmare from a Wes Craven film.

"… and I could die happy." Ted said.

"What?" Susan asked. "What did you say?"

"Oh, nothing, just thinking out loud. I said, if I could just sleep for about twelve hours and get some Top Sirloin from the lodge, I could die happy."

"Don't talk like that."

"Like what? Susan, are you sure you're okay, because you're really out in left field. Did you hurt your head in the crash? You're not seeing double are you?"

"No, Ted, I'm fine. I just don't want you to talk about *dying*. Please."

"We're all going to die, baby, just a fact of life. We might as well enjoy it while we're here and still young enough to make the most of it."

"I'm not enjoying it right now. Not any of it. My feet hurt, my legs are killing me, and I'm starting to stink."

"You're still beautiful," he said. "A little sweat and road grime aren't going to change that."

"It's a bit more than that."

"There might be a massage in this for you," he said, winking. "I know I could use one."

"You have a deal."

Ted squeezed her hand and carried on as the first cold droplets fell from the sky and pattered the surface of the road.

"Come on," Ted shouted. "We can make it before it gets bad."

They jogged the rest of the way, reaching the parking lot just as the sky opened. They stood there, silent and motionless as the sky cried frigid tears.

It wasn't anything like they'd hoped.

Susan felt the remainder of her energy drain from her body like blood from a wound.

"What is this?" Ted asked.

Susan didn't have words to answer.

***

The parking lot was completely empty and covered in layers of dead leaves. Brown shoots of tall grass hugged the concrete foundations of long-dead light poles, swaying in the wind that suddenly whipped across the lot. The log cabin used as the admission office had been punched flat by a massive tree that had fallen across its roof. The branching roads and paths leading to the camp sites, cabins, and lodge, were barely discernible in the thick weeds and brush that had grown through the crushed-gravel roadway.

Ted scratched his head and sighed shakily. "What's going on here?"

Susan peered into the forest, unable to shake the feeling they were being watched. She saw shapes out of the corners of her eyes, hiding behind trees and in the overgrown brush. Dark shapes with human forms. When she tried looking at them directly, they vanished. She questioned if they were there at all.

"Ted, do you see this?"

"This isn't right," he said, ignoring her. "It can't be."

At the dark edge of the parking lot, eyes suddenly blinked open, flickering like candles, watching them intently. Susan counted over forty sets of eyes of all shapes and sizes; some huddled in groups while others were spread out over the entire width of the tree line.

"This is *crazy,*" Ted said. He was so focused on the condition of the resort he hadn't noticed they'd acquired an audience.

"Come on, let's find the lodge. Maybe there's someone who can help us." Susan didn't believe it, but losing Ted now wasn't an option. He was already far too close to the edge.

"The lodge? Sure. There should be a phone there." He spoke quietly, swaying in the wind gusts that threatened to blow him over. "I don't understand, Suzie. I don't get it."

"Don't worry about it now," she said. "Let's go, okay? I don't want to be out here in the open."

"In the open? It's just a parking lot."

"Is it really? Where are the cars, Ted? Where are the people? I'm not talking about the ones hiding in the bushes either."

Ted scanned the forest but saw nothing. Their visitors had gone. "What are you talking about?"

Susan groaned and shook her head. "Nothing. I just want to move, okay?"

"Could the storm have shut the place down? Did they evacuate?"

"Ted, please, listen to me. Something is wrong. I know you don't believe me, or you don't *remember*, but you have to listen to me. We need to go!"

"Go? Where? This doesn't make any sense. *You're* not making sense."

"Now is not the time for you to be stubborn," she shouted. "If you need to check the lodge, let's go. I'm not going to stand around and wait for something to happen."

Another of the balls of light shot into the air, followed by the now familiar siren. The pale, white light illuminated other buildings that lie hidden behind the thick growth. The overall sense of rot and ruin was only solidified. Pained cries echoed from the forest. Screams. Howls. Whispered mutterings. The ball of light faded and slipped beneath the tops of the trees, sizzling and crackling with dying energy.

"There," Ted shouted. "There's someone else here!" He took off running, leaving Susan to struggle behind. An overgrown path led deeper into the campground. Ted followed a chorus of mumbling voices, calling out to them, pleading for help. The voices kept changing direction, making it impossible to judge their location, but still Ted continued on, tripping over rocks and tearing his skin open on low-hanging branches.

"Ted, please!" Susan shouted. "Wait for me! Don't leave me behind!"

"Susan, come on. They're here! Somewhere. I can hear them!"

"Stay away from them! Don't go near them, please!"

"Come on! They're just ahead. They're right over the hill."

Susan didn't realize she'd been crying until her vision blurred and doubled. She felt *them* closing in around her, whispering what sounded like warnings. She got turned around as her vision trebled.

She tripped over a fallen tree and fell face first into the layer of wet leaves. The bushes reached out and grabbed her clothing like clutching fingers, and no matter how hard she struggled, she only became more confined. In the darkness, hands reached for her, brushing her clothing and the feverish skin of her face. They grabbed her, pulling her deeper into the shadows. Somewhere ahead, Ted called out to her frantically, but she couldn't find the breath to respond. A freezing cold hand covered her mouth as she was tugged further and further away from the path.

Bright lights exploded overhead; a supernatural fireworks display. Susan couldn't help but stare into the night sky, as one after another, the balls of light bellowed their shrill song. The cacophonous swirl of sirens mixed with the light, raspy mutterings of her captors lulled her into a pleasant darkness. Her eyes fluttered and closed as the night claimed her. She thought of Ted. Then nothing.

***

Ted rushed to the top of the hill, flailing wildly to keep his balance. He fell to his knees and caught his first glimpse of the resort laid out below. The voices stopped, plunging the circle of cabins into silence.

"did you go?" he wailed. "I know you're here! Why are you hiding from me?"

Someone laughed nearby; a deep throaty chuckle that was carried away on the wind.

Panting, he got to his feet and descended the small hill. Blackened fire pits dotted the overgrowth, cold and dead. The cabins were in various states of abandonment; some of their doors were left open, swinging in the wind. Dry leaves skated across their porches and collected on the dusty floors of empty rooms. Not a soul moved.

"Susan!" Ted screamed. "Susan, where are you?"

He remained motionless, listening for the sound of approaching feet, but heard nothing. *Where the hell did she go?*

"Susan!" he repeated. "Here! I'm over here." Nothing.

Ted called for her over and over again, his voice growing raspy and harsh

"She was right behind me," he said aloud. "Right fucking there!" His voice rolled over the hills and dissipated, carried away on the wind, but it was the *other* voice he heard clearly. A woman's voice. "Suzie, is that you? Where are you, baby?"

The female voice was repeated, but it didn't sound like Susan.

It was so familiar.

"Who is that?" he called. "Where are you?"

"Come closer..." it beckoned.

"Where? Susan? Who is that?"

"Closer..."

"I need to find my wife," he cried. "Where's Susan? SUSAN!" he wailed. He stood in the circle of darkened cabins and felt the world spinning around him. Two hundred yards to his right, Ted saw a dim, yellow light flicker to life on the expansive porch of the Pine Lakes Lodge. He sped off into the night, oblivious of the shadows that crept in around him from all sides. He tripped over a large rock and tumbled to the ground, slamming his head hard enough on the packed dirt to see stars. He stood and fell back, his head swimming with dull pain. He reached a hand to his scalp, and it came away covered in a thin coating of blood. He battled unconsciousness. The shapes of the trees and cabins were outlined with a dull pinkish-white aura as multi-colored bursts of light flashed before his eyes.

"Stand up, Ted. Ever so close."

He stood several times, only to collapse to the forest floor. The pain in his skull made him dizzy and disconnected; his stomach rolled with bitter acid. He planted his feet and stood slowly, fighting the urge to vomit. He steadied himself against the trunk of a giant oak tree and shook his head as a thin trickle of blood dribbled from beneath his hair and down the back of his neck.

"You can do this," he said. "One step at a time."

Ted dragged himself forward, staggering on the open path leading to the lodge's steps. A bright light flashed before him, and in its glow stood a large, ragged-looking man holding a rusty machete. The man growled and held his weapon above his head as Ted raised his hands to block the incoming blow. The light flashed again, and the man disappeared just before the blade could slice through Ted's flesh.

"What the fuck?" Ted whined. "I… *know* you. What is this?"

"The Path of Memory," a female voice said.

"Memory," he whispered. "Memory of what?"

"Everything. How you got here."

In another flash of light, a pale, gangly creature with unseeing eyes shambled toward him from the dark. It screamed with rage, bounding toward him in a blur, a vision seen through a cloudy pane of glass. "The sewer," Ted whispered as the creature vanished. "Oh my God. Jack, the town, Emma. It was all real."

"All real, Ted." A naked woman stood along the path, smiling sadly.

"Julie? I *remember*. Susan was right about everything." Ted cried harshly, loud fitful sobs that made the pain in his head throb with new life. "I'm so sorry," he whimpered. "I'm sorry we left you behind."

"You have your path to follow, and I have mine." Julie blackened and crumbled into a pile of thick, black ash that blew away on the wind.

"I don't understand," he wailed. "Where's Susan?"

Off the path, a pair of red taillights glowed brightly, flickered, and went out.

"*Come...*" the female voice demanded.

"I need to find my wife," he screamed at the disembodied voice. "I'm not leaving without Susan."

"*That is not up to you.*"

Dogs howled in the distance. An awful, sad, pitiful bray.

"I remember it all. Every second."

A group of children appeared on the path ahead, smiling sweetly; pale faces turned to watch his advance. They were quickly replaced by the vision of an old woman, sitting in a rickety rocking chair and sipping at a cup of steaming liquid.

"You just keep moving along," she said. "There's no point staying where you're not wanted."

"Not wanted? Emma? Where's Susan? Where's my wife?"

"I don't have all the answers, Ted. No one does."

The vision faded and rose into the air in a puff of white mist. The path was dark, stretching out before him to the foot of the lodge. His head throbbed and his skin was slick with foul-smelling sweat. Ted's feet had grown heavy, dragging in the leaves and clumps of moss and mud.

It felt like an eternity had passed when Ted finally reached the wide, wooden stairs at the front of the lodge. A single candle burned on the railing, illuminating the porch in a pleasant, orange glow. The tall, double doors remained closed.

"What do I do?" Ted cried.

"The choice is ultimately yours," the voice said.

Ted crawled up the remaining steps on his hands and knees, panting and sick from the pain in his skull. He propped himself up against the banister and tried to catch his breath.

"Is Susan in there?" he asked.

He received no reply.

The trees were whipped into a frenzy as the storm arrived in earnest. Sheets of rain spattered the lodge and quickly soaked through Ted's clothing. He slid away from the edge of the porch and sat against the wall next to the entrance, cocking his head, listening closely for any signs of movement inside.

Ted wiped tears from his face and slowly stood. He grabbed for the brass handles and pushed the latch. The doors screeched open on rusty hinges, revealing the dark, musty interior of the giant hall. Ted crossed the threshold and walked inside as the doors clacked closed behind him.

The darkness enveloped him.

***

Susan opened her eyes to the sound of distant crying.

Far away, thunder rumbled and shook the foundation of the building. As her eyes adjusted, the small room came into focus. Rain pattered the dusty floor through a broken window; a rusted bed frame sat on her left, devoid of sheets or mattress; the mounted head of a large buck stared at her from the wall, its rack festooned in cobwebs.

She stood and wiped thick dust from her palms as the shrill cry repeated. The sound was muffled, but close. Where the hell was Ted? The building groaned around her as she slid along the wall, feeling in the dark for a way out. The room was claustrophobic, and for just a moment, Susan panicked. She was trapped. What if Jack had caught up to her after all? What if he'd taken her prisoner for the perverse use of his twisted clientele?

Susan's hand bumped the doorknob with a metallic rattle as she exhaled a relieved breath. She turned it in her sweaty hand and the door opened silently into a dimly lit hallway. Lights flickered along the walls; electric candles coated in dust. Doors were lined up on either side as far as she could see, dozens of them extending the length of the hall in both directions. Various noises emanated from the rooms, from the commonplace to the truly bizarre.

One of them *must* be a way out.

The first door she tried was locked; behind it, dogs barked and wailed and moaned in the distance. Behind the second locked door, scattered mutterings and hushed warnings; the sound of children hiding from their parents to escape punishment. After several more tries, Susan found an unlocked door. She cracked it open and put her ear in the gap, but heard nothing more than falling rain. She pushed the door open further and stared out into the rain-swept darkness. Gasping, Susan stepped back and shook her head.

It was the main street of Pine Lakes.

Across the flooding street stood a group of figures in tattered clothing, huddled around a flaming barrel. One turned and smiled through broken teeth, its head nothing but a skull covered in fine wisps of greasy hair. It reached out a skeletal hand and pointed as laughter echoed hollowly from its fleshless mouth.

"So you've come to your senses," the skeleton cackled.

"Oh my God," Susan moaned. "Jack?"

"In the flesh," he joked. "Well, not exactly."

The group of skeletons turned and clattered across the street on filthy, splintered phalanges; an army of the long-dead. Susan slammed the door and backed away, bumping into the wall behind her. Through the door came the sounds of angry cries and the light, papery scratching of their skinless fingers. The door shuddered in its frame, but held.

Susan stumbled down the hallway, trying the knobs on other doors as she passed, but most remained closed. After a dozen attempts, another door opened into the darkness. The gassy, rotting stench of the sewer assaulted her senses. Her eyes burned and watered at the swampy stink. In the recess of the shadowy cavern, shiny, waxy faces turned in her direction and began running toward her, tripping over one another in their enthusiasm for warm meat.

The cavern trembled and filled with the crescendoing roar of water and the approach of something most foul and ravenously hungry. On a wave of filthy, turgid water, swam the bloated, slime-coated abomination that had taken Julie into the sewer's depths. The sewer dragon, Fang, guardian of the underworld.

It swept forward on the surge of water, lightning fast, reptilian eyes burning with orange flame. With a massive head, it swept bodies aside like toys, pausing briefly to crunch on the bones of those in the way. The reeking water reached Susan first, bursting through the doorway and filling the hall, turning it into an indoor river. She splashed away, sputtering as the soupy torrent filled her mouth and choked her. She struggled to her feet and braced herself for the monster's thick jaws to crush her into paste, but the death blow never came.

Susan peeked through her fingers and shuddered. The doorway was filled with a single, giant eye. The creature squinted at her, its diamond-shaped pupil dilating. The sour odor of stagnant water wafted through the door and filled the hallway with a thick, noxious funk. Water continued pouring through the doorway and sloshing around her ankles, running in either direction like a storm-clogged gutter. With a grunt and a splash, the reptile god turned and made quick work of the albino monsters cowering in the shadows.

Susan splashed away from the door, confident she wouldn't be followed. Whatever this place was, it seemed these doors were one way glimpses into the *other*. Now if she could only find a way out of here before the hall flooded.

The next door opened on nothing. Not precisely nothing, but a noticeably barren landscape devoid of life. A red sky swirled over rocky fields; a black ocean of oily water lapped at a broken coastline as lightning forked across the alien sky. Susan slammed the door quickly, afraid the pure emptiness would suck her in and rob her of what sanity remained.

Susan sloshed down the hall, checking doors quickly, afraid of what she'd find waiting behind them. The rank water had risen to her calves. Behind the next working door was the interior of Emma's cabin. Pleasant heat drifted into the hall and warmed her skin; the spicy aroma of the woman's tea was a welcome one compared to the water's cold, bitter tang. For a second, Susan thought of how easy it would be to cross the threshold and step into the warmth and comfort of Emma's safe place. But at what cost? How would Ted ever find her if she escaped into one of these rooms, into the places beyond? She held out hope that there was still a chance they'd be reunited. This could not be the end.

The hallway creaked and groaned and twisted, canting beneath her feet like the deck of a sinking ship. The lights behind her sputtered, one by one, and went dark. There was no going back. If there was any way out of here, it was ahead.

The Hall of Choices carried on.

13

TED INCHED FORWARD INTO THE DARKNESS, HIS FOOTFALLS echoing off the high ceiling. He sneezed in the cloud of swirling dust, awakening the throbbing in his skull. An overhead chandelier crackled to life, illuminating the lodge's main hall. Neglected furniture sat beneath wrinkled sheets turned yellow with age. The carpet squished beneath his feet where puddles of green water had collected from the leaky roof. On his left, a long wooden counter ran the length of the room. The first ten feet were for check-ins, identified by a large wooden sign hanging overhead from lengths of chain. A thin partition separated this from the lodge's bar, where bottles of murky liquid lined a set of bowed shelves.

He ran around the edge of the check-in counter, slipping on the slick carpet, and found an old rotary-dial phone. He picked it up and put it to his ear, hearing only faint static. He disconnected the call and tried again, but the white noise persisted. Faint voices swam just beneath the surface, calling to him, mocking him. Ted grabbed the heavy phone from the desk and threw it across the room where it landed with a heavy jangle. He looked around for another phone, but saw nothing, not even a pay phone.

From the dead receiver came throaty laughter and squeals of static; it grew louder, filling the room like a loudspeaker. He reached down to pull the phone cord from the wall, only to find it wasn't connected. Frowning, he ran to the phone and kicked it, hurting his toes. Still, the noise persisted. Grabbing it in his hands, he heaved the phone toward the front doors, where it shattered the thick glass and bounced onto the porch. The room became quiet; the silence broken only by Ted's heavy breathing.

"What do you want from me?" he shouted.

Ted's ears had started ringing, doubling the pain in his injured head. He pressed his hands into his temples and tried to massage the pain away, but it did little good. He needed to find Susan and get out of this place.

The air crackled and sizzled with unseen energy as Ted stumbled across the room, driven by pure need. All he wanted was to lie on one of the lodge's dusty couches and drift away, but Susan was still here somewhere, and he couldn't bear the thought of her wandering these ruined halls, aimlessly searching for him and for a way out. He wanted to feel sorry for himself, wanted to curl up in his mother's embrace and let her take away his pain, but he was on his own. For the first time in his life, he was completely and totally alone. Emptiness consumed him.

"Ted," a voice called. Upstairs. "Ted, where are you?"

Susan.

Ted lurched to the staircase and looked up into the darkened hallway of the second floor, pausing briefly to shake off a bout of dizziness. "Susan? Where are you, baby?" No reply. "Just stay where you are. I'm coming for you."

He took the steps two at a time until he reached the top. Peering into the darkness, Ted searched for any sign of movement. Any sound. Rain beat on the lodge's roof; wind whistled through broken windows. Doors stood open on either side of the hall, offering glimpses into rooms where only spiders lived. Each room was a barren square, devoid of furniture. There was nowhere to hide, so where the hell was she?

"Susan, I'm here," Ted called. "Tell me where you are."

The thunder grumbled a response, shaking the building. He'd come too far to lose her now.

"Help me!" he shrieked. "Where's everyone now when I actually need them? Julie? Emma? Anyone?"

Ted stood perfectly still in the middle of the musty hall, holding his hands over his face and crying harshly. It felt like this place went on forever, and every room was just more of the same. He didn't know how much longer he could go on; it felt like his head was about to split open and spill his brains onto the carpet; each peal of thunder another nail in his coffin.

Somewhere ahead, a door squealed open, spilling brilliant white light into the hall. Ted couldn't look at it; he shielded his eyes with his hand, creeping toward the source of the light, as a steady wind blew toward him, pushing him back. He fought against the gale, grabbed at the walls and door frames, pulling himself forward one step at a time.

With a loud crack, the same white light blazed from every door, every window, every split in the lodge's old timbers. It washed over him, bathed him in its purity. His aches and pains were lifted from his body by warm, probing fingers. He collapsed to the floor, surrounded by heat, feeling his consciousness slip.

"Ted," a voice whispered.

He heard Susan's voice, but his body wouldn't respond. He reached out a hand, waggled his fingers toward the sound of her voice. The light swept him away.

***

The hall appeared to stretch out for miles.

The water had risen to Susan's waist, making it harder to move. Her legs were burning from the strain; her toes had gone numb.

She continued trying doors, many of which remained locked. Those that were unlocked opened onto scenes of horrifying creatures, barren landscapes, broken cities. Each desolate vision pushed her mind closer and closer to the brink of collapse.

Susan turned the knob on the next door and opened it cautiously. Thick, choking smoke blew into the hall on a hot wind. She pulled her shirt collar over her nose and mouth and squinted into the orange glow as her eyes watered and dribbled over her cheeks. She stared down a wind-swept street clogged with abandoned vehicles. Rows of houses stood on either side, engulfed in flames; hot ash skated across broken, blackened sidewalks.

In the distance stood the tall, steel silhouette of an unfamiliar city, spires pointing to a crimson sky. The inferno raged with an unsettling roar, twisting the skyscrapers into unnatural, hunched monsters. Susan slammed the door and wept. There was nothing left. The world she'd known was gone, swept away like trash on the breeze.

The river of filthy water tugged at her legs and pulled her down, swiftly carrying her forward. She no longer had the energy or the will to fight. There was no escape. She listened as doors slammed behind her, booming in the blackness, hiding the atrocities that lurked just beyond their thresholds. Nightmares couldn't hide behind closed doors; Susan knew they were there. The visions would shamble around in the dark corners of her mind every time she closed her eyes.

But hopefully not for much longer.

Water sloshed over her face, spilling into her mouth and burning her sinuses. She welcomed it. She thought of Ted as she floated away, wondering what had become of him, hoping he'd found a way out of this madness. Susan was nearly there. Death could only be a blessing.

Susan's ass scraped the carpet beneath her; she realized the water had begun receding. She reached beneath her and scraped her fingers along the carpet, slowing her forward motion. She stood, shook the water from her clothes, and hugged herself to keep from shivering. A lone light flickered on above a closed, white door. It was the only light left. She turned to look behind her, but there was nothing but a plain wall. A picture frame hung crookedly from a single nail; a photo of her and Ted on their first visit to the Pine Lakes Resort. Arms around one another, beaming, standing before the wide expanse of the lake behind them.

Susan reached out and touched the dusty glass, rubbing a finger over Ted's smiling face. For a brief second, she thought she heard his voice. Soothing her, reassuring her, loving her. Just that quickly it was gone. The frame fell to the floor and shattered as the photo withered and faded.

"Nonono," she cried, "you can't have him." She lifted the photo from the frame and hugged it tightly to her chest, feeling it crumble and fall through her fingers like sand. The overhead light exploded in a shower of sparks, leaving her in total darkness. She slid down the wall and wailed, the final exclamation of her broken heart.

She huddled in the dark, waiting for everything to go away.

Susan heard noises from behind the solitary, closed door. The floor creaked under the weight of someone's passing; hushed voices whispered back and forth. She looked up at the door, wiped her eyes, and watched as thin, white light spilled through the cracks around the frame. She heard a muffled cry, the same cry she'd heard upon waking. Whatever it was, it was right behind the door, but she couldn't bring herself to find out. Time after time, doors opened on unspeakable horrors. One more and her already fragile mind would snap like a rubber band.

The cry came again, louder, clearer.

Susan stood and listened as light steps approached the door. The knob turned slowly. Susan tensed, knowing there was nowhere to run. Inch by agonizing inch, the door opened in, revealing more of the brilliant glow. At first it hurt her eyes to gaze inside, but little by little, her vision adjusted, and the room became clear.

It was immediately familiar.

It was she and Ted's spare bedroom. The one they'd cleaned and painted and decorated over long hours of laughter and excitement and long talks about the future. It was a room full of hope and love. A room that was soon left behind to collect dust, to be forgotten, sealed off behind walls of painful memory.

Their unborn child's nursery.

***

In the dim glow of their past, Susan and Ted sat on the floor of the bedroom, covered in splotches of paint, watching as it slowly transformed into something beautiful. Ted munched on a bag of raw carrots and looked over their handiwork. It was really coming together. Their child would soon fill these walls with laughter and light. Susan would sit in her rocking chair as warm breezes blew off the lawn, holding a new life in her hands, planning the millions of possibilities spread out before them like a glittering sea of diamonds.

"Do you think he'll like it?" Susan asked.

"*He?* You mean will *she* like it?"

Susan laughed and ate one of Ted's carrots. "Do you want to know?"

"No. Absolutely not. I want it to be a surprise."

She thought it over and smiled. "So do I. Can you believe it? We're going to be parents, Ted."

"We are? I was wondering why we were doing all this work."

"It'll be well worth it."

"The kid better appreciate it," he joked. "I don't want to get callouses for nothing."

"Your hands will recover." She grabbed his hand and rubbed it tenderly. Ted put the bag of carrots aside and pulled her closer. She sat between his legs and rested her back on his chest as he wrapped his arms around the small bump of her stomach. So tiny, yet large enough to fill them both to the brim with unbridled joy. Ted held her, smelling the fresh, wonderful scent of her hair.

"We need to get cracking on names, mister," she said. "We can't wait until we're on the way to the hospital."

"Robert," Ted said, "if it's a boy. I want to name him after my grandfather."

"And if it's a girl?"

"Girls' names are a trap," he laughed. "The older we get, the more pretentious the names become. What ever happened to Mary and Martha and Minerva?"

"Minerva? I would never do that to my child."

"You know what I mean," he said. "In the eighties, everyone started naming their girls after cars. Expensive cars. Mercedes, Lexus, Shelby. No one ever named their daughter Dodge or Datsun, did they? These guys couldn't afford a stylish ride, so they named their kids after one."

Susan snorted laughter and nodded. "There was a girl in my elementary school named Porsche."

"Porsche? Was she *fast?*"

"She got pregnant in junior high school, so what do you think?"

"See what happens when you put a label on someone? You have to live up to your name."

"What about June?" Susan asked.

"The months are worn out too. January, April, May, June. Same with the seasons. There are a million Summers and Autumns running around out there."

"You're a tough nut to crack," she said.

"I want something pretty to match the most perfect child the world has ever seen."

Susan laughed. "That's a lot of pressure to put on a child."

"I don't think so. Pretty name for a pretty girl. She'll wake up every morning feeling beautiful."

"She'll feel beautiful no matter what we name her. We'll make sure of that."

Ted hugged her and kissed her neck. "That's why you're going to be a great mother."

Susan smiled, feeling completely at home in Ted's embrace. They were actually doing this. They were a few short months away from becoming parents. It thrilled her and scared her to death, but she wouldn't change a thing.

The silence stretched out before them. Susan dozed off as the sun warmed her face.

"Victoria," Ted said.

"Victoria," Susan repeated, letting the name roll off her tongue. "It's perfect."

"It is, isn't it?"

"Victoria."

***

"Victoria," Susan whispered.

The room was as she'd remembered it: rocking chair by the window, crib in the corner, changing table nearby. It was a perfect replica. The pale light bled the color from the room, giving the appearance of an old black and white movie. It smelled of fragrant flowers.

"What is this?" she asked cautiously.

"You remember," a voice said pleasantly. "You remember everything. Every detail."

"What is this doing here? How is this possible?"

"After everything you've seen and heard, you question the one thing that should give you the most hope."

"No, I don't mean it like that. I don't know what I mean, it's just, I don't understand."

"In time, Susan."

"Where are you?" she asked. She turned in a slow circle in the center of the nursery. The walls were hidden in cloudy, white light, and in the glow stood a half-dozen figures, shadows. Human shapes. They remained still. "*Who are you?*"

"That's not important, dear. What's important is that you're here."

"I don't know where *here* is," she cried. "This could be another trap. Haven't I suffered enough?"

"Yes. You *have* suffered enough. It's how you came to us, how you found this place."

Bright, beautiful laughter emanated from the crib in the corner. A mobile of butterflies spun overhead, playing sweet, tinkling lullabies. A tiny arm reached up with small, groping fingers, and Susan stepped back, expecting any number of horrifying abominations. It was just a hand. A perfect little hand with perfect little fingers.

Susan sighed, relieved, and stepped forward. She was terrified. She approached the crib with trepidation, fearing another trick, another trap, but nothing happened. A child cooed playfully out of sight and Susan's heart filled with calm.

"Is that… is it… a baby?"

"What else would it be, Susan?" the voice snickered.

"But here? In this place? Why?"

"This is a safe place, Susan. Your trial is over. You can rest."

"Whose baby is this? Why is it here?"

"I think you know the answer to that, Susan."

The baby squealed, waving two chubby fists in the air.

"My baby?"

"Your baby, Susan. A sweet, healthy little girl."

"No. No! What kind of trick is this? My baby is dead. DEAD! Why would you do this to me?"

"She's not dead, Susan. Nothing ever truly dies. She's been waiting for you."

"Waiting? For me?"

"Yes. We've taken care of her for you."

"I don't understand what's happening? How is this possible?"

"You know the answer to that as well."

Susan rubbed her forehead with a shaking hand. "Why won't you tell me?" she shouted. "Why all the riddles?"

"You have the answers you need. It's not our place to offer you explanations."

The infant giggled.

"Can I *see* her?" she asked.

"Of course you can. She's your *daughter*."

Susan didn't move. Her mind buzzed with questions.

"She's not going to come to you, Susan," the voice tittered.

"I don't know what to do," Susan cried.

"Yes you do. Go to your daughter. She's waited such a long time."

Susan sobbed uncontrollably and fidgeted with her shirt. Her daughter. The perfect life that had been taken away from them lie only four feet away in the same crib Ted had built with his own hands. It didn't make sense. Nothing made sense anymore.

She moved forward. One tentative step, then another. When she reached the edge of the crib, she closed her eyes and took a deep breath. Was she ready for this?

After a moment, Susan placed her hands on the smooth, wooden crib rail and opened her eyes.

"Oh my God," she whispered.

A plump little girl stared up at her with the bluest, most beautiful eyes she'd ever seen. The infant smiled a toothless grin and reached for her, legs pumping, babbling happily. Thin, blond, wisps of hair covered her shiny scalp. After all the horror, and all the death, Susan stared at *life* at its most innocent.

"What do I do?" she sobbed.

"Embrace her. Isn't that what you've always wanted, what you've dreamed of since the day you found out you were pregnant?"

Susan reached down, cradled the infant's head, and lifted her from the crib. She held her, feeling her warmth, smelling her skin, looking at every inch of her tiny body from the crown of her head to her ten, amazing toes. The baby girl reached up and clapped a hand over Susan's lips, laughing and wiggling in her arms. It wasn't another dream that Susan would wake from in tears, it was real. It had weight.

"Victoria," Susan whispered, running a finger over her baby's silky cheek.

"It's a beautiful name," the voice said. The soothing voice was actually many voices speaking in unison. Musical. Genderless. "When you're ready to go, Susan, say the word."

Susan hugged Victoria, afraid to squeeze her too tightly. "Go where?"

"Anywhere. Everywhere. It's your choice."

Susan nodded as understanding flooded her being. The undulating forms stepped closer, surrounding her. She had no fear.

The door behind her opened. Susan stared into the hall and saw a shadowy figure crawling across the floor. It raised its head, their eyes met.

"Ted?"

***

"Ted?" the voice whispered.

He forced his eyes open against the glaring light and stared into the room.

"Susan? Is it really you?"

If Susan answered, he couldn't hear her. Her lips moved, but made no sound. Ted crawled to a sitting position just outside the door and watched as tall, shadowy figures surrounded her, wrapping long arms around her waist. They formed a misty circle of light around Susan's body, partially obscuring her from view.

"No!" he shouted weakly. "Leave her alone."

Susan wasn't struggling. She smiled at him as tears coursed over her cheeks.

"What's happening?"

Again, Susan's mouth moved silently. She looked peaceful. Serene.

"Susan," Ted cried. "Please don't go."

"He's not ready," a voice said.

Susan nodded.

"Not ready for what? God damn you, leave her alone!"

Something wiggled in Susan's arms, but the glare was too bright for him to make out any detail. He squinted into the light as the room grew fuzzy, like a television with bad reception. The air crackled. Ted realized he could see *through* Susan's body. She was simply fading away.

"Susan, fight it! You can't leave me here!"

Ted reached across the threshold and pulled his hand back with a hiss. The light stung his flesh as tears leaked from his eyes. Like a sprinter at the starting gate, Ted tensed and prepared to run. Susan's form flickered and vanished with a crack as light poured from the room, knocking Ted back against the wall. He cried Susan's name over and over, but she was gone. The light faded. The room was empty.

"No!" Ted screamed. "Susan! Come back to me. Don't leave me like this."

Lightning flickered through a broken window. The room was in ruin, just another forgotten space in this desolate land of shadows. Ted put his head in his hands and wept like a child. The emptiness in his soul threatened to crush him beneath unforgiving hands. Pain flared in his chest and extended out. The pervading feeling of loss consumed him.

"Why?" he whined. "God damn you, why?"

Ted jumped with a start as a howl pierced the darkness. It was close, just down the hall. The hounds had returned.

Heavy footfalls rushed toward him. Above, the roof rumbled beneath the scrabbling of clawed feet. Ted stood and ran down the never ending hall as it twisted around him; doors flung open and tore from their hinges as orange eyes peered hungrily from empty rooms.

A taloned hand reached from a doorway and tore a jagged hole in his thigh.

"I just want my wife," he bellowed. "Go to hell!"

Laughter surrounded him, mocking, warbling laughter.

Ted turned a corner and felt the floor disappear from under his feet. He tumbled end over end, crashing off the banister, bouncing over risers. He hit the floor on his back as air exploded from his lungs. He remained motionless, waving at the stars that burst in his vision. His body ached. His racing heart thundered in his ears as the blood rushed to his head. He rolled over and took a deep breath, clutching at the soggy carpet. Dim, gray light poured through the main entrance forty feet away. He had to get outside. Maybe he had a chance.

Maybe he could still rescue Susan. Somehow.

Ted crawled the first ten feet, unable to find his balance. By the time he reached the center of the room, he was able to stand and stagger the rest of the way. He opened the front door and burst onto the porch, nearly tripping over the phone he'd tossed through the window. Kicking it aside, he descended the stairs and stumbled down the rocky path toward the circle of cabins below. He turned and looked up with a gasp. The roof was lined with hunched, black shapes. Dozens of them. Snarling, gnashing their teeth, growling deep in burly chests.

"I'm going to find Susan," Ted stated. "Nothing on Earth will stop me from finding my wife, do you understand me?"

"Your wife is long gone," a voice shouted from the forest. Ted saw Jack's silhouette standing along the path. "Why don't you come with me, friend? You can have a whole new life in Pine Lakes."

"Fuck you," Ted shouted. "I'll wait here forever before going back to that graveyard."

"Interesting choice of words, Ted. Maybe *our* graveyard is exactly what you need."

Jack's laughter boomed over the rain. Ted turned and carefully walked the path, keeping his feet from touching the edges, afraid of wandering too close to the black shapes that lingered just out of eyesight. Jack bellowed behind him. Promises. Lies. Furious outbursts of undisguised rage. Ted carried on, so tired he could barely keep his feet moving. If not for the hope of finding Susan, he'd let them take him. Rip him apart. End this nightmare once and for all.

After several minutes of wandering, Ted stood in the center of the clearing, surrounded by the private cabins that Susan had loved so much. Cabin 105, *their* cabin, stood directly ahead. If she was anywhere, waiting for him, it would be there.

He mounted the steps, reached out, and opened the door.

***

"It's *quaint*," Susan said. "Charming."

"You like it?" Ted asked.

"I love it. It smells so *fresh* up here."

"I'm so glad," he gushed. "I was afraid you wouldn't like it. I spent so much time with my parents here it became like a second home. Cabin 108. Right over there," he pointed.

Susan nodded and sat on the bed, testing its firmness. "This is 105," she stated.

"I thought it was time to start a new tradition," he smiled.

"That's very presumptuous," she laughed. "What makes you think

I'd want to come up here every year, huh? Do you expect us to get married and have kids and a house with a view?"

"What's wrong with that?"

"Nothing," she said quietly. "Absolutely nothing."

Ted sat next to her on the bed and put his arm around her shoulders. "Wait until it gets dark and the crickets come out. It's *magic*."

"It's just a resort, Ted. They're all over the place."

"I know, but this one is, I don't know, *special*. Can't you feel it? It's like a current of energy runs through here and just makes you feel at peace. I know it sounds silly…"

"No, it doesn't," she interrupted. "It shows your romantic side."

Ted laughed and squeezed her shoulders. "That's me. The hopeless romantic."

"What now?"

"Well, we can grab a bite to eat at the lodge, maybe take a boat out on the lake. Later we can roast marshmallows, hot dogs, huddle up by the fire."

"You have this all planned out I see."

"Sort off," he giggled. "I want you to love it as much as I do."

"I'm sure I will. I love you after all."

"How does it get any better than that?"

Susan leaned in and kissed him tenderly on the lips, exhaling a sigh of absolute contentment. Ted was right, there was magic here. She felt it tingling in her fingers and toes. Outside, children played cheerfully, giggling and calling out to one another. A sweet, warm breeze blew through the window and ruffled the curtains.

"Hey, look at this," Ted said, jumping from the bed excitedly. "Come here."

Susan stood and followed him to the window. From their cabin they had a perfect view of the lake. Paddle boats dotted the surface; people swam in the shallows, splashing each other playfully; the sun turned the slight ripples into shining points of glittering light.

"Oh Ted, it's gorgeous."

He elbowed her arm as if sharing a private joke. "Right?"

"I can see why you like it here."

"I'm glad you approve."

"I do. I love it." She wrapped her arm around his waist and hugged him tightly.

"I claim this cabin as the property of Ted and Susan for now and forever," Ted shouted.

Susan giggled and slapped his arm.

"I have an idea." Ted broke from Susan's arms and began stalking around the cabin, peering into corners, ducking his head into the small bathroom. "There has to be somewhere decent."

"What are you talking about?" Susan asked.

"You'll see."

After another minute of seemingly senseless wandering, Ted shouted loudly and squatted next to the bed. "Perfect," he muttered.

"What in God's name are you doing?"

Ted braced his hands on the side of the bed and slowly slid it across the floor, grunting from the effort. Susan stood back, hands on her hips, watching him amusedly. He pulled something from his pocket, got down on his hands and knees, and diligently began scratching at the wooden floor. Susan stepped forward and Ted reached up a hand, stopping her in her tracks.

"Hold on, just a second," he said. He went back to work, muttered a few words, and leaned back to admire his work. With a laugh he stood.

"What did you do?"

"Take a look," he said.

Susan walked to the spot on the floor and bent down, smiling so widely that her face hurt.

"Oh, Ted. You didn't have to do *that*."

"Yes I did. Every year we come here, from now until we're old and gray, we'll add another mark to signify the anniversary of our first vacation together."

Susan felt tears come to her eyes. It was the sweetest thing Ted had ever done. Carved into the rough wood was a large heart with their initials and a single line. Year one.

"Who else would deface property just to tell you he loves you?"

"You're one of a kind," she whispered. "And you're all mine."

"Until you get sick of me," he laughed.

"Never." She hugged him and kissed him passionately, grabbing the back of his neck and running her hand through his hair. "I'll never get tired of you. Ever."

Ted smiled and wiped a single tear from his eye.

They never made it to dinner, never made it to the lake. Instead, they stayed in bed until after sundown, passionately making love as everything else melted away. They fell asleep in each other's arms to the sounds of crickets and the breeze quietly soughing through the trees.

Magic.

***

Ted collapsed to the floor as the door shut behind him. He pounded his fists on the wood and screamed into the empty room until he tasted the warm, salty tang of blood in his throat.

Susan wasn't there. No one had been there for ages. The cabin smelled of rot and mold. The room had been stripped of all furnishings except for a tattered, stained mattress resting on a rusted box spring. Ted shuffled to the bed and rested his hands on the cool fabric. He'd lain with Susan on this very bed. Tickled playfully, discussed their past and their future, made love in each other's warm embrace.

All gone, just like Susan. A life blown away like icy snowflakes in an unforgiving gale. How had their lives come to this? A stained mattress in a distant corner of oblivion. He laid down, shifting away from springs that poked into his flesh. He longed to feel Susan's warmth, feel her presence beside him.

There was nothing here but the void of loss.

Ted couldn't keep his eyes open, and every time they closed, he saw her face coming out of the dark. He had no more tears to cry. His mind raced with a lifetime of little moments, sacred memories. He kept them close as he felt himself slowly slipping away.

Days passed. Years. Centuries.

The life he'd known, the one he shared with Susan, collapsed into ruin. Cities toppled to be reclaimed by nature. The human race vanished from the Earth as the Sun went quiet and still, plunging everything into an endless midnight.

It was always you, Ted thought. *Only you. My love.*

Ted's ancient, hunched body stood, grabbed the edge of the bed, and pushed with the last of his waning energy. He got to his knees and brushed a thick layer of dust from the cabin's floor, revealing scratches in the old wood. Eighteen individual hash marks.

With a long, cracked fingernail, Ted dug into the wood, scoring the surface with another bright line.

Number nineteen.

He smiled and collapsed, running his gnarled hand over the wood's surface; the last remaining vestige of he and Susan's fleeting life together.

Ted felt his body growing lighter. His vision faded. A million years passed in the blink of an eye as the planet spun around a dead star and the cosmos flickered and died.

The cabin door creaked open, spilling bright light across the floor. It took Ted the last of his energy to raise his head and squint into the blinding glare.

A shadowy form stood there, motionless.

A smaller figure came forward and extended a hand.

The shape giggled, the sweetest laughter Ted had ever heard.

"Are you ready?" a voice asked.

"Susan?"

"Come on daddy. We have so much to show you."

Epilogue

"They've been here for about a week," the officer said. He stood in the wet soil next to the wreck of a twisted Plymouth Barracuda. Others milled around the accident scene, poking at wreckage, prodding at the trail of items that were flung from the car's trunk during its descent from the road.

"Hell of a wreck," the man's partner muttered. "Any chance they lived through it?"

"None," he replied. "Not after a fall like that."

Another man joined them, smartly dressed, and announced himself as the Medical Examiner.

The officers stood nearby as photographs were taken of the scene and of the two lifeless bodies sitting in the vehicle's cabin. It was laborious work for some, as others leaned against trees, sipping at steaming coffee; just another day at the office.

"Do we know who they are?"

"Theodore and Susan Merchant," the officer responded. "Married. Mid-thirties. No kids. The man's mother reported them missing last weekend."

"What a way to go," he whistled. "Can you imagine a drop like that?"

"No sir, and I don't want to. At least it was quick."

"We're going to have to cut them out," a voice called. "They're both pinned beneath the dash."

"Christ. Even if they'd survived the fall, they would have been trapped here."

The officer mumbled and popped a stick of gum in his mouth. "I don't want to be here any longer than I have to be. It's *creepy*."

His partner laughed and clapped him on the shoulder. "You afraid of the woods all of a sudden?"

"Not the woods, but what *lives* there."

"Oh! Big, scary monsters."

"No, asshole. Big, scary bears, mountain lions, wild dogs. Woods this deep tend to hide their secrets."

"Bigfoot?"

"Maybe you'd be surprised. Why don't you spend a few nights here and let me know?"

In the distance, an animal bellowed a long, whining howl. The officers broke out in goosebumps and laughed nervously.

"When the Coroner gets here, I'm out."

"Now who's scared of the woods?" his partner laughed.

"Well, it *is* creepy. You're right about that."

They turned and walked away from the scene, allowing the Examiner to do his job.

"Hell of a way to go," the officer repeated.

His partner grunted, turned, and shook his head. "Yeah, it sure is."

"At least they died together."

A Few Words About "Pine Lakes"

!!!WARNING!!! This section contains spoilers. If you haven't read the book yet, do not continue reading!

Let me be the first to tell you: this book didn't turn out as I'd expected.

After the warm reception to my first novel, "The Darkening," I was immediately back at my keyboard trying to craft another story. I wanted it to be different from my first book, but yet carry on a similar tone of love, loss, and things that go bump in the night. I had nearly thirty thousand words when I hit a dead end and filed my tale away for another day. It went into that special folder that all writers have, the one full of questions, but nary an answer to be seen. It's still there, waiting for my return.

To get the creative juices flowing again, I sat down and tapped out my second release, "The Farm." This novella was meant to bridge a gap between full-length releases and give me extra time to formulate a proper follow-up. That one came out pretty quick, and although I'm sure it has its flaws, I was very happy with it. I spent time promoting, advertising, appearing on internet radio shows, doing interviews for local newspapers. Little by little, reviews started coming in for both books, positive reviews. Suddenly, the shit I'd spent my time on was reaching an audience of *actual* readers. Paying readers! Offers for anthology submissions came my way; collaborative efforts presented themselves. It was all very new, very exciting, and completely terrifying.

I needed to get working… and fast!

When I got back to it, I thought maybe the safest and quickest way to go would be to release another novella. Twenty-five thousand words, in and out. I got a lot of work done on several concepts - all stories that will reach you throughout the upcoming year or so - but it was a single photograph that turned it all upside down. A picture of an old car, lost and left to rot in the woods. The first several chapters popped into my head immediately, just from that one photograph.

How had that car gotten there?

Who'd been driving when it reached its final resting place?

What would I see if I sat in the driver's seat, peering through a broken windshield into the gloom?

Ted and Susan showed up to take charge before I had any details to offer. Ted took the wheel and began driving into an uncertain future. This novel suddenly took flight, in this case, off the side of the highway and into the forest. What's in the forest you ask? I'm not sure. It's so goddamn hard to see down there.

I wanted to take Ted and Susan on a journey. One that would test them as a couple, one that would bring up painful memories, but one that would ultimately show what they were made of, and how far their love for one another could carry them.

I hope I pulled it off.

Maybe you'll see a little of yourself in Ted and Susan, and maybe you'll wonder how far you'd go for someone you love.

Just be careful. The road ahead may seem straight and narrow, but there's always the possibility of a blind curve taking it all away.

If you meet Ted and Susan somewhere out there in the dark, rest assured, you've gone too far...

... and there may be no coming back.

Christopher Motz - May 15, 2017

About The Author

CHRISTOPHER MOTZ LIVES IN SMALL-TOWN PENNSYLVANIA with his wife, step-daughter, and miniature Morkie, OY. Other works include his novel, "The Darkening", and novella "The Farm." Christopher is an avid reader, musician, and collector of rare books and vinyl.

YOU CAN REACH CHRISTOPHER ON THE WEB AT:
CHRISTOPHER-MOTZ.COM

Made in the USA
Middletown, DE
02 June 2017